Written, Directed, and Produced by
Christopher Robertson

A Note From the Director

The following presentation contains scenes of violence, horror, heartbreak, and zombie carnage.

My Zombie Sweetheart is set in a fictional 1950s world often portrayed in movies, television, and other media. Fictionalized and stylized, it nevertheless contains elements inherent to that period that some readers may find upsetting.

Also from
TerrorScope Studios

Get the Rockin' Soundtrack Here

SCAN ME

Or search My Zombie Sweetheart on Spotify

Dedicated to sweethearts everywhere.

Once Upon a Time at a Drive-In

Imagine a world presented in the soft pastels of a colorized black-and-white film. A world presented in TerrorScope! A world only glimpsed as it's projected on a screen fifty feet high. One you look into as you sit in a car you borrowed from your folks. Maybe you're there with someone special, waiting for the chance to slip your arm around and pull them in close?

Outside your car, other kids hoot and holler. They toss popcorn like it's confetti. Part carnival, part theatre, welcome to the drive-in—a palace of young love, Friday night dreams, and wonder. There will never be anything quite like it again.

The trailers are done, the popcorn's warm, and the colas are cold, so settle down and watch as the credits roll and…

We open on a perfect night, the sky full of stars. The kind you only see from a backyard when you're ten years old. The kind that only ever shines over quiet little towns with white picket fences and treehouses strewn with half-read comic books and discarded candy wrappers. It's the start of the summer, and the magic is at its most potent. On nights like this, if you look up at the heavens, you might just see something truly out of this world.

"Woah!" shouts a boy as his hand shoots up into frame. He traces a trail of light that zips across the infinite, twinkling sea over his head. "D'you see that!?" The star disappears, and his fingers mime an explosion.

"Yeah!" says a girl lying on the grass next to him, and she giggles at the silly noises the boy makes.

1

"D'you know that all the stars in the sky are dead? Been for like years?"

"You are such a nerd," the girl replies, and they both laugh in that genuine, wholesome way you can only do when you're a kid. When you're a boy who doesn't care if a girl thinks you're square, and when you're a girl who doesn't care if a boy hears you snort like a pig.

This is Buddy and Suzie at ten years old. Two years till junior high would split them up. Before a cruel and heartless world would find pointless reasons to tear them apart. This is Suzie when she doesn't care that she's got Band-Aids on her knees from falling out of Buddy's treehouse. This is Buddy before he discovers the world isn't kind to boys like him. This is back when the two of them could lie on the grass, stare up at the sky, and not have a care in the world.

They giggle in spits and bursts until they simmer down to a quiet, contented hum.

Buddy, with his thick, black-framed glasses and the gap between his two front teeth that his parents say will go away eventually, even though he's already moved onto his adult teeth. Buddy, with the unfortunate bushy hair that even Suzie with her monogrammed pearl-handled brush can't tame. Buddy, lying on the grass next to his best friend in the whole world, Suzie.

Suzie, with her goofy, boyish smile that her mother says lacks the demure gentleness that befits a young woman. Suzie, with the pretty dresses all torn and grass-stained, and, yeah, her mother doesn't think this is ladylike either. Suzie, with the baby blue eyes that sparkle like the night sky. At least that's what Buddy has started thinking when he lies in bed at night. Suzie, lying on the grass next to her best friend in the whole world, Buddy.

The rush of giggles dies completely, and Suzie turns her baby blues to Buddy, but he doesn't notice. Against the soft caramel tone of his skin and the starlit night, his eyes seem wonderfully alive with joy. For a second, she's lost in the expansive brown of them. It makes her feel something flutter in the pit of her stomach. "B-u-ddy?" she asks.

"Yeah?" Buddy says, and when Suzie doesn't follow up, he takes his eyes off the sky and casts them at her. "Huh?"

Suzie just smiles. "Nothin'."

Buddy squints at her, and when she keeps smiling at him, he says, "Girls sure are weird."

Suzie pulls an over-dramatically hurt face, acting as though she wasn't trying to provoke him. "Nuh-uh, boys are the weird ones!"

"Nuh-uh," Buddy counters.

"Yeah-huh," Suzie insists.

"Nu—" Buddy tries to say, but Suzie shuts him up as she shoves a handful of grass into his open mouth.

Buddy sits up as he spits and tries to get the grass out. Suzie just laughs as her friend splutters away with little success.

"See! They eat grass," she says. "Boys are W-e-i-r-d weird with a big ole capital W like a cow! Moo!"

Buddy wipes his mouth, the remaining strands of grass getting in the way of his comeback. "You don't," he blows a straggler stuck to his lips away, "you don't spell cow with a capital W!"

"Moo! You'd know, Cow Boy!" Suzie says while she tosses a few more blades of grass Buddy's way. "Moo!" she snorts and thinks it's the funniest thing in the world, even if it makes no sense to anyone but her. She didn't

3

know what she wanted to say to Buddy, but she sure wanted his attention.

"Only 'cause some WEIRD girl went an' shoved it in my mouth!" Buddy attempts to explain and then thinks changing the subject might work better. "Girls are all, all sissy—" he stammers.

"You got a bug on you," Suzie says.

Buddy abandons his point and panics, slapping around his arms and legs. "Where? What is it, a tick? Ants? Please, God, don't let it be ants! Where!?"

Suzie just about dies laughing. She laughs so hard she falls onto her side and rolls around, not caring that she's wrecking the dress her mom just bought her.

Buddy gets the joke and gives her an "oh, ha-ha" look, but he knows when he's defeated, so he drops all arguments and gives up. Having been thoroughly debunked, he lies back down. After a few more unashamedly goofy giggle-snorts, Suzie joins him.

"Funny. Very funny," Buddy concedes after a moment of silence.

Suzie giggles, just a single victory snicker. "I know," she says.

"But, no foolin', girls can be sissy," Buddy says, and as he enters dangerous territory, Suzie raises an eyebrow. "Not you, though," he adds quickly, and Suzie relaxes that eyebrow. "I mean, you're hardly a girl." Both Suzie's eyebrows go up at that, but Buddy doesn't see the warning sign and plunges on. "And they like to scream at movies and are afraid of the dark and stuff. You know, sissy stuff."

Suzie props herself up on her elbows. "I'm not! You're scared of getting a shot! And, and you're scared of Mr. Frederickson's cat."

"That's different," Buddy says.

4

"How's that?" Suzie dares him to answer.

"That thing's evil! Like from outer space or something," Buddy explains, and Suzie can't see a fault in his argument, so she lets him have that. She tries not to think of the sheer number of times that cat has gone for her. Or how it's gotten her into trouble on account of how much it likes to tear up clothes. Or the time it chased Mrs. Willkes' Doberman down Oak Street. There's barely a kid in the whole neighborhood who doesn't live in fear of that tortoiseshell demon.

It's getting late, but the night's still warm, and neither of them wants to be anywhere else.

"Hey, Suzie?" Buddy says.

"Yeah B-u-ddy?" she answers back.

"How come you're not scared of the dark?"

"Huh?"

"Most girls are, I think," he says. "I think most kids are, actually. Not you, though. How come?"

Suzie shrugs. "I dunno…I never thought much about it. How come you're not, eh Cow Boy?"

"'Cause—shut up—my dad once told me," he points to the brightest star in the sky, "the thing about the dark is it lets you see what really shines."

Suzie drops her hand, and it lands right next to Buddy's. On instinct, both Buddy and Suzie's fingers crawl through the grass, moving to close that gap. Suzie's pinky finger grazes Buddy's. It's soft and sticky from the peanut butter and jam sandwiches Buddy's mom made them earlier. That's got to be why her mouth feels so dry, she thinks; the peanut butter, right? Buddy feels her touch, and it tickles him all over. He curls his little finger, and just as it closes around Suzie's—

"SUSAN CASSANDRA PALMER!"

The voice is shrill, yet it sounds like it erupts from the depths of Hell. It carries with it the pure, unbridled rage of a livid mother's indignation.

Both Buddy and Suzie sit right up with the backs of their necks on fire.

"How dare you!" the woman shrieks as she marches around the side of Buddy's house. She pushes open a low gate like she owns the place and demands again, "How dare you!?"

The kids quickly put some distance between themselves, for all the good it'll do.

"Imagine the disgrace, for Mrs. Goodman to tell me, to my face, where you were?" The woman rounds the corner, and we see that none of it shows for all her fury and bluster. She's beautiful, elegant, and poised; when her mouth is closed. "No, not my Susan, she's at her Girl Scouts meeting. Do you have any idea how degrading it was for that smug, fat little wretch to delightfully inform me she saw my daughter—*my* daughter—cavorting around with the negro boy on Sycamore!"

"Momma," Suzie tries to protest, but her mother's flat-out palm silences her.

"What's all the commotion?" says a warm voice from inside the house. A beat later, its owner steps out—a round, jovial man with his shirt untucked, suspenders hung free, and his gut in full repose.

"Mr. Day, were you aware my daughter was out here with your son?"

"Well, ma'am, I guess I did. Don't see the harm in it. They're just kids," Buddy's dad says. The inevitable parental conflict is a dance familiar to all kids, and both Buddy and Suzie are grateful for the temporary respite.

"For now, they're just kids, but what about when they grow up? What about when people start to talk?" Buddy's dad has this effect on people; he puts them at ease, but even with the wind taken out of her sails, Mrs. Palmer still has concerns.

"People generally do two things, Mrs. Palmer. Talkin' is one of them. The other I don't care to mention in polite company," the man says with a chuckle. Buddy's dad then remembers his manners. "Would you like to come in for a drink, ma'am? The wife's making this Chinese tea they say is good for the heart." He doesn't need to add that she sounds like she needs it.

"No," Mrs. Palmer says and then also remembers her manners. "No thank you, Mr. Day. Susan and I must be going."

Suzie's mother pats her thigh like she's calling for a dog to heel. Knowing she best do what her mother says, Suzie stands without protest, though she hides a sad goodbye wave to Buddy.

As mother and daughter leave, Buddy's dad calls out, "Goodnight!" with a kindhearted wave.

Somewhat flustered she's been called out on her etiquette twice in so many minutes, Suzie's mother returns the sentiment and resumes dragging her daughter away. She gets about halfway, then feels the need to go back and clarify. "Mr. Day, I want you to know I have no problem with your son being, um—"

"Black?" Mr. Day helps her out.

"Yes. Quite. I'll have you know that my husband and I both enjoy the music of Ray Charles."

"I see," Mr. Day says with a smirk, and the joke goes way over Mrs. Palmer's head.

"It's others, you see. Some people won't take too kindly to a young black man being seen around a young white girl, alone. I hope you understand?"

"I hear you, Mrs. Palmer, really I do, but maybe we should just let the kids be? Maybe they don't need to grow up like that?"

"I'm afraid we live in the real world, Mr. Day, and whether they know it or not yet, it doesn't matter. This is the way things are."

"Could be kids like them change that?" Mr. Day offers. "Kids who don't care one way or the other? Maybe that's the way things ought to go." He puts Suzie's mother in a tight spot. There's nothing he suggests that she personally finds all that objectionable, but the other mothers on the PTA and the Church Social Committee on the other hand...

"Buddy," Mrs. Palmer says and acknowledges the boy for the first time this evening, "you may play with Susan when other children are around and supervised."

"Okay," Buddy says, and for all his smarts, he's completely lost.

"I know you're a good boy, but there's been talk," she says, and it means nothing to Buddy, but he agrees anyway because she's Suzie's mother, and that's what you do. He doesn't want to get Suzie in any more trouble.

Done digging a hole, Mrs. Palmer bids Buddy and his dad good night and takes her daughter home.

Mr. Day watches his son wave goodbye to the pretty little blonde girl and lets out a heavy sigh. His boy's heart is on course for a hard break one of these days. It pains him to know it and to know he can't do a thing about it either. Despite it all, he can't help his optimistic nature, and the sight of those kids together does more for his overworked heart than any Chinese tea ever could.

Buddy, though, he's as oblivious to all that like only a ten-year-old can be. He lies back down on the grass and watches the twinkling lights dance across the night sky.

8

Oblivious, also, to the single pinprick of gleaming light that burns from something that very much wants us to think it's just a rock. It, like how he truly feels about Suzie Palmer, is years off from hitting home. Make no mistake; both are coming, and they each spell their own kind of doom for the boy.

Then and there, though, all Buddy cares about is the gentle summer night's breeze that feels welcome on his skin and the singing of the cicadas that sits just right on his ears. It's a good night and, given what's to come, we'll let him have it.

So let us pan up to the stars as, out of shot, Buddy's father turns up the radio and the soothing baritones of a barbershop quartet sing while words form from the burning, distant starlight:

The title card burns, along with all the stars, and night fades into day. A bright, sunny day…

FAST TIMES AT WOODVALE HIGH

A FEW YEARS LATER.

Not much has changed for Buddy Peter Day. He's still on the ground, looking up and seeing stars, though this time they come courtesy of Teddy Duchamp and Gordy Garcia.

We fade in, then pull down from one hell of a beautiful sky, robin's egg blue with wisps of white fluffy clouds, to a yellow school bus that pulls up outside Woodvale High. A few kids get off before we see Buddy step out. White button-down shirt, thick-rimmed glasses now held together by tape, and a backpack strapped way too tight. Not a bad looking kid; his eyes have only gotten kinder since we last saw him, though not that most people can tell with those thick glasses and the way he keeps his head down as he moves. Buddy's about two steps from the ground as Teddy saves him the effort with a quick shove he calls an accident before even making contact.

Buddy feels the pen in his shirt pocket crack. The ink seeps through to his skin as Teddy's sneakers land on the ground next to him. Buddy tries to get up, and he sees Gordy's hand reaching out to help. Not thinking, Buddy takes it only for Gordy to let go right away, causing Buddy to land hard on his ass. "Least that's already cracked," he says to himself.

10

"Sorry, man, fingers slipped," Gordy says as he wags his fingers with his hands held high. "My bad," he laughs as Teddy high-fives him.

"Real funny guys," Buddy mutters, though not quite quiet enough.

"Yo, you hear that, Ted? Buddy here reckons we're foolin' around with him," Gordy says with a pantomime of innocence.

"Let's help him up, show there's no hard feelings," Teddy says. He and Gordy hold a hand out for Buddy to take.

Buddy hesitates and weighs his options. He knows the two aren't genuine, but he figures it's easier to let them have their fun and move on. If he keeps up the fight, they'll just make it worse. So, prepared for what comes next, Buddy takes each of their hands.

The smirks on both of their faces come as no surprise as they yank him hard up off the ground and let go, sending him stumbling forward on his momentum. Two, three steps, then Buddy slams hard into a tree.

Teddy and Gordy walk off, looking from the back like twins in their matching blue and yellow Woodvale Hornets letterman jackets. They share another high-five as Buddy slumps down against the tree. He lets the dizzy spell pass as he casts an eye up at the sky. Through the leaves, he sees stars in bright daylight, and he can't decide what hurts more, his backside or his head. His shirt and mood already in ruins, and the day's only just begun.

Still, though, the sky looks pretty from down there.

That's a typical start to the day for Buddy. Want to know how it's going for Suzie Palmer? Cross-cut to: the halls of Woodvale High—full of girls in poodle skirts and boys with crew cuts and slick-backs. Paper pumpkins and skeletons line the walls with posters advertising Woodvale High's Halloween costume party in two weeks.

Just as Buddy gets helped off the bus outside, Suzie is at her locker, and boy is she pretty! The kind of pretty that just makes you smile to see it. She's like bottled sunshine in bobby socks, and she's forgotten to do her English homework again.

Of course, it doesn't even occur to Suzie to try and sweet-talk Mr. Jessop into letting it slide. It bothers her; she let herself forget, but it was a pretty eventful weekend. As she thinks back on it, she forgets she's forgotten her homework all over again. You see the problem here?

Suzie shuts her locker door, and there's the unashamedly mischievous smile that could only belong to Betty Blacker. Betty's the kind of girl that no matter what her name is, you spell it t-r-o-u-b-l-e, and boy does she know it. Betty works damn hard to make sure people know it too. Like the way she teases the lollipop she has in her mouth. Betty has no intention of eating it, but she learned that if she does that, then boys and teachers, mostly the male kind but not always, will do whatever. Some people say she's like Suzie's evil twin, right down to the contrasting jet-black hair.

Betty pops the lollipop out of her mouth. "Hey dolly," she says as she holds her head high and gives Suzie a look that says, "You got some 'splaining to do."

Suzie doesn't know what Betty's getting at. "Hey?" she says, but Betty wants to savor this, so she pops the lollipop back in, smirks, and raises her eyebrows in a way that says, "You know damn well what you did." Suzie knows this game, and she isn't up for playing. "Betty

12

Blacker, you spit that lollipop out right now, and while you're at it, whatever it is you're dying to say too."

Betty gives in. Usually, she'd milk this a little longer. If it were any of her other friends she'd make them squirm, but this is Suzie Palmer. Sweet Suzie, the keenest girl in school, and there's nothing Betty enjoys more than seeing a good girl, or boy, go a little bad. With great satisfaction, she says, "So I've been hearing that a certain Rock 'n' Roll Queen was playin' backseat bingo with a certain baseball stud last night…"

Suzie turns a shade of red usually reserved for stopping traffic and swings a fist playfully into Betty's arm. Betty acts wounded, but the look of pure joy on her face shows through. "I did not!" Suzie protests.

"Don't give me that same old Saint Suzie bit," Betty laughs. "We all saw you two go off together to his car. Now a good friend kisses and tells…"

"So? He just gave me a ride home. Big deal. Quit buggin' me!" Suzie explains, hoping nobody is close enough to hear what Betty's saying or, by lunchtime, all the kids, the teachers, the janitor, and his hamster will have heard about it.

"Uh-huh," Betty says with an eyebrow arch that says, "I'm not buying it."

"Seriously," Suzie insists.

"Uh-huh," Betty says again, more of a question this time. Suzie just nods, and Betty's hopes fall. Boy, was she looking forward to getting a few questions answered about that specific baseball stud. "But you were wearing his letters. You're jacketed, right?"

Suzie shrugs a "Who knows," and she spins on her heels as she heads off to class.

Betty follows. "Oh, come on! Quit being such a drag. I told you the day after Teddy 'n' I necked out at the drive-in, so come on, spill!"

"Sure, then you also told me about doing the same with Gordy Garcia. Not to mention that time with Stan Pearce at camp, and Bill Weiss during study hall." Suzie runs down the list as she walks ahead of Betty.

"See! There's my point; you owe me! Come on, Suzie! Come on!" Betty begs, but Suzie doesn't give in. She's starting to see why Betty enjoys teasing people so much. It's kinda fun, and she thanks her lucky stars Betty didn't see the jacket hanging in her locker, the yellow and blue lettered jacket with the name Dash emblazoned across the back.

Cut to: outside Woodvale High as the school bell rings. A 1932 Ford Deuce roars up to the school, and the driver kills the engine after it pulls into a parking space marked for teaching staff. The driver doesn't care; he knows nobody is going to make a thing of it. Same deal with the bell, sure he's supposed to be sitting in Mr. Cormac's science class, but that doesn't mean he can't take the time to finish his smoke. It's precisely that attitude that simultaneously makes him one of the best ballplayers Woodvale High has ever seen and keeps him held back two grades, but that's not so bad all things considered. Not with that cutie Suzie Palmer in class with him.

Cut to: Mr. Cormac's science class. Buddy walks in with his glasses askew and a splat of black ink over his chest. He catches the eye of Johnny Freemantle, his friend and fellow lifetime resident of Woodvale High's unofficial outcast society.

14

"The hell happened to you?" Johnny asks.

"Got shot by an angry squid. Would have got him back, but he gave me the slip," Buddy says as he finds his seat, then he goes about unpacking his books.

Some of the girls behind him are chatting, and Buddy can't help but overhear. When the first one says, "D'you hear Suzie Palmer's going steady wi—" Buddy's heart drops, and when the other girl interrupts with, "Yeah, oh my gosh, can you believe it," his heart sinks right down. "Asked her out right after the Rock 'n' Roll Ball, I heard. Right after—"

Suzie walks into the classroom with a slightly out of breath Betty hot on her tail. Their sudden appearance shuts up all the gossip. Most of the kids in the class have their eyes on Suzie. Not Buddy, though; he tries not to look at her much at all these days. "Hey Bud—" she goes to say before she's almost deafened by Betty's squeal calling out, "Teddy! Teddy, stop!" as her current boyfriend puts his arms around her from behind. Teddy goes right for all her ticklish spots with precise familiarity.

Mr. Cormac enters the class and puts a stop to all that. "This is a classroom, Miss Blacker, Mr. Duchamp, not a county fair. Please take your seats." They both do but not without Teddy trying to sneak in a few more grabs at Betty, who dodges most of them but lets the guy goose her just a little. The teacher begins roll call, and without looking up says, "Blacker, we know you're here. Please get rid of that thing in your mouth, this is a classroom and not a candy store." Mr. Cormac being one of those teachers her tricks don't work on, Betty does as she's told.

Suzie sticks her tongue out at Betty. She gets her back by nodding towards the empty seat at the back of the class and blowing some taunting kisses. Buddy sees the exchange, and it all clicks into place as Mr. Cormac calls out, "Day?"

Buddy doesn't respond. The idea of Suzie and Dash together makes him feel like blowing chunks all over the place.

Teddy takes advantage of the silence and coughs, "Queer," though he doesn't hide it all that well. Most of the class giggles.

"That's enough, Mr. Duchamp," Mr. Cormac demands. "Domico?" he calls, but there's no answer. He looks around the class and spots the empty seat in the back. "No Danny today?" he says without any concern. There might even be a hint of well-reserved relief.

"Here," says Danny "Dash" Domico as he strolls into the classroom.

"So nice of you to join us, Mr. Domico; class starts at nine, you know?"

Dash shrugs. "Coach needed to see me," he lies, knowing full well Mr. Cormac doesn't buy it and that it doesn't make a difference either way. As long as Dash keeps carrying the team up the league, he's got a golden ticket to do whatever the hell he wants. And though resigned to this fact, Mr. Cormac had hoped the boy repeating his class twice would have picked up enough to manage a pass. A part of him worries he's died, gone to Hell, and his torture is trying to make Danny Domico understand biology for all eternity. From the number of pretty young things hanging from his arms over the years, it seems he's got the basics down, at least.

"Fine," Mr. Cormac says. "Just take your seat if you will."

Dash walks past Buddy's desk, but he's so preoccupied with winking at Suzie that he accidentally knocks Buddy's books to the floor. "Careful where you put those," he says, and then he catches Buddy's eye. There's something there, a hint of fire that burns for just a moment. Buddy Peter Day isn't much more than another little bug that he occasionally enjoys pulling the legs off of, but suddenly, this nerd gives him a look that he wouldn't take from anyone. Least of all, a kid with the muscle tone of a wet paper towel. It passes, but just for a second there, it looked like Buddy was going to start something. Dash thinks that maybe he ought to put Buddy in his place again before he gets any ideas.

Mr. Cormac goes through the rest of the roll call. "Palmer?"

Suzie calls out, "Here!" and Mr. Cormac looks up.

"I hear congratulations are in order, Miss Palmer. Good job."

"Thank you, sir!" Suzie says while ignoring the faces Betty pulls at her.

Bridge and fade a little later into class. Buddy stares at an ant farm with Johnny beside him. There's the clack of chalk on board as Mr. Cormac writes up his lesson.

"Moron," says Johnny, though Buddy's not paying attention. He's lost in thoughts about how much easier life would be if he were an ant. Of course, he realizes they all serve a single queen, and most die for her, so maybe not. Plus, the damn things creep him out.

"Mr. Oh-I-can-hit-a-ball-with-a-stick."

"Huh?" Buddy says, looking up from the ants.

"Dash," Johnny answers.

"What about him?" Buddy asks.

"He's a moron," Johnny explains.

"Oh," Buddy says, "yeah."

Johnny is a little concerned for his friend. "What's up with you today?" he asks, but Buddy doesn't answer. Johnny follows Buddy's line of sight right to Suzie and her friends as they horse around, minus Dash, who needed the bathroom a half-hour ago and left without a hall pass, and it isn't hard for Johnny to get the picture. Johnny might be slow on the track, but he gets the drift as far as matters of the heart are concerned.

Teddy tries to scare Betty with one of their ant farms, and she squeals like it's the scariest thing though it's more than a little put-on. "Teddy! Teddy, don't!" Betty screams. "You know those things give me the creeps after that stupid movie."

Teddy laughs while pretending to take the ant farm away. "What movie you talkin' about, babe?"

"The one with the damn ANTS—NO-GET-IT-AWAY!" Betty screams as Teddy whips the thing back into her face. She grabs the ant farm from him, and her whole body tenses up as she delicately puts it down, away from Teddy, making as little contact with it as she can. "The one we saw last weekend at the Paradiso. With the giant freakin' ants!"

"Babe, I ain't seen that one yet…" Teddy says, and Suzie bites her tongue, knowing all too well who took Betty to the drive-in.

"Oh," Betty says as she remembers it was Gordy who took her out to that movie. She kicks herself for forgetting. His car even broke down racing some fools on the way back, and she ended up having to walk back into town just so the tow truck guy didn't see them together. Just in case word got around. "Must have been with my folks," Betty says like butter wouldn't melt, and Teddy, luckily for her, is dumb enough to buy it.

18

Dash picks that moment to strut back into class, and even from across the room, Buddy and Johnny can smell the waft of cigarette smoke that follows. He walks right over and puts his arm around Suzie, and Buddy dies a little inside as she leans into him. It's not that he's jealous, he tells himself, it's that he thought Suzie knew better.

"Yeah," Johnny says, "so it's Suzie Palmer he's goin' steady with this week...hey, weren't you guys—"

"Okay, class!" Mr. Cormac interrupts and saves Buddy from answering. "Mr. Domico, Mr. Duchamp, stop that please, leave Miss Blacker alone and listen up! Today we're finishing off our study of hive-minded insects. I want you all to..."

The class goes on without much else of note happening till the bell rings, and most of the kids are out of there before Mr. Cormac can plead for them to tidy away the ant farms. Buddy and Johnny are the only ones who bother to clean up; they stay behind to help Mr. Cormac put away the rest. As the two of them leave, they find Dash waiting for them down the hall.

Dash doesn't mess around. He's not like Teddy or Gordy; he's not foolin'. No, he grabs Buddy by the back of his shirt, spins him around, and slams him hard into the closest lockers. "You eye-ballin' my girl?" he says. "Huh, Four-Eyes?"

"C'mon D—" Johnny attempts to plead.

"This doesn't concern you, Square. Leave. Now." Dash commands. Johnny looks to Buddy for permission, and Buddy nods. No sense in the two of them getting their butts kicked after all. Johnny, wracked with guilt but grateful as all get-out, gets the hell out of there. Dash turns his attention back to Buddy. "I saw you eye-ballin' my girl. I saw that look you gave me." Dash takes

Buddy's pen from his shirt pocket, and Buddy makes a mental note to stop keeping them there. "Do it again and see this pen—" Dash shakes Buddy. "Look at the pen, dipshit!"

Buddy looks down his nose at the pen.

"I'll take this pen and stick it so far up your nose your mom will think you've grown a horn." Just to drive his point home, Dash pushes the tip of the pen up into Buddy's nose, just a little, but enough to nick, and Buddy feels a few drops of blood run down to his lips. "Got it?"

Buddy nods, as much as he can, and Dash lets him go. With his back to the wall, Buddy doesn't know where to go with Dash still in his way. Dash looks over the fine, well-crafted fountain pen and figures it must be worth a few bucks even with the monogram. "Nice pen," he says as he pockets it. Dash pats down Buddy's shirt with a condescending harshness and notes the ink spot. "Need a new shirt, don't ya Nosebleed." And with that, Dash leaves Buddy alone with his shame.

Johnny slinks back round the corner just as Buddy wipes a tear away from his cheek. "Hey man, you okay?" Johnny asks.

"Yeah," Buddy says, "I'm just boss."

PAPER-SHAKERS AND HEART-BREAKERS

Want to know what else is boss? Cut to: a sweet home run from Dash during gym class at the end of the school day. If Eisenhower wants to get us into space so bad, he should give that boy a call. He could send us to the moon with that arm.

Pull back from the field, and we have the girls, Suzie and Betty, and they sit with another two on the bleachers. All four of them in cheerleading uniforms. The other two, they're Connie Grayson and Christina Cole. Connie's a fuzzy duck, the kind of girl who doesn't step outside the shadow cast by her social circle's leader, and that leader is unquestionably Christina Cole.

The best way to describe Christina is to take the well-cultivated bad girl attitude of Betty, strip away the underlying lack of self-confidence so all that's left is bad, and mix it with Suzie's looks without the sugar. Yeah, Christina's got an attitude you can just see by looking at her. She was on a specific trajectory in life. See, Christina was always the prettiest, the center of attention, the Queen of gosh-darn everything.

Then something happened. Suzie stopped wearing grass-stained dresses to school. She stopped having perpetually skinned knees and learned how to brush her hair. People noticed Suzie Palmer, and suddenly Christina Cole was forced to share her limelight. What makes things worse is Christina can't find much she can use to bring Suzie down. Suzie's light shines too damn bright to cast any real shade, and if you think Christina is to Suzie what Dash is to Buddy, you're half-right. A guy like Dash will tell you to your face he's gonna mess you up. A girl like Christina is more likely to slip a little poison in your ear until you do it yourself.

Christina's still pissed Suzie kicked her ass at the Dance-Off, walking away with the prize that should have been hers, and we're not talking about any trophy. We're talking about Danny "Dash" Domico.

Speaking of the devil, here he comes. Dash steps back up to the plate without a care in the world. Secure in the knowledge that he's the lord of the diamond and the King of Woodvale High. He throws a nod over to his Queen on the bench.

All the other kids on the field, you can see it in their faces—they know trying to catch a ball hit by Dash is like a mortal trying to grab a bolt of lightning sent by Zeus. None of them even want to try, but Coach won't stand for that, and Dash, he's as bored with it as can be. It's routine. The only person on or around that field who cares is Suzie, who jumps up to her feet right as the ball hits the bat, and an echo of wooden thunder rips out.

Suzie sits back down. "Woo!" she says. "That was unreal."

Christina rolls her eyes and chimes, "A bit of advice, don't seem too eager."

Suzie looks confused; she's generally a pretty eager person, so she wasn't too outside herself cheering and whooping like that. Okay, maybe a little. Perhaps Dash's casual strut around the bases while Tim Dorothy searches the bushes out by the parking lot for the ball makes her feel all kinds of funny in her stomach. Still, there was no need for Christina to put her down, and

22

Betty agrees. "Come on, let the girl have her kicks!" she says and gives Christina a playful shove.

Christina ignores her. She's fine with Suzie having her kicks, just not *her* kicks.

So, where is Buddy right now? Do you want to take a guess? Yeah, he's in the school library, cut there and get your no-prize. He's got a science book open, but he's not reading—he's doodling on a sheet of paper instead. And wanna know something? His doodles are pretty good, a skinny little bug-eyed nerd getting lifted off the ground by a gorilla in a baseball cap. They're pretty relevant, too.

Johnny comes in and dumps his backpack on Buddy's desk, scattering a few papers, but Buddy doesn't notice. "Hey man," Johnny says, but Buddy's way too into his drawings. "Hey?" Johnny reaches over and grabs Buddy's paper, and that gets his friend's attention. Buddy shields his work as Johnny says, "So you're alive then!"

"Yeah. Yeah, I'm just…" Buddy says the rest without a word.

"Hey man, don't let it get to you," Johnny says as he makes himself more comfortable. He looks around, checks there's no teachers or librarian about, then he slips a couple of Pixy Stix from his backpack. He downs two before offering Buddy one, but Buddy declines, and Johnny pours the rest down his throat with a shrug.

"Way I see it is, so what if Dash wants to cream you. Big deal. He's been doing that on and off since forever. It's, what d'you call it? Poutine! No, wait, that's Canadian fries. Routine! It's routine," Johnny says as he pontificates with the Pixy Stix.

"Johnny," Buddy says as he gives his friend a look. "Anyone ever tell you you're a big tickle?"

"All the time, my friend, all the time. It's a curse, sincerely," Johnny says, and Buddy doesn't have anything to add to that. Mr. Jessop, the English teacher, does though.

"No, boys, the only curse around here goes by the name Johnathan Freemantle," he says, and Johnny tries to slide deep enough into his chair that he disappears. "Now, hand it over."

The teacher holds his hand out, and Johnny reluctantly gives him the few Pixy Stix he has left. That's not enough for the teacher, though, who keeps his hand out and says, "What about the rest?" Very reluctantly, Johnny takes the rest of his stash, including a bag of potato chips and some Hot Tamales out of his backpack and hands them over. "You know, Mr. Freemantle, a little less of these and a little more time out in the sun, and maybe your shirt would fit," Mr. Jessop sneers as he slips Johnny's confiscated candy into his coat pocket. He seems satisfied with his work until the teacher catches a glimpse of the inkblot and speckled blood on Buddy's shirt. "Young man, I have no idea what your standards might be at home, but at Woodvale High, we have decorum. Clean yourself up, or don't bother showing up in my class."

Buddy knows no adult at this school, with any kind of influence, gives a crap what the boys in blue and yellow do to kids like him, so he apologizes for the state of his clothes and nods along. His dad once told him sometimes people are just bad news, but they ain't so bitter with a side of apple butter.

Mr. Jessop walks off, and once he's safely out of earshot, Johnny hits out with, "Yeah, and maybe if you undid that bowtie a little, your hot head would deflate."

Buddy snickers. "You should totally say that to his face."

"One of these days I'm gonna," Johnny says. "One of these days I'm gonna rip that stupid bowtie off his neck and watch his head whizz around the room like a balloon."

The boys laugh.

"I'm gonna get that candy back even if I have to bust open his guts," Johnny adds, and, when he's sure the coast is once again clear, he opens up a zippered pocket inside his backpack and takes out a well-worn, beaten up candy bar. Johnny looks over its mangled shape before shrugging, ripping it open, and shoving it in his mouth.

"How long has that been in there?" Buddy asks, and Johnny gives him a mumbled, mouthful response that roughly translates as "Who knows."

"So," Johnny says as he picks the leftover chocolate from between his teeth with his tongue, "you wanna hang tonight?"

"Nah," Buddy says. "Not really in the mood."

"You sure? Cousin's out of town, so I borrowed," which means without permission, "his car. Drive down to Cherry Lake and catch the spookshow?" Buddy stalls, trying to think up an excuse. He's been running out of them lately, but he just can't find the drive to get out and do anything. Johnny seesaws between Boris Karloff and Vincent Price impressions as he acts all spooky and says, "Come wiv' me, Buddy, to witness the Creature from the Black Lagoon!" Then he laughs like a madman, not caring a bit for the dirty looks the other kids give him.

Buddy, deadpan: "Nah, it's cool."

Johnny, defeated: "Yeah…I suppose watching a beauty queen get pawed at by a slimy monster is a bit close to home." The words come out and he regrets them immediately. Buddy quits on him right there, gets his stuff together, and shoves it into his backpack. "Shit, man, Buddy, I didn't mean that." Buddy just ignores him. "Sincerely, man, I'm sorry," Johnny pleads.

Buddy lets go of a little tension. "It's okay Johnny, I'm just…"

"We cool?" Johnny asks.

"Yeah," Buddy says, but Johnny can tell he's not feeling it.

"Sincerely?" Johnny asks with puppy dog eyes, and he puts his hand up for a high-five. Buddy hits it, the earnestness of his friend defusing him, and he even manages a smile. "I hate to be a pill, but did you finish zat shtuff for Herr Schneider?" Johnny asks as he slips into an awful German accent and he gives Buddy a big, chocolate-stained grin.

Buddy rolls his eyes. "Sure," he says as he takes some papers out of his bag and hands them to Johnny. Too late, he realizes he's handed over one of his drawings, and Johnny gets a good eyeful of it. It's a drive-in not unlike the Paradiso over in Cherry Lake, only the giant ant on the screen is stepping out of it with a few crushed cars under its feet and a hapless teenager in a blue and yellow letterman jacket clutched between its mandibles.

"Wow, man, that's awesome!" Johnny says. Buddy pulls his drawing away and shoves it back into his backpack with little concern for keeping it intact. "You gotta show me more of that stuff, sincerely, man, please."

Buddy ignores that. "Just change enough of it so Schneider doesn't catch on."

"Will do, thanks, man!" Johnny says. Then, as Buddy stands up: "Where you goin'?"

"Didn't you hear Jessop?" Buddy says. "Gotta go see about a sink before he has another hissy fit."

Buddy leaves Johnny to copy his homework and makes for the nearest bathroom. No amount of splashing and soaking his shirt does the trick, though, and the brick-hard bar of soap only seems to make things worse. So he says, "To hell with it," and takes his shirt off and jams it into the bin. There's no saving it, and he doesn't want the questions his mom will undoubtedly ask if she sees the state of it. He'd rather drop dead twice than let her know what's going on. He's not keen on just wearing a t-shirt to school, even if most of Dash's crew do just that, but he figures it'll do for the rest of the day. Not even a moldy old teacher like Mr. Jessop says boo to them—even with a deck of Luckies tucked into their sleeves.

When Buddy catches sight of himself in the mirror, he notices that a few blood spots made it onto his t-shirt. This day, he's drowning in it, and Buddy thinks it can't get any worse. He's dead wrong on that one.

There's a squeak of shoes on the linoleum outside and the squeal of a girl laughing. It sounds very much like whoever the noises belong to are on their way into the bathroom. Buddy does a quick check to make sure he's actually in the boys' room and, if the smell wasn't enough, there are the urinals to confirm it. His instincts tell him to hide, so Buddy slips into one of the stalls, shuts the door, and pulls his feet up just in time.

"Wait-wait-wait!" It's a girl's voice, and Buddy recognizes it. "Gordy, wait!" It's Betty Blacker, but as far as Buddy knew, she's been goin' steady with Teddy Duchamp since forever.

"Baby, you know I can't when you're lookin' so good," says the guy she's with, and there's no doubt it's Gordy Garcia.

27

Damn, sure there were rumors about Betty being kind of a runaround, but Buddy never gave much credence to gossip. Would Teddy still give his brother in letters a high-five if he knew that paw had been all over his girl?

"Gordy, we can't! Not here!" Betty pouts. Despite her protests, she doesn't sound like she minds all that much.

"Baby, there's less chance anyone's gonna see us here than at the passion pit, and you weren't so frazzled there," Gordy says, and Betty giggles.

"Just—" Betty cuts herself off with a kind of moan Buddy's never heard a girl make before.

Then the school bell cuts in.

"Shit," Gordy sighs.

Buddy can hear a quick ruffle of clothes, and then Betty says, "Come over on Sunday night. I'll have the house to myself after eight."

"What about Teddy?" Gordy asks, and there's more in his voice than the fear of getting caught. Jealousy?

"What Teddy doesn't know," Betty doesn't finish, but Buddy hears her blow Gordy a kiss and then duck out of the bathroom. He waits for Gordy to leave, but the guy sticks around a bit. Through the crack in the stall, Buddy sees Gordy go to the sink and stare at his reflection.

"The hell are you doin' man," Gordy asks himself. "You ain't no bird dog. She's Teddy's girl…"

Any ideas Buddy might have had about letting this news slip out vanish as he listens to Gordy. There's something in his voice—honesty, and a sense of regret. It speaks to Buddy, and even though he'd like nothing more than to get back at Gordy, Teddy, and the rest of Dash's crew, this isn't it. With his heart hardened as much as it is, Buddy's not ready to accept that the real reason why is that he feels sorry for Gordy. Because, all things considered, he can relate.

It plays on Buddy's mind for the rest of the day. All the way up to when the bell unleashes a bunch of screaming kids out into the world. Out into the wide-open wonderland of Friday night. Date night.

The school day ends with Dash and his boys whooping as he pulls out of the parking lot in his Deuce. He honks at the girls as he rips past them. Suzie and Betty wave the car off as they head home together. Then there's Buddy, who walks home alone because he missed the bus while trying to stay out of Dash's way.

On his walk, Buddy tries his best not to think about Suzie. Specifically about the stupid thing that idiot Johnny said. Specifically because maybe it wasn't so dumb after all. It's not like Suzie was ever his girl. Yeah, they were friends—best friends, or so he thought—back when they were little, but that was before. This past year, she's only said half a dozen words to him, and most of them were just things like, "Hey, Buddy."

That's not her fault, though, and Buddy knows it. He's done all he can to keep the distance between them despite hating himself for it.

Suzie wasn't his girl, never was, and never could be. He never even thought of her like that. So why does it burn him that she's with Dash now? Why should he care? It's not like he was into her or anything; at least that's what he tells himself. But if that were true, why would he even have to say so? Why would he have to keep the thought from bouncing around like a rubber ball inside his head if she wasn't just the bee's knees? If he wasn't secretly, in the very core of his heart, madly in love with Suzie Palmer?

DATE NIGHT

Cut to: the Day house, a blue and white box where everything looks just a little off. Buddy walks in through the front door and dumps his backpack. The smell of his mom's cooking hits his nose, but even that does nothing to lift his spirits.

"That you, Buddy?" she calls from the kitchen.

"Yeah, mom…" Buddy answers as he walks into the lounge and freezes. That's not his mom on the couch; it's Mrs. Frederickson with a beehive on her head and a snarling cat on her lap.

"H-hi," Buddy says, and the cat yawns, showing off its fangs.

"Hello Buddy," she says with a smile, but Buddy can't get past that cat being right in the middle of his living room—where he and his folks watch TV—and just about flips his wig.

Mrs. Day peels some oven gloves off as she comes out of the kitchen. She's the kind of mother who doesn't realize she's every boy's not-so-secret crush. There's a reason why Johnny Freemantle is always happy to come over for dinner, and it's not just the cooking. Mrs. Day doesn't go in for fancy clothes or trendy hairstyles. She keeps it simple, lets her bouncing curls do whatever, and that just so happens to frame her golden honey, smiling face perfectly. Her preference for simple dresses and skirts show off her heart-breaking curves with zero distractions. Buddy hears, "Say hi to your mom for me," a hell of a lot. Usually, from Johnny.

The Fredericksons' cat flexes its claws.

"Dana, I'm sorry, but it appears the cat's gotten Buddy's tongue," Mrs. Day says, and the look on the cat's face says it thinks that's a swell idea.

His mother gives Buddy a look that says: I know you have better manners than that. The shame of being a pill hits, but at least it keeps her from asking what happened to his shirt. He doesn't need his mom going out to fight his battles or, worse, telling him some dumb line about how all the other kids are just jealous.

"Sorry. Hi, Mrs. Frederickson," Buddy says as he walks over to her and kisses his mother on the cheek. She wears a red blouse that matches her lipstick, which is dressing up for her. Because tonight, after all, is date night.

"Say hi, Mr. Dinkles," Mrs. Frederickson says and forces the cat to wave its paw. She puts on a silly baby voice. "I just stopped by with my Mummy to use the oven because Daddy broke it lighting his pipe!"

"Okay," Buddy says. "Hi"—the cat gives him a look that implies he'll regret this—"Mr. Dinkles."

"Tough day?" Mrs. Day asks her son.

"Just a day," he answers as she ruffles his hair playfully.

"Think it's about time you got a haircut, sweetie?" she asks, and Buddy pushes her hand away. "I'll drive you down to Red's tomorrow if you like."

"Cut it, mom. I don't want to."

"Okay, sure, I've got some scissors around here. I guess I could just—"

"Mom!"

Buddy's sudden forcefulness sets Mrs. Day back a bit. It's not like him to lash out. "Okay, okay," she relents. "You kids, I'll never," she sighs. "Dinner in an hour. If your father's late again, he just gets it cold, and we'll just have a little date night at home without him."

"Mom! No."

Mrs. Day smiles at him in the hopes of embarrassing him out of his mood. It doesn't work.

"Can I just go to my room and read some comics?" Buddy asks.

"Sure," Mrs. Day sighs as she gives up.

Buddy heads over to the stairs when Mrs. Frederickson says, "Oh, I saw that friend of yours on TV today!"

"What friend?" Buddy asks with genuine wonder. It's not like he's got a lot of them.

"You know, that girl. The pretty one with the blonde hair?"

"Dana—" Mrs. Day tries to cut in.

"Sally? Sandy? Something like that. You know the one? You two used to be such good..." Mrs. Fredrickson trails off. "Anyway, she won some dance-off with that crazy man on the radio. Howling Bill? Is that his name?"

"It's Rockin' Hill Billy," Buddy answers and shudders on the inside. Suddenly the wild man DJ doesn't seem so cool anymore.

"Yeah, that's the one," Mrs. Frederickson says. "What was your friend's name again?"

"We're not friends," Buddy says.

"Oh? But I'm sure you two—Sarah? Was that it?"

"We're not friends!" Buddy lashes out. "Just cut it out!"

Mrs. Frederickson recoils, and Buddy's mom steps in. "Buddy Peter Day, you watch your tone!"

Buddy tenses up, tears forming in the corner of his eyes. "Just," his voice wavers, and it seems impossible that all that fight from just a moment ago came from him. He looks on the verge of breaking, and it cuts his mom deep. "Mom, please just…can we leave it?"

Full of guilt and concern, Mrs. Day just nods. "Okay…okay," she says. "Maybe you should go for a lie-down."

"Okay, mom," Buddy says, but he just stands there. His mind's full of stuff he doesn't understand, nor does he want to. He doesn't get why the mention of Suzie sets him off so. It's not like they've been close recently, it's not like they've hung out in years. Besides, it was his idea to put the freeze on their friendship. Still, it's biting him, and he feels like a real heel for snapping at his mom like that.

"Okay, on you go," Mrs. Day says, and Buddy takes a few steps towards the hall, then stops.

"Mom," he says as he turns to face her. "Sorry." To their guest, "Sorry, Mrs. Frederickson."

Mrs. Day smiles, happy to see that sweet, caring boy of hers once again and nods as Buddy heads to his room. She watches him go, and in the silence that follows him a newscaster's voice fills the house from the TV.

"Isn't that something? Now, folks, you might want to look up at the sky a little later on. Those boys up at the college reckon there's gonna be a spectacular show up there for us tonight."

Mrs. Day isn't paying attention, though. All she can think is that it's a girl, of course, it's a girl. A pretty white girl, and not just any girl at that—it's got to be *that* girl. She lets out a heavy sigh because she knows that no matter how any of this plays out, it's not going to be good for her son.

While Buddy slams himself face-down on his bed and waits for the rest of the world to disappear, cut to: Suzie

33

as she looks herself up and down in a full-length mirror that commands her corner bedroom. It's like something out of a fairy tale, complete with the princess it reflects. She holds a yellow summer dress up against her body; it's so new it still has the tags and the cinnamon and clementine scent of Sal's Boutique.

Suzie's so lost in whatever daydream the dress is sparking that she doesn't notice her mother, standing in the doorway looking at her daughter like a proud momma bird. "What's the tale nightingale?" she asks her little girl, and Suzie turns and smiles.

"What do you think, mom?" Suzie asks.

Mrs. Palmer enters the room and takes a good look at her daughter. It fills her with so much pride to see her like this. Her hair in a cute little pageboy cut instead of matted with mud and tangled up with bits of grass. It's enough to bring a genuine, flawed smile to her prim and proper face. "I think," Mrs. Palmer says, "my Baby Girl's got herself a date, and she's not told her dear old mother a thing about it!"

Suzie gasps, "Mom!" as her mother feigns outrage.

"I'm heartbroken, I am. My little girl," Mrs. Palmer says. Though she only wipes away a pretend tear, she's not that far from the real kind.

"Aw mom, don't," Suzie says as she puts the dress down. "Mom, seriously, I'm just going to the All-Night with Betty, then Connie's gonna drive us down to Cherry Lake."

"Uh-huh," Mrs. Palmer says, and it's clear she's not buying what Suzie is selling.

"Mom," Suzie insists though she doesn't know that her mother has acquired a bit of an inside scoop.

"And if a certain Mr. Danny Domico happens to be there, then it's just a coincidence, huh?" Mrs. Palmer

34

smirks with a self-satisfied delight, like she's a cat that got all the cream there is.

Suzie gasps and feels the burn of her cheeks as they turn red. The embarrassment has her flustered like she's never been before. "Mom! How did—"

"Betty called while you were in the shower," Suzie's mom interrupts.

"I'm gonna kill her," Suzie says as she pictures that face-wide grin Betty would have had after making that call. "I'm, I'm—"

"Now, now. At least your friend understands that a mother worries," Mrs. Palmer says, though she can hardly contain herself.

"I'm gonna—" Suzie just knows Betty's on her back, legs in the air, kicking as she laughs. She can practically hear her, and even though she feels the need to, Suzie can't think of a way to get even. She just doesn't have that in her, and Betty's made such a name for herself that there's not much you can say about her she won't wear as a badge of honor just for the fun of it.

"Worries herself to death," Mrs. Palmer continues as she delights a little longer in her daughter's embarrassment. "Imagine the scandal! My daughter, runnin' around with all sorts of boys…"

"This! This is why I didn't say anything, oh god—" Suzie sits on the chest by her window.

Mrs. Palmer decides she's finally had her fill, so she joins her daughter by the window. She puts her arm around her and says, "He's a lucky boy, you know."

"Mom—" Suzie tries to speak, but her mother interrupts her.

"Shh," she says as she brushes aside her daughter's hair and looks into the soft, baby blue of her eyes. "Where did I get such a pretty daughter from?" Suzie scrunches her face up to look ugly, but it only makes her look cuter, and her mother ignores it anyway. "You used to be such a tomboy. All muck 'n' mud. You and that Day boy playin' spacemen—now look at you!" Tears of real, honest pride well up in her eyes.

"So, can I still go out?" Suzie asks, and her mother hugs her tight. Suzie hugs her back just as hard.

"Of course you can, dear," Suzie's mother says. "Let's not tell your father, though."

After that moment of sweet mother-daughter bonding, we cut to: Buddy as he lies on his bed reading a comic book. There's a knock at his door, and after waiting a moment, Buddy's dad slides into the room. Even though he's built like a dock worker (who went on to become a pie-eating champion), Mr. Day is as gentle as a church mouse and moves with an unexpectedly sensitive grace.

"Hey there, my best Buddy," he says, using some of that patented dad humor to disarm his son.

"Hi, dad," Buddy says.

"The Boss Lady sent me. Dinner time," Mr. Day points his thumb out of the room.

"Okay," Buddy says as he puts his comic down and gets up off his bed. The quiet compliance confirms what his wife told him when he got in.

"Say…anything buggin' you?" Mr. Day asks his son.

"I'm okay, dad," Buddy answers, though he doesn't really sell it.

"You sure?" Buddy's dad asks.

"Uh-huh," Buddy insists.

"Listen, the Boss Lady said you got a bit, a bit…when Susan Palmer…" Buddy's dad dances around the idea.

36

"I'm…fine," Buddy says, hoping if he keeps saying it, it'll turn out true.

"Okay," Buddy's dad says all cheerful-like, hoping it'll catch. "If you say so, kiddo. Come on, let's eat."

While the Day family sits down to Friday night dinner, we cut to: Suzie as she walks down the stairs wearing that yellow summer dress, her dad standing at the bottom. He watches her like a big papa bear; his hands tucked into his belt like they're in tight competition for real estate with his gut.

"Howdy Pardner," Mr. Palmer says. "Boy howdy, don't you look purty Miss, I tell you what!"

Suzie giggles. "Stop it, dad," she says even though she loves it when he puts on the pretend cowboy act. Mr. Palmer might be an accountant in life, but he's a high-plains drifter at heart.

"Headin' out?" he asks.

"Yeah, just waiting for—" The doorbell interrupts. "Betty."

Both Suzie and her dad laugh while outside the door, Betty mumbles, "Don't leave me hangin' here, girl!"

"Gotta book, dad," Suzie says, then kisses him on the cheek. "See you later," she says, and Mr. Palmer doesn't know it yet, but those six innocuous words are ones he'll never forget.

Suzie heads out the door to greet Betty, who wears a long, gray pencil skirt and a suspiciously buttoned-up jacket. The two of them link arms and giggle on their way down the drive.

"Have fun, Missy," Mr. Palmer calls after his daughter.

"Will do, dad!" Suzie calls back.

Mr. Palmer is joined by his wife, and the two watch till their daughter and her friend are out of sight. Even though it's the most normal thing in the world, that moment will play on repeat in their heads for the rest of their lives.

THE INCIDENT AT
MAKE-OUT POINT

While Buddy's eating with his folks and Suzie's on her
way out with her friend, we cut to: Dash's 1932 Ford
Deuce.

Rockin' Hill Billy craws through the radio:

*Aw yeah, kids, it's Friday night, and you know what that
means. Grab your sweetheart and head on down to the drive-in, hit
up the All-Night, or just cruise on up to Make-Out Point, because
it's date night! Just whatever y'all do, don't touch that dial! Rockin'
Hill Billy's got you covered all night with all the tunes you're ever
gonna need!*

The Deuce speeds along way over the limit. It kicks
up dust and roars like a devil as Rockin' Hill Billy lets Bill
Haley & His Comets do some shakin', rattlin', and a bit
of rollin' too. Dash drives one-handed, with the other out
the window holding his cigarette. He's got Teddy in the
passenger seat and Gordy in the back. Gordy's swapped
his Hornets jacket for a boiler suit style uniform with a
nametag.

"So?" Teddy asks Dash.

Dash takes a draw from his cigarette before he
answers. "Made in the shade, my man. Made in the
mother-fuckin' shade."

Teddy drums on the dashboard with excitement.
"She's fast?"

Dash smirks. "Fast as this car," he says and revs the engine to prove his point.

"Christ!" Teddy howls.

"Man," Gordy says from the back, "she is the most!"

"Hey," Teddy asks, "what about that other paper shaker?"

"Which one?" Dash asks back.

"Blonde and stacked." Teddy uses his hands for emphasis.

"Like that narrows it down!" Dash says, and all three boys laugh.

"Man, she was right there today when you had your arm around Palmer. Had her peepers all over you both, man. Didn't look cool with it," Teddy says.

"Like I care." Dash takes a drag of his smoke.

"What I'm saying is, this other chick, she free for grabs or you got dibs?" Teddy asks, and in the back, Gordy doesn't like where this is going, but neither of the boys up front notice.

Dash takes another drag and answers, "Knock yourself out."

Teddy claps his hands with another whoop.

"Hey, ain't you and Betty goin' steady? She ain't gonna like you canoodlin' with some other chick," Gordy says.

Dash and Teddy slow-turn and give each other a look before they burst out in wild, rowdy laughter, and both of them say, "Like I care," at the same time. The whole thing is a hoot for Dash and Teddy, not so much Gordy, who's more than happy when Dash pulls over to drop him off at the Stop-n-Go for his shift.

Gordy watches the Deuce tear away into the distance, kinda glad he's not in it with the boys, though he feels as left out as a bug that he's not going to the All-Night with them. Except maybe it's not that he feels left out; perhaps it's something else, and he's not quite ready to start thinking too hard about what that might be.

Cut back to the Day house, and dinner was wholly uneventful. That in itself is something unappreciated.

Mr. Day looks up from his plate. "How was school today, Buddy?"

"Okay, I guess," is all Buddy wants to say, so Mrs. Day tries to spike his interest with something she heard on the news.

"The man on the news said there might be a meteor shower tonight."

"That's cool," Buddy says. He pushes his mostly untouched plate away. "May I be excused, please?"

"Buddy…" Mrs. Day starts, her eyebrows knitted with concern.

"I'm finished," Buddy says without making eye contact with either parent. "I don't feel so good."

"On you go, son," Mr. Day says before his wife can say anything else. Once his son is safely out of earshot, Mr. Day answers the stares he could feel his wife giving him. "I'm going, I'm going," he says as he stands. "I'll talk to him." He kisses his wife on the head.

In his room, Buddy slumps down on his bed. He stares up at his ceiling and sighs. A suspicious creaking calls his attention over to his slightly open closet. He climbs over his bed, approaches it slowly, and then pulls the door fully open, and…nothing.

Like a yowling vampire, the Fredericksons' cat hisses and jumps past Buddy. It runs to an open window, then stops, turns, and stares back at Buddy with a pure concentrate of feline contempt. Buddy tries to scare the cat away, but he's learned from experience not to get too close. The cat hisses, claws at him, and then eventually leaves of its own accord, but only when it's good and ready to do so. Buddy shuts the window fast and hard.

While Buddy fends off the devil's kitty cat, cut to: the All-Night Diner, where it's jumping with kids and cars all over the place. Rockin' Hill Billy blasts out of half a dozen radios simultaneously.

Alllllllll right and hey there kids, how y'all doin' this fine, fine evening? Rockin' Hill Billy here sayin' heads up tonight, 'cause there's gonna be some show up there in the heavens above. Lordy me! This one goes out to Suzie Palmer, WVRK Radio's very own Rock 'n' Roll Queen!

As Chuck Berry sings about how sweet it is to be sixteen, we head into the diner where a waitress carries a tray of milkshakes over to a table where Suzie, Betty, Christina (who wears the same kind of uniform as the waitress), and Connie sit around talking.

The waitress places the tray down and shoots Christina a dirty look. "You're supposed to be working, Christina," she says.

"I'm on break," Christina hits back.

"Break was over twenty minutes ago," the waitress snaps.

"Get bent," Christina says and takes one of the milkshakes from the tray. The other waitress shakes her head and walks off, not in any mood to be dealing with Christina's bullshit at this particular moment. Suzie and the rest of her friends all take their drinks.

"You'll lose your job, you know," Betty says as she puts her shake back down and looks around the diner to make sure there are enough eager eyes for her big reveal.

"Like I care," Christina says, and nobody else does either.

Betty unbuttons her jacket and slips it off with a knowing smirk as she reveals a black, sleeveless bodice top that plunges so deep she looks like a lily-skinned flower with a bad attitude. Her friends and most of the diner go slack-jawed at the sight of Woodvale's own Bettie Page.

"My god, Betty," Connie says.

"What's holding that up?" Suzie asks playfully.

"The hopes and prayers of her parents," calls Rick, the cook from behind the bar. He makes the sign of the cross with a spatula, then adds, "Christina get your ass back on the floor. We're swarmed in here!"

Christina shouts, "I'm on my goddamn break," and sips on her milkshake as Rick waves her off.

"What are we doing later?" Connie asks.

"The drive-in?" Betty suggests.

"Yeah, and have to sit through you guys necking all night? No thanks," Connie says. "Why am I the only one here without a date!?"

Christina shoots Connie a dirty look that makes the girl shy away almost instantly.

Betty screams with shock and delight as Teddy grabs hold of her from behind. He finds plenty of naked skin for him to tickle while Dash pulls a seat over, takes his place next to Suzie, and puts his arm around her without a word.

"You always gotta be such an actor?" Dash says to Teddy, who just shrugs and starts kissing Betty's neck—she squeals for him to stop, but it's obvious she doesn't mean it.

"Hey, where's Gordy?" Betty asks, and Teddy's taken aback, doesn't see why she'd care.

"He's working tonight," Teddy says.

"That makes two of us," Christina tuts. "Some of us gotta, you know," and she heads back to work without so much as a goodbye.

"What crawled up her butt and died?" asks Teddy.

"Who knows," says Suzie.

"Teddy, stop," Betty giggles. "You're making Connie jealous!"

"Are not!" insists Connie.

"How so?" Teddy asks.

"'Cause we're all coupled up and here's Connie all on her ownsome tonight," Betty says as she sticks her tongue out at her friend.

"Aw man," Teddy says. "That's a shame Gordy had to work then."

"Uh, nope, that's not a good idea," Betty says and then has to think fast to cover her ass. "Gordy's way too dumb for Connie. She likes 'em smart."

"You into nerds then," Teddy teases. "How about that Buddy kid? He's a whole bottle of nerd."

"Ew, god no," Betty and Connie say in unison, and Suzie suddenly feels very uncomfortable. Hearing people say things like that about Buddy really gets to her. Sure, she thinks, we've not been friendly lately, but he's still Buddy, and it's not right.

Dash cuts through the laughter and says, "Let's get out of here" to Suzie, and she's more than happy to go. She suddenly doesn't want to be around her friends so much anymore.

Cut back to Buddy's room, where the kid lies on his bed, above the sheets; eyes closed tight as he tries to squeeze all thoughts of Suzie from his mind. There's a knock at the door, and his dad calls his name from outside.

When Buddy doesn't answer, Mr. Day enters anyway. He pretends to casually survey the room before awkwardly sitting beside his son. Mr. Day picks up the comic Buddy was reading earlier.

"*Vault of Horror*, huh?" Buddy's dad asks. "Just in time for Halloween."

"I guess, I dunno," Buddy says, not wanting to get dragged into a conversation.

"So," Buddy's dad says, "the Boss Lady was saying that she mentioned your friend Suzie and you got a little…"

Buddy sits up, sharp. He's had enough of this. "We're not friends! Not anymore. Not for a long time."

Mr. Day makes himself comfortable. "You know, when I was about your age, I wasn't exactly a ladies'—"

"Dad. Please don't. I'm fine. Please!" Buddy insists.

"You're not, though. You barely say two words to your mother and me. You're sitting at home on your own on Friday night when I know good and well there's a sci-fi flick on at the Paradiso. So what is it? What's going on with Susan Palmer that's suddenly got you like this?"

"Dad, I just want to read my—"

"No." Mr. Day snatches the comic away from his son. "None of this till you tell me what's going on."

Buddy bites his lip and holds back from saying something hurtful to his dad. He stops himself from speaking a truth he doesn't want to admit to, let alone say aloud. The thing with the truth is it wants out, and if it can't get out one way, it'll find another. Buddy's eyes water, and that's it—he's overcome, and it all spills out. "She's dating this…he's just the worst and…"

"Ah…" Mr. Day gets it. Buddy realizes he's right in his dad's face and backs off, again confused about how

Suzie has him acting. "You know, son…you can't win 'em all."

Buddy's taken aback by his dad's sudden forwardness and honesty. He'd expected a whole bunch of comforting but useless advice. What his dad said to him felt like asking a doctor how long you have left to live only for him to start saying three…two…one…

"You can't make people like you or dislike someone else. All you can do is be who you are, and soon enough, you'll meet people who're drawn to what you have to give."

"Dad," Buddy says, "it's not even that. This guy's no good. He's bad. Real bad."

Mr. Day hugs his son. "Sometimes people see good where others don't. Sometimes people see good where it isn't. The thing is they have to see it, or not see it, with their own eyes—you can't make them. If this boy's as bad news as you say, she'll figure that out quick enough."

"Yeah?" Buddy asks, and the thought gives him hope.

"Yeah, and the thing is, you know there's a lot of folks that don't like it when her sort and ours get together. You get what I'm saying?" Mr. Day says and hopes to God he doesn't have to have that talk with his boy this evening.

"I know," Buddy says, and he does. More than his father could ever realize. Despite all that, he still carries a torch, and no amount of rain on his parade seems to be able to put it out. "But grandpa and grandma—"

"Had to deal with a lot of stuff you don't want. Could be it's all for the best," Mr. Day says and hates himself for it. There's nothing he'd like to see more than his boy and Susan Palmer holding hands and not a soul caring about it. "Say, how about we grab some gloves and have a game of catch…" Mr. Day says, then he trails off as he sees Buddy's reaction to the mention of baseball. "Ballplayer, huh?"

Sometimes he wishes his son was less like him, that the boy was more athletic. It's a lot easier to find acceptance when you're helping bring glory to your team. His boy isn't, though. He's smart. Real smart. He was reading the paper well before he started school, and it scares him sometimes because he knows his son won't find it easy to be accepted by either half of his heritage. Mr. Day gets that. He used to hide his books in his boots lest the other kids on his street think he was putting on airs, or the rich ones who lived near the library across town accuse him of stealing. To this day, the odor of stinky socks still makes him think of Washington Irving and Edgar Allan Poe.

Buddy looks away. "I'm okay, dad. Really. Think I might just lie out on the grass and watch the meteor shower everyone keeps talking about."

Mr. Day pats his son on his thigh. "Sounds like a plan to me."

Cut to: someone else with a plan as Dash races his Deuce one-handed again, though this time his free arm is around the seat with Suzie sitting in it. She's got his Hornets jacket on and just about drowns in it. It smells of cedarwood, either from his aftershave or from his baseball gear, and, either way, she likes it.

"I like your car," she says, looking to start a conversation. It occurs to her that they haven't talked much since he gave her a ride home last week. Since they kissed out by the diamond and he asked her on this date.

"It was my dad's," Dash says, and when he catches Suzie looking at him, wanting more, he adds, "he died."

"Wow, Danny," she says, "I'm so sorry."

47

"It's cool," Dash shrugs. "Not like it just happened or anything."

"Were you close?" Suzie asks.

Dash removes his arm from her and places it back on the wheel. He shrugs but still makes some distance between them despite the tough guy act. "I guess. He was deployed a lot, so I got used to him not being around as much, but sure. I never knew my mom, my real mom, so back when I was little, it was just him and me."

"Danny..." Suzie trails off. She doesn't know what to say. The idea of losing one of her parents is unthinkable to her; losing both is beyond comprehension. She doesn't know how she'd go on after something like that, but here's Dash, not only getting by, but pretty much the King of Woodvale High.

"We fixed this car up after he got remarried. Just a pile o' scrap when we started. Think he wanted somethin' that was just me 'n' him, you know?"

Suzie puts her hand on his leg as an act of sympathy, and Dash smirks. He knows good and well that if he lowers his defenses, it's much easier to lure someone in, and once they're there, he can lock it down. Dash casts his eyes down her hand and then follows her arm up to her baby blues. He smiles at her, then looks ahead at the road with a grin. It's not that anything he said wasn't true, but Dash learned long ago that lots of girls just can't resist a wounded puppy. Even if it's a wolf.

Confident he's going to get some tonight, Dash makes the turn off to Make-Out Point instead of driving down the road to Cherry Lake.

Just as Buddy makes himself comfortable on a picnic blanket in his backyard, Dash pulls his car over into a secluded spot overlooking the town and takes the top down.

It couldn't be a finer night, not that Dash notices. Not that he sees that one star that glows brighter than the rest. The one that seems to be getting bigger and bigger. Suzie sees it though, only because as Dash kisses her on the neck, she rolls her head back, and when her eyes open, she's looking right at it.

"Wow! The stars are gorgeous tonight," she says and gets the strangest sense of déjà vu that pulls her right out of all the tingly feelings Dash's kisses were giving her. Dash continues to kiss her and doesn't respond. "Aren't they, Danny?" and still Dash goes at it without paying her any attention. Suzie pushes him away.

That makes him take note. "What's the matter, baby?" he asks.

Suzie wraps her arms around herself, suddenly feeling very exposed, all the tingles gone, and even when Dash strokes her shoulder, they don't come back.

"Can't we just sit for a while, look at the stars?" she asks.

"Sure, baby," Dash says, and he puts his arm around her, pulling her in closer.

Suzie likes the way that feels, so she leans in herself, and for a minute, they just watch the stars. That big one seems strange. Suzie recalls what Buddy used to tell her when they looked up at the stars together, but she can't remember him saying anything about them getting bigger. Still, she thinks it's beautiful.

Dash starts trying to kiss her again, and Suzie pushes him away. "Danny, come on!"

"Don't be like that, Suzie," Dash says as he leans into her and puts his hand on her breast. Suzie struggles; she pulls away and slaps his hand.

"Danny, no!" she demands as she protects her chest with crossed arms.

"C'mon Suzie," Dash says with a smirk as he runs his hand through his hair. "Quit bein' such a tease. You don't gotta worry," he says as he slips the strap of her dress off her shoulder with one quick flick. "I ain't gonna tell anyone you're fast or nothin'."

Dash slides over and pins Suzie against the door of his car.

"I want you to take me home, Danny. Right. Now," Suzie insists.

"Suzie," Dash scoffs.

"Take me home!" Suzie yells loud enough, hoping someone else will hear and interfere if he decides not to.

Dash takes the keys out of the ignition and tosses them out of the car. He gives Suzie a look that says "Your move," though he can't imagine she'd make the one she does. Suzie gets out of the car and starts walking back down the road to the highway.

"Suzie, come on," Dash says, bored of this game now, but Suzie keeps on walking. "Shit," Dash says, punches the dashboard, and then searches for his keys. He didn't throw them all that far, so it doesn't take him long. He's back in, on the road, and catches up with Suzie within a minute.

"Suzie, get back in the car," Dash says, but Suzie marches on.

"Just leave me alone, Danny."

"You're not gonna walk home. It's miles away."

"I'll hitchhike," Suzie snaps back.

Dash loses it, and he revs up, pulls ahead, then turns hard in front of Suzie, blocking her path. He reaches over and opens the passenger side door. "Get in."

Suzie walks around the car, nearly slipping down the sharp decline that runs from the road to the foot of the forest. Dash punches his steering wheel, kicks his door open, climbs out of his car, and goes after Suzie on foot.

"Jesus, Suzie! Get back in the damn car. I'm sorry, okay? Jesus!" Dash calls after her. Suzie ups her pace and puts some more distance between them. "I'll give you a damn ride home, just get back in the car for Christ's sake!"

Suzie doesn't believe him.

Dash picks up speed to a half-run and catches up to Suzie. He grabs her by the shoulder, flips her around, and accidentally rips her dress. It scares the life out of Suzie, and Dash knows there's no saving this now, so he goes all in. Suzie tries to shove him off, but he holds on, his grip too steady for her to break, and she can feel her skin bruise already. There's violence and pleasure in his eyes. He squeezes her hard, and in the struggle, Suzie rips his t-shirt at the collar.

"Danny...you're hurting me," she begs, "please—"

An all-consuming roar and wave of heat sucks up all sound around them as a meteorite cuts through the sky overhead. The flaming rock decimates everything in its path and comes crashing down, not far from the two of them. The whole forest reverberates with a violent tremor that causes Suzie to fall forward into Dash but, at the same time, causes Dash to stumble into her. His weight overpowers her, and Suzie falls backward over the drop. Dash can't do anything but watch as Suzie flips and rolls like a broken doll down into the forest, and if all that wasn't enough, she whams her head hard against the thick old roots of an ancient jack pine tree.

"Suzie!" Dash screams. He slides down after her and drops to her side, stumbling with little concern for his well being, but it's too little, too late. "Suzie! Oh god, no!"

he begs, and when he tries to lift her head, his hand comes away sticky and red.

Suzie's eyes twitch and flicker, one of them barely open, the other wide and bloodshot.

"Shit! No, Suzie, I didn't mean to, I didn't…" It might have been an accident, a freak of nature, but she wouldn't have been right there if it wasn't for him. Dash knows this. He knows it's what the police will think, even if they buy into his story about the meteor. They'll never believe he didn't mean it. He didn't mean it, right?

Dash stands up and looks around. "Shit," he says again and makes up his mind. He bends down and carefully takes his Hornets jacket off her body.

"D-d-d-Dash," she stutters.

He looks down at her; his jacket clutched in his hands. "Suzie, I-I'm sorry."

It's too late, the blood, there's too much, he says to himself. He can't do anything for Suzie anymore. It's for the best, Dash tells himself as the Deuce peels away into the night as he leaves Suzie in the dirt to die.

It does not happen fast, though. Suzie lies there, staring up at the same stars as Buddy does just a few miles away back in town.

Cut to: the forest, to a baseball-sized rock that sits in the middle of a smoking crater. Sure, it looks like a rock, but only because there's no other way to describe it. No rock is that perfectly shaped, though, and the way it glows, it's more than just the heat from the burning entry into our atmosphere. Even as the heat dissipates and the chilly October night air cools the surface, a subtle luminescence persists, and there's a hum, hidden by the panic of wildlife and the crackle of burning wood.

A small section breaks off and falls to the ground. The small chunk moves around, clicks and cracks, and unfolds into something like an ant crossed with a wasp, but the shape is all wrong. It flies off with sharp little wings in search of something, and it isn't long before it finds what it wants.

The strange bug lands on the bruised and scratched face of Suzie, and the very last thing she sees before she dies are two massive, impossibly black insectoid eyes that don't belong in this world.

SHE WAS A TEENAGE BEAUTY QUEEN

While Suzie lies dead, and a malignant horror from beyond the stars burrows deep inside her still warm, yet lifeless body; we fade to Buddy as he watches the skies. The infinite expanse above and the eternal void inside makes Buddy feel utterly alone. Later on, he regrets that self-pity party, but at the moment, all he does is sigh, get up, and head inside as he hears the opening monologue to *The Twilight Zone* starting up.

Meanwhile, cut to: Sam's Stop-n-Go gas station about half a mile out of town, where Gordy struggles to stay awake. He's seen three cars in total come through all night, and from experience, that's busy for a late shift. There's a reason mean, old Sam pays a "jackass high-school moron" to mind the register on Friday nights. It's "'cause it's cheaper than hiring an illegal!" Every time Gordy clocks in, he has to listen to some variation of that while Sam laughs and thinks it's the funniest thing in the world. Gordy's father once told him there are only two occasions when white folk don't see his kind as something other than a "wetback." When they're mowing their lawns or kicking ass on the field.

Gordy doesn't know about that; Betty doesn't fit into his pa's worldview for one. Still, it's a good thing for Gordy that he knows his way around the diamond. It's enough for folks who might otherwise be inclined to hold their tongues around him; that and the fact that

Dash once kicked the ever-living shit out of three Cherry Lake kids for asking him if Gordy was his gardener. And while his pa will complain, he'll also in the same breath say all kinds of wrong things about Italian Americans. Don't even get him started on the Irish.

Gordy snores a little. The opening monologue from *The Twilight Zone* comes to an end, and Gordy just about craps his pants when there's a hard, sudden full-body slap against the window next to him.

"Jesus Christ!" Gordy yells as the racket yanks him clear out his nap, and he has to grab hold of the counter to keep from falling right off his seat. It takes him a few seconds to process the fact that it's Dash at the window because the King of Woodvale High doesn't look like himself. He looks scared. Damn scared. His pompadour's gone full flop, his collar is ripped, and is that blood or mud on his t-shirt? "Dash, the hell you doing—"

Dash doesn't let Gordy get another word out. "Man, you gotta do something for me. You gotta."

"Sure man, just come around," Gordy says. Dash runs to the front of the store and just about knocks the doorbell off its hook as he enters. "Ain't you supposed to be down the passion pit with that birdie?" Gordy asks.

Dash grabs Gordy by the shoulders instead of answering and demands, "Promise me. Promise me!"

"Dash! Chill!" Gordy says as Dash grips him hard enough to leave a mark. He removes himself from Dash's grasp. "Just tell me what's happened."

Dash wipes the sweat from his forehead. "No, you gotta promise me first. Promise me you'll tell anyone who asks that I was here all night with you."

"Dash, man, that don't make no sense," Gordy says.

"Shit! Promise me! Swear to me, Gordy, swear! Swear that I came by for gas with Suzie and I had car trouble. Yeah, we came by, and I couldn't get the Deuce to start, so she decided to walk back to town." Dash's panic is something new for Gordy. Never saw anything like it before, never even close. "We tried to stop her, didn't we Gordy, but she just wouldn't listen…yeah, that works." Dash never loses his cool, even when the whole game comes down to him; he never seems to care—seeing Dash's hand tremble, seeing him sweat like this puts Gordy on edge. "Swear! Swear to me, Gordy, you'll tell them!"

"Okay! Jesus, man, okay. You got it," Gordy agrees, and it's fifty-fifty if it's out of loyalty or fear at this point. It seems to calm Dash down a little either way. "Dash, man…you in trouble?" Dash doesn't say anything, but the ripped shirt gives Gordy a hint. "What've you done, Dash?"

"I ain't done nothing!" Dash yells and slams his fist down on the counter. "Goddamnit, I ain't done nothing," he insists, and he kicks over a rack of newspapers. "It was an accident," Dash winds down. "An accident, I swear," and he lets himself fall to the ground. Then Dash does something Gordy never thought he'd ever see.

Danny "Dash" Domico cries.

All Gordy can think to do is put his hand on Dash's shoulder and say, "It's cool, man, it's gonna be okay," and wonders what the hell Dash has dragged him into.

That night, as most everyone in Woodvale says howdy doody to the land of nod, Suzie's parents lose their cool progressively as the clock ticks on past her curfew. What starts as indignation and frustration at their daughter disobeying their rules starts to get supplanted by a gnawing dread that something's terribly wrong. Mr. Palmer hides his fear with loudly spoken threats of tanning his daughter's hide whenever she deigns to show herself while praying on the inside that he gets to plant a kiss on her head and tuck her into bed by the end of this.

Eventually, the scales tip and the Palmers can't hide from the truth anymore, especially when Mrs. Palmer confesses to her husband that their daughter was out on a date with a boy. Seconds later, Mr. Palmer is on the phone with the Sheriff's department and rousts the one deputy on duty into waking Sheriff Keyes. Five minutes later, Keyes is on the road and getting filled in by his deputy, and from what he learns from the game of telephone, he decides to stop at the Blacker house on his way to the Palmers.

Cut to: Betty as she enjoys one last cigarette on her way home, a big smile on her face, and a hickey on her neck—both courtesy of Teddy. The sight of Sheriff Keyes' black-and-white car in her driveway wipes away that smile and gives the still fairly full cigarette a one-way trip to the ground.

"Shit," Betty says as she quickly buttons up her coat. Her mother would kill her if she saw what she was wearing and, as a bonus, it covers up the hickey. There's no getting around the trouble coming her way, but at least Betty can minimize it. Since there's no point in trying to sneak back in, she goes for the front door instead of the backyard trellis. At least I don't got to figure out how to climb in these damn heels, she thinks as the porch light comes on, and Betty winces.

She's no more than set her foot on the path when the front door is thrown open, and her mother, in her full

57

bathrobed and curled-hair glory, comes storming towards her daughter like a furious mud-masked, robed sultan in fuzzy slippers.

"Hi, mom," Betty says and winces in anticipation of the slap that comes. It's not as harsh as expected, as experience would dictate, and when Betty opens her eyes, she sees nothing but terror and relief on her mother's face. Betty's confused; this doesn't feel right, and the sight of Sheriff Keyes at her front door doesn't help.

Betty's heart sinks as her mother asks, "Honey, where is Suzie Palmer?"

Not long after Betty tells him everything, Sheriff Keyes spots Dash's 1932 Ford Deuce parked up at Sam's Stop-n-Go as he makes his way out towards the drive-in outside Cherry Lake, where the Blacker girl told him Suzie and Dash were heading after they left the All-Night. He pulls up and sees Danny "Dash" Domico slide himself out from under the car, his torn t-shirt sodden with oil and grease.

No, something isn't right, Keyes can tell, but only in the vaguest of ways. He doesn't buy the story Dash gives him, not in the least. The Domico boy has always been trouble as far as he's concerned, but when the kid behind the counter gives him the same story, he's not left with many options—even if there was something off about the boy. Far too alert for a kid working at a gas stop at nearly one in the morning.

Keyes doesn't have any choice but to call in his deputies, and a few from Cherry Lake just to help out, and start making plans to search the woods all the way from the Stop-n-Go back to Woodvale.

It's not Sheriff Keyes or any of the deputies that find the body of Suzie Palmer, though. No, that grizzly discovery comes courtesy of a little Jack Russell Terrier with a defiant streak by the name of Eddie.

Eddie lives with his family on a farm not too far from the road that high-school kids of Woodvale and Cherry Lake call Make-Out Point, and on this morning, the youngest of his humans, a pup named Willie Wilson, walks him out by the point. Eddie catches the scent of something not quite right and follows his nose to a small crater. He whines as the gray sphere at the epicenter gives off both heat and an odor that doesn't make sense; he's never smelled anything like this before, and Eddie's made it his business to sniff a lot of things in his life.

"Here Eddie!" his human calls him from the road, but Eddie ignores the command. He catches another scent, one that's vaguely familiar, and follows it away from the crater.

"C'mon Eddie! Here boy!" the kid calls, but Eddie's on the trail of someone. It almost smells like the kind girl who sometimes gives him a pet and a cookie whenever he's in town guarding his family as they pick up food from the store. It does smell like her, Eddie's sure, and he picks up speed in hopes of potential treats, but as he gets closer, the scent becomes twinged with rot, and it raises his hackles.

Eddie sniffs his way to the girl, to the body of Suzie Palmer, and knows right away why she smelled wrong. His human needs to see this, and so he barks.

"Eddie! Come on!" the boy calls as he catches up with the dog. "Mom'll have a bird if we miss breakfast…" The boy emerges from the forest and sees the girl who works at the grocery store, only she's not moving. Only her mouth hangs open, and she stares into nothing. Only she's not breathing, and when the boy realizes this, he screams.

We fade from that to the Eternal Gardens Funeral Parlor a week later as the corpse of Suzie Palmer lies in her open casket in a pretty blue dress with a peaceful smile painted on her face by a mortician. Though the Palmers wanted a quiet, personal funeral, the outpouring of love from the town moved them. Seeing how much their daughter's death impacted everyone, they consented to a memorial to let them all say their goodbyes on the day before they'd bury their only child.

The town pastor stands before a packed room as he delivers a eulogy. "Susan Palmer was, in anyone's eye, a remarkable girl." The "was" makes Mrs. Palmer wail, and her husband holds her tighter. "A talented, bright young lady," to which Betty weeps openly. "And yet she knew not pride nor vanity. She greeted each day with a smile on her face and a song in her heart." Teddy, who sits next to Betty, holds his girl's hand just as tight as his tears.

Meanwhile, Gordy bows his head in his hands and struggles to keep his cool. His right foot taps a beat; he doesn't notice.

The pastor continues, "She was, in essence, the best of all of us."

Dash sits with his stepmother on one side and his sister on the other. He can feel the eyes of the whole room on him even though nobody is looking. He tells himself not to, but Dash can't help casting a sideways eye at Gordy every few minutes.

"She will be missed," the pastor concludes.

Buddy sits with his parents. He hasn't spoken much since the whole town came to a standstill last week after the discovery of Suzie's body by Make-Out Point. Principal MacKay canceled all classes, and the Halloween dance, too, which gave Buddy a lot of time to think. To think about how sure he was that Dash was behind this, even though the Sheriff had cleared him. Sure, he has an alibi, but Buddy doesn't buy it. Dash's goons lie for him all the time. Buddy regrets not speaking up earlier, not saying something. He regrets not socking Dash in the face; even if he took a beating for it, it'd have been worth it. Maybe Suzie wouldn't have gone out on a date with him if he had a big shiner ruining his pretty face. Most of all, though, Buddy regrets ever listening to Suzie's mother.

He thinks about how things were with Suzie, how they'd been the best of friends. Then about how Suzie's mother took him aside during Suzie's fourteenth birthday party and told him exactly what happens to black boys who get too friendly with white girls. That, it's not her, of course, but some people don't take it lightly. She showed him newspapers with photos that made him sick to his stomach. It wasn't so much what might happen to him though. Mrs. Palmer told him that these kinds of people would punish Suzie in ways that would make her wish she was dead. They were starting high school after the summer, the perfect opportunity to make new friends. "To be with your own," she said. "It's for the best." And as much as not being with Suzie tore him apart, Buddy couldn't let anything happen to her. If that meant cutting her out of his life, so be it. He remembers all of this, clear as day, as the best friend he ever had lies dead in a casket, regardless of his good intentions and efforts.

As much as he wants to blame Mrs. Palmer for forcing Suzie and him apart, Buddy knows there's only

61

one person honestly responsible for the way things were between them. All week, Buddy works up the nerve to say what he has to say, and when the hall has emptied, he walks up to the casket.

"Suzie," he says, and can hardly see her for the tears in his eyes. "I'm sorry. Sorry for not being there, for being a coward. I'm sorry..." and he can't think of anything else to say, so he just takes her delicate, ice-cold hand in his and lets it all out.

Cut outside, as Gordy does his best to avoid Dash. He sees Betty standing by herself under the shade of an unkempt tulip tree. The life and the spark has just gone from her. Gordy gulps down his nerves, feels them churn in his stomach, and heads over.

"Betty, I gotta tell you—" Gordy says but then stops himself as the thought of what'll happen to him if the truth gets out. He doesn't know what's worse, the law or Dash. Either way, he's screwed, so even though every decent bone in his body wants to talk, Gordy silences himself. "I'm sorry," he says, "I'm just so sorry," and he leaves it at that. Betty's just too overcome to process how strange he's acting.

Over by the road, Buddy kicks a rock around while he waits for his folks to pull up. They'd gone to get the car while he said his goodbyes. Johnny casts an eye over, sees his friend, and then asks his folks to give him a minute. He walks over to Buddy, and since he's not sure what the right thing to say is, he just goes with "Hey."

"Hey Johnny, how's it hanging?" Buddy asks with all the enthusiasm of an inert electron.

"A little to the left today, my friend. These threads might kill, but they're sincerely cutting off the boys!"

Johnny fixes his pants with a shuffle, bringing the slightest hint of a smile to Buddy's face. Johnny notices and lands another one with, "Guess we know how Roy Orbison does it, huh?" Johnny smiles like a total goof.

Buddy smirks and then falls into an all-out laugh. Johnny feels pretty proud of himself, till Buddy starts getting hysterical. Till the chuckles turn into sobs, and Buddy slumps back against a tree. He slides down to the ground and says, "Why Johnny, why her?"

Johnny takes a seat on the grass next to his friend. "I can't tell you, man. World's full of stuff that don't make sense. Like tomatoes."

"Tomatoes?" Buddy raises an eyebrow.

"Yeah, like, they ain't a vegetable, they ain't a fruit, makes no sense."

"They're a fruit," Buddy says.

"What?"

"They got seeds. Fruit has seeds; even if you can't see 'em, they're there."

"Shit..." Johnny's mind implodes. "You mean like, even a banana?"

"Yeah, those too."

"No way..."

"Yes, way. They get eaten then pooped out, natural fertilizer."

"That's disgusting!" Johnny's whole world rocks and his friend's dumb reaction is just the distraction Buddy needs. "That's it, man, from now on I'm only eating candy and burgers, I ain't no human fertilizer machine! Sincerely!"

"Well—"

"Okay, man, since you're so smart, 'splain this one. Why do folks wear shades, even in the rain?"

"Huh?"

"Like that cube over there." Johnny points to a man across the street and a little down the road. Dressed just like someone would draw an accountant or a county clerk, he sits on a bench like he's waiting for a bus. There are two odd things about him. First is that he wears jet-black sunglasses even though the sky's overcast and gray, and the second is that, even though he's not looking their way, Buddy can't help but feel like he's watching them.

"Could be he's blind," Buddy says. "That happens, you know."

"Well, yeah," Johnny says. "But how come he ain't got no stick then?"

Buddy doesn't say it, but this is one of those rare times that Johnny has a point. "My dad says sometimes folks wear shades to hide reefer eyes."

"Does he look like a beatnik to you?" Johnny asks, and Buddy has to agree. "And, if he is blind, why does it feel like he's staring right at us?" Johnny makes the ooo-wee-ooo sound of a theremin as he waggles his fingers in the air.

"Maybe 'cause we're staring at him?" Buddy suggests, but it does nothing to fight the growing creep both boys feel. Neither can bring themselves to look away despite the mounting unease the solitary, unassuming man in sunglasses causes. The sound of a car horn makes them both jump out of their skins.

"Jesus!" Johnny yells as both boys turn and see the Freemantles in their grody old station wagon. The state of that brown dirt magnet pretty much explains why Johnny has to "borrow" his cousin's car anytime he talks some poor girl into going on a date with him. "Gotta go, man, gimme a call if you want to catch a flick or something," Johnny says, and he means it, but he knows Buddy won't. Especially not for a while.

Buddy waves goodbye to his friend, and a few moments later, his folks pull up. As the Day family drives home, Buddy can't help but notice that the man with the sunglasses still sits on that bench, even though the bus just went past.

Night falls in Woodvale, and even as the porch and streetlights come on, darkness hangs over the town. It persists in the communal sadness, and parents hug their children especially tighter that evening.

As the funeral parlor grows dark, odd sounds echo around the hall. Muffled thuds and disjointed clicks; they're soon drowned out as someone tries to force a window open from outside. The frame jumps and shakes, then pops open. A few seconds later, Teddy climbs in through, and then he unbolts the front door. Betty stands in the doorway with all her attitude gone. She cradles herself and seems so much smaller and delicate in the dark.

"I still don't think this is a good idea," Teddy says as Betty steps inside.

"I...I just wanna see her again," Betty says. "Before they bury her."

Teddy holds out his hand, and Betty takes it. Their eyes meet, and he nods. He'll do this for her, whatever it takes to make her happy. This last week has made him take a cold, hard look at himself. He always knew Betty was a bit of a runaround girl; the fact is, that's one of the things that drew him to her, and he had his suspicions about her and Gordy after that night, but when Suzie died, it made him realize how fragile life was. It made him realize that none of that stuff mattered. He loves Betty, and that's that.

Betty wraps herself in his arms for protection. The loss of her friend has done the same thing for her that it did for Teddy. The two of them have done a lot of growing up this past week.

Hand in hand, Teddy and Betty approach the casket.

Teddy carefully lets go of Betty but keeps eye contact till he reaches the now closed casket. He lifts the lid open gently then holds his hand out for Betty to come. She steps up and takes it. Teddy puts his arm around her as Betty looks down at her friend. What they say is true, Betty thinks, she looks so peaceful. Like she's just sleeping. Except for her eyes, open and wide (were they open earlier?).

The sight breaks Betty, and she buries her face in Teddy's chest, her sobs muffled by his shirt. She grows weak, and her knees fail her. Betty falls, but Teddy stops her, helps her sit on the floor, and kneels to keep her close.

"It doesn't make any sense," Betty says as the tears let up. "It just doesn't!"

Teddy holds her in his arms, but something distracts him. A sound…coming from the casket. "Betty…" he trails off as he becomes more and more convinced something is moving inside.

Betty looks up at him, wipes tears from her eyes, then screams as Suzie's hand grabs hold of the side of her casket.

"Suzie!" Betty yells and just about pushes Teddy over in a rush to get to her feet. "Oh my god, Suzie!"

"Betty, wait!" Teddy says as Suzie sits up.

Betty wraps her arms around her friend. "Oh Suzie," she says with absolute joy, such joy she doesn't notice that her friend is cold as ice. "Thank God!" Betty cries.

Suzie sits there, awake and yet somehow not. At least, that's how it looks to Teddy. It's her eyes, he realizes—they're cold and gray, and she doesn't blink. It's the way she stares too, like a bug. It gives him the creeps and then some.

"Betty!" Teddy screams as Suzie sinks her teeth into the neck of the girl he loves.

Betty pulls away from the dead girl, and Teddy watches with open-mouthed awe as Suzie rips a full mouthful from Betty's neck. Betty flounders and grabs onto the side of the casket for balance. All she does is pull the thing, and the dead girl, down with her. The blood pours from her wound, and Betty loses consciousness as it flows across the black and white tiled floor.

Suzie turns her attention to Teddy as he skitters backward on all fours. "Jesus! Suzie!" he calls out as she takes slow, heavy steps in his direction. He gets to his feet and sees his window for escape closing as Suzie moves to block him in, the bloody body of his girlfriend on the floor behind her. "Oh Jesus, Betty…"

The look on Suzie's face, it's like a hungry fox cornering a wounded rabbit. It's not Suzie at all, but whatever it is, it's coming for Teddy.

He goes for it, dodges past her like he's on the field and running for home plate, only to slip as his foot lands in a pool of blood hidden in the shadows. Teddy cries in pain as he hits the ground hard and tastes his girlfriend's blood on his lips. Somehow that's worse than the pain, so he screams at the disgusting, debased horror of it.

The Suzie-thing catches up, and the last thing Teddy sees is her empty, inhuman eyes and lupine snarl as she descends on him. Instinctually, his hand, twitching and trembling, flops to the ground and fumbles its way towards Betty's. He can't reach her though, and Teddy dies inches from the girl he'd only recently realized meant everything to him.

Sometime later, after all the screaming dies down, a pretty dead girl in a blood-splattered blue dress stumbles out of the funeral parlor. Eyes that are and aren't hers survey the world around like they've never seen it before.

A sound forms inside her, a buzzing and clicking sound. Like something both mechanical and organic coming to life. The noise modulates through frequencies the body of Suzie Palmer can and can't hear till it finds one that works. Something between a buzz and a cackle, and it searches for the right combination of sounds to give what used to be Suzie the correct instructions. It finally settles on one combination, on one word, and it comes through everywhere and nowhere all at once.

FEED.

A spark occurs in response to the command from somewhere deep inside the volumes of data compressed inside Suzie's mind. The closest association. A neon-lit sign that reads: All-Night Diner.

FEED.

It commands, and the thing that used to be a teenage beauty queen obeys, shuffling off towards the edge of town.

Sometime after that, as Betty and Teddy lie dead on the floor, their hands, inches apart, begin to twitch.

THE ALL-NIGHT DINER MASSACRE

While death walks out of the Eternal Gardens Funeral Parlor, cut to: the Domico household, which stands atop a grassy hill with a rusted, metal shack of a garage at the bottom, just off the main road into town. Dash lies on his back, his legs sticking out from underneath his 1932 Ford Deuce.

In messing with the car enough to make his alibi all the more believable, Dash inadvertently proved to be a better saboteur than he expected. Sure, he was able to drive it home after Sheriff Keyes gave him the third degree, but it hasn't been running right ever since. The silver lining is that Dash has something to focus on, something to keep his mind from coming back to that question: Did he push Suzie to her death, or did she fall because of whatever the hell it was that crashed into the woods?

Preoccupied with trying to find a way to eliminate that infuriating rattle his baby has picked up, Dash doesn't hear his stepmother calling from the porch of the house on the hill. "Daniel? Daniel, sweetheart?"

He's not spent much time in the house since Suzie…since that night. Something about being around his stepmother, his sister, and the wholesomeness of it all is too normal for him. He's been sleeping in the cot his father once set up in the garage, for nights when his wife kicked him out for one reason or another.

Danny slept in that cot a lot after his dad died. Danny, not Dash. Danny was a crybaby brat who could do nothing to help nobody. Dash was born on that cot, and he was born to kick ass. So Dash doesn't respond when his stepmother calls; he stays focused on his car, because doing something is better than doing nothing.

"Daniel, sweetheart, dinner's on the table!" Mrs. Domico calls out as she wraps her arms around herself against the evening chill. She knows the boy's not coming in, but she tries anyway, just like every night for the past week.

Inside the house, Jessie Domico sits at the kitchen table. A tiny little thing with jet-black hair down her back and a big old ribbon pinned on top. Mrs. Domico enters and shuts the door behind her but makes an effort not to lock it. She's been leaving it unlocked all night despite there being a murderer somewhere out there. She needs Daniel to know he can come in from the cold whenever he wants.

"Momma?" Jessie asks as her mother peeks through the curtain.

"Yeah, sweetie?" she answers without looking at her daughter.

"Is Danny going to be okay?" Jessie asks with the pure-hearted sincerity of a five-year-old.

Mrs. Domico turns away from the window and takes a seat at the kitchen table. She meets her daughter's hopeful eyes, and can't bring herself to be anything but truthful. "I don't know, sweetie," she sighs. "I just don't know."

"He's pretty bummed, huh?" Jessie asks.

"Jessica Domico, you watch your language at the dinner table!" Mrs. Domico snaps and just about brings her daughter to tears. The second she realizes how harsh

70

she was, Mrs. Domico is off her seat, across the table, and has her arms around her daughter. "I'm sorry, sweetie, I'm sorry," she says as she cradles her little girl. "Momma's just worried about your brother."

"Why's Danny so sad, momma? Is it because that girl died?"

"Yeah, sweetie," Mrs. Domico says with tears running down her face into her daughter's hair. "He was pretty sweet on that girl."

The roar of the Deuce shotgunning to life outside kills the moment. By the time Mrs. Domico gets to the window, all she can see is a cloud of dust and black smoke as the car tears away from the drive and turns onto the road to town. She watches till the dust settles, and the car's rear lights are just pinpricks on the horizon.

Cut to: Dash as he drives angry, both hands on the wheel with a grip so tight he might just crack the mahogany. His eyes are focused forward but not on the road. So as the Deuce speeds into town, kicks up dirt, and roars like a dragon, Dash doesn't notice as he tears right past Suzie—all bloody in her pretty blue dress.

Something about the car makes Suzie stop her march. It lights her up on the inside—breaks the hold of the thing controlling her for just a second. Then, from everywhere and nowhere, the command:

FEED.

Suzie snarls and bares hungry teeth. Strings of reddish drool dangle and swing from her lips down to her jaw. Once again she succumbs to the command, and this time, the neon sign for Rick's All-Night Diner isn't just in her mind. It's right there, just above the tree line a little further down the road.

Cut to: Rick's All-Night Diner's kitchen, where the eponymous Rick's hand twists as he flips a burger like he's mixing a cocktail. He presses it flat with the spatula—it sizzles as it tears, and Rick sprinkles his secret spice concoction over the meat.

Meanwhile, Christina, in her waitress uniform, leans up against the counter. Connie sits on a stool at the other end, sipping on a strawberry milkshake. They're mid-conversation, and it's probably best we've missed most of it.

"It's not like she was that special, you know?" Christina says while her friend dutifully nods along. "She shouldn't have won," Christina says, and Connie keeps on nodding. "God, and, like, everyone's acting so, so…"

"Sad?" Connie offers.

"What? No, shut up," Christina says. "It's worse than that. They're all so…wounded!"

Connie gives her a look that says she doesn't get it, and Christina turns her back on her friend, looks through into the kitchen, and rolls her eyes as she watches Rick dance over the grill. With their backs to the main door, neither of them notices the bloody girl in the blue dress stumble out of the shadows and stagger closer in a herky-jerky way that looks like neither leg knows about the other.

"Her folks, you can understand, you know?" Christina goes on. "But, just…urgh!" She growls in frustration. "'Least they'll bury the bitch tomorrow. That'll be the end of it."

72

Connie doesn't know much, but she knows better than to say boo to Christina, so she just sips through her straw and nods.

"And, I'm grateful for her getting us a week off school and all, but did they have to cancel the dance? I was going to put that little runt right in her place and win the costume contest for sure," Christina says, and the thought of it makes her smirk. "Instead, here I am, wearing this goofy thing."

"I think you look great," Connie says like a trained puppy.

"Jesus Christ, Connie, that's not what I was getting at," Christina huffs. Of course, I look great, she thinks, but what's the point if you can't rub it in the faces of other girls who haven't learned their place yet?

Rick pops out of the kitchen with a fresh burger on a plate and slides it down the counter to Connie. He casts an eye around the nearly empty diner and whistles. "Dead in here tonight."

"Suzie Palmer went and died, so now the whole town has to sit at home and cry," Christina says and makes a boo-hoo face to ram the point home.

"Nice, Christina," Rick says. "Real nice. Empty or not, you're still on the clock. Take the trash out back."

Christina sighs and rolls her eyes. "I swear, one day I'm gonna walk right on outta here."

"Uh-huh," Rick says, having heard that particular threat on many occasions before.

"You wait and see," Christina says.

Rick dives headfirst into a painfully awkward imitation of The Crickets: "You say you're gonna leave, you know it's a lie, 'cause that'll be the daaaaay when I die!"

Christina gives him a stone-cold silence and a glare to match.

Rick pulls the garbage bag out of the trash can and holds it up for her. "Just take out the trash, then you can get back to your little pity party with your friend there."

Christina grabs the bag from him and waits till he's back in the kitchen and safely out of earshot before she tells him to "Get bent!"

Jump-cut to: the back door as it swings open violently, then bounces back hard and hits Christina right in the face.

"Damn it!" she shouts and gives the door another kick. Some of the jagged metal bolted to it, half-loose after years of abuse, slices through the trash bag, and causes all the rotten leftovers and paper cups to spill out. Gunk slops all over Christina's brand-new white tennies.

"Goddamnit!" Christina curses as she feels the burger grease infused milkshake dregs seep into her socks. She shakes the majority of the filth off her shoes and yanks the garbage bag away from the broken metal. Christina decides that whatever's on the ground is for the raccoons and tosses what's left in the dumpster. She wipes her hands on her apron and turns to head back inside, only to stop when she notices something. A figure standing just outside the reach of the back door light. The sight gives Christina the fright of her life. "Jesus!"

The shadow doesn't move, and for a second, Christina thinks it's just a trick of the light. Except tricks of the light don't growl all low and guttural like a hungry stray.

"Who's there? Goddamnit, that better not be you, Rick, or I swear to god..." Christina goes uncharacteristically silent as Suzie stumbles into view.

"...Suzie?" Christina notices all the red splattered across Suzie's blue dress and takes a step back instinctually.

Suzie matches Christina's pace, and her eyes lock onto the pale, exposed flesh of Christina's neck.

It's a prank, Christina thinks, the whole damn thing was a stupid Halloween prank. "Su—" Christina tries to say as Suzie lunges, grabs hold, and pushes Christina through the door and down onto the tiled floor inside.

Christina screams for help, and Rick comes out of the kitchen a few seconds later. "This better not be 'cause you saw another goddamn..." Rick trails off at the sight of Christina on the floor with another girl on top of her. "Roach..." he finishes as Suzie bites deep into Christina's shoulder. The girl howls in agony as she reaches up for Rick's hand, begging him to save her. Her eyes are big and pleading, the venom replaced by desperation.

"Help," Christina manages to spit out with a gurgle of blood, and when all Rick does is turn and run, she whimpers at the unfairness of it all. Her mucky tennis shoes kick out randomly as her body goes into shock.

Out in the front, Connie backs away from the kitchen door, the screaming enough to tell her something's terribly wrong. Rick bursts in, and Connie yelps. "Wha—" she tries to ask as Rick grabs ahold of her.

"Come on!" Rick shouts and takes her by the arm. He pulls her towards the front door, and they both skid to a halt the second they see what's just come through it— Betty Blacker with half her neck gone. Teddy Duchamp with only one cheek. And the both of them staring with cloudy gray, unblinking eyes.

Neither Rick nor Connie have the time to think about anything. Not about what the hell is going on. What's wrong with their eyes, why they're not blinking and, strangest of all, why just before they both lunge, Betty and Teddy were holding hands.

"What in the hell?" Rick shouts as Connie screams. Rick pulls her back the way he came, but stops dead as Suzie emerges from the kitchen.

Connie feels teeth sink into her other arm, and the shock lets Teddy pull her away from Rick. Betty comes into the gap between them and bites into Connie's cheek. "Rick!" she screams as Betty and Teddy drag her away.

This time, instead of just running, Rick jumps into action, and he grabs a stool from the bar. He uses it to push Betty back, all the way to the wall, and then pin her there. He manages to hold her, but barely.

Connie pulls away from Teddy and leaves a chunk of her arm between his teeth. She grabs hold of the wound, but it's too large for her to staunch the blood flow. There's nowhere for her to go. Suzie blocks the way to the back though; for some reason, she just stands there, dead gray eyes watching the scene unfold without even a blink. Rick has Betty pinned by the door, and Teddy's already on his way to her.

"Teddy, stop!" Connie pleads as she stumbles backward, the blood loss and lightheadedness getting to her. "Please Teddy, stop!" As the back of her knees brushes up against the seat of a window booth, she slips and falls back into it.

Rick can barely keep Betty at bay, so there's not much he can do as Teddy closes in on Connie and crawls into the booth on top of her. All he can do is watch over his shoulder as the girl's legs kick wildly till they don't anymore. The horror of it drops his focus and weakens Rick's grip enough for Betty to push free.

Betty falls forward and pushes Rick back to the counter, slams him hard against it. She hangs on to the front of Rick's shirt. He tries to push her off, but she holds fast. Her nails dig into his skin through his clothes, and Rick's mind automatically recalls the time a tortoiseshell cat on Sycamore Street latched onto him as he tried to pet it. It's an odd final thought to have, and there's not much more he can do as Betty sinks her teeth into the flabby meat of his upper chest. Rick sees the faint presence of something wholly inhuman in the cloudy gray of her eyes just before he loses consciousness.

This whole time, Suzie hasn't moved from the other end of the diner—something's got her attention, and it's not the cannibalistic carnage or jet of blood that sprays from Rick's neck all over the jukebox as Betty goes in for the kill. Nor is it the new frequencies she can feel take root inside the freshly dead bodies scattered across the diner. The thing inside her is so focused on those connections that Suzie, the real Suzie, slips through. She stares at something on the side of the counter.

It's a carving, just a few letters, etched into the wood—some dumb kids' initials inside a badly shaped love heart. The letters, they—

Hard-cut to: years ago, a rainy summer day, and a much younger Suzie Palmer sits in the middle of a bedsheet fortress in the basement of Buddy's house, surrounded by a scattering of comic books and candy wrappers. With a rainbow of colored Band-Aids on her knees, Suzie watches as Buddy comes down the stairs— he carries something wrapped in cloth.

"You got it?" Suzie asks.

"Yeah…" Buddy says as he unfurls the cloth and shows her the knife his grandfather had given him as a birthday present. "It was from my grandpa. From the war. Dad doesn't like it, but he let me keep it anyway."

Suzie picks up the knife and catches her reflection in the blade. It looks a lot bigger in her hands than the knives she's seen in the cowboy movies she watches with her dad. The weight surprises her too. Buddy is a little awestruck at the sight of her holding it, unafraid and unintimidated by the danger it poses. He watches as Suzie carves her initials into one of the wooden support beams that holds up the ceiling and their fort's main sheet.

Suzie passes the knife to Buddy. He takes it carefully and carves the letters B and D just underneath Suzie's initials. "Now everyone knows this is our hideout," Buddy says as he finishes. "Just hope my mom doesn't see it."

A quiet moment passes between them before Suzie asks the question Buddy hoped she wouldn't. "So, how do we do it?"

"Johnny says we both gotta cut ourselves first," Buddy answers, and the look on his face says he's not looking forward to that part.

"Johnny Freemantle!?" Suzie asks with more than a hint of doubt.

"Yeah," Buddy answers.

"Johnny...Freemantle?" Suzie asks again.

"Yeah," Buddy says. "He says he an' his cousin did it last time they went camping with their folks."

"I've seen Johnny cry from a splinter. Ain't no way he's done this," Suzie points out.

Buddy smirks, remembering another conversation from a million years ago, all the way at the start of the summer. "Look, if you're too sissy, then we don't need to..."

Suzie scowls at Buddy and, in one swift motion, closes one hand around the knife and pulls it down. She winces at the sound of her skin tearing and the sudden, wet warmth. The knife comes away shiny and red—blood wells between her fingers and drips to the floor.

Buddy just about goes green as Suzie shows him the cut on her palm. "What's-a-matter B-u-ddy? You've not gone all sissy, have you?" She waves her bloody palm in his face. "It's just a little blood," she taunts him. Not about to take that from a girl, Buddy grabs the knife and then pulls in a deep breath before he slices his palm.

"It's just a little blood," the words run through her head as Suzie watches her younger self and Buddy place their bloody hands against the post. It runs together and mixes as both kids let the blood flow into the grooves made by their carvings.

"It's just a little blood," the words run through her head as we fade in, and Suzie finds herself standing, once again, in the middle of a blood-splattered diner.

Suzie watches as the things that used to be her friends stumble back together and then get stuck as they try and move through the front door at the same time. The two go back and forth, with no real thought process, just a singular drive.

FEED!

The whole scene is comic, but there's not even a twitch on Suzie's lips, not even a hint of laughter in her bug-like unblinking eyes.

Inside Suzie's pretty, dead head though, something's waking up. She turns and stumbles back behind the countertop and through the kitchen door.

On her way out of the diner, Suzie steps over Christina. Her eyes twitch as she gurgles on her blood. Still not dead. Suzie looks down at the girl, and as Christina slaps at her weakly, Suzie begins to feel. Somewhere inside, neurons fire, and the other thing within her panics.

FEED!

Suzie kneels next to Christina and bites into her almost mechanically. Christina gives one last slap and goes limp. Suzie pulls up from the dead waitress, a chunk of skin in her mouth that she chews without any enthusiasm. In death, Christina's trademark scowl and indignantly flared nose relax. The girl looks sweeter, more innocent than she ever did in life, and seeing her like that, without that essential Christina quality, brings that strange sensation back. It's guilt. Suzie feels guilty.

A great buzzing bounces around inside her skull, and Suzie grabs hold of her head, tries to shake it off, but it's no use. The sounds bring with it pain, such pain, and beneath it a single impulse.

FEED!

She won't do it, though; she won't feed on another person. Not with this new thing, this guilt. The sound of the burgers sizzling on the grill sparks a compromise. Suzie climbs to her feet and staggers over. She almost falls face-first onto the blackened, grease-smeared surface but manages to brace herself against the frame. Suzie scoops a burger up with her bare hands, sears herself but doesn't seem to notice, and tears into the burned meat. After a few chews, a wave of lightning-hot stabbing sensations hit, and each commands her to:

FEED.

FEED.

FEED!

Something forms in her head, though, something almost human. A single word:

NO!

A sliver of herself returns. Suzie glimpses the light for just a second, but it's enough to get an idea of what this thing inside her wants. It doesn't want her to feed; she's dead. No, it wants her to kill, needs her to. It needs more bodies. She doesn't know why, but it does, and it's hijacking her instincts to make it happen.

Kill—the thing inside Suzie takes this word and searches for what it means, and when it understands, it adopts a new tactic. It knows how to make Suzie kill.

With a white-hot stab of pain, it forces Suzie to see something that will drive her to do as it commands. The image of a good-looking boy, face twisted in shock and horror as he stands over her—the sweat and panic-stricken Danny "Dash" Domico. The last thing Suzie saw was the self-centered panic of a boy scared not for her, but for what her death meant for him, and this thing inside her uses that. The command comes again:

FEED!

And then it changes, comes through the static like it just found the right station.

KILL!

Suzie does not fight it this time. She wants this, and it's getting so hard to stay awake. So much easier to give in, go back to sleep, and let the other thing retake control. So that's what she does.

Revenge of the Rock 'n' Roll Zombie Queen

Cut back to the Domico house, to the garage doors as Dash pulls them open from outside. He's a pompadoured silhouette in the headlights of the Deuce that idles behind him. Dash pushes both doors wide enough, hops back into his baby, and drives her slowly forward till she comes to a stop inside the garage. He treats his car with the kind of care a mother reserves for a newborn.

Dash climbs out and wrestles off his jacket, with no care whatsoever, and it catches on a thin metal chain that sticks out from under his t-shirt. He doesn't notice the snag, and as he throws the jacket aside, it takes the chain with it; the metal snaps and a pair of dog tags lands in the dirt.

"Shit," he says.

Dash is pissed and curses again as he picks them up, and even though it's just the easily fixable chain he broke, it still sits sour. He cleans the dirt off them and feels a little better for it. His fingers trace the name Domico, Francis, and a series of numbers. The touch of the metal, cold on his fingers, warm in his heart, brings a smile to his face. Dash slips the tags safely into the pocket of his jeans then shuts the garage doors. He runs his hand through his hair with a sigh. The drive didn't do much to clear his head, but at least his car runs fine again. That's something, at least.

It's pretty late, but the light in the kitchen window from the house on the hill still shines. Not that Dash cares to notice.

Dash opens a small beer fridge and takes a Ballantine longneck out. He sits on the old army cot, pops the cap off the bottle, and takes a drink. He casts an eye to the table next to him, to a picture of a man who looks like an older, broader version of himself in army fatigues. A much younger woman with sad eyes stands next to him with a baby boy in her arms.

"Here's to you, dad," Dash says as he raises his beer to the photo then downs the rest of the bottle. His hand finds the tags in his pocket, and a single tear forms in the corner of his eye. He takes another beer, then another and another till he falls asleep, face down, in the old army cot.

Dash jumps awake sometime later to a hell of a racket. At first, he thinks it's just rain on the roof till he sees the doors almost jump off the latch. Someone's out there, banging on the door, rattling it like they need to get in.

"I'm up," he says as he rubs his forehead, the noise outside almost indistinguishable from the pounding of his hungover migraine. Whoever's out there doesn't stop, though, and at hearing Dash call out, they rattle the corrugated iron doors even harder. "I'm up!" he shouts at them, "Jesus!"

The banging keeps on till Dash yanks the doors open wide. "What…" is all he says as he takes in the sight of Suzie in a bloody blue dress, a clown's smile of blood smeared across her lips. Her unblinking eyes are cold, devoid of life and yet so, so hungry.

Dash doesn't have time to wonder if he's dreaming or just so drunk that he's seeing things. He only manages to get "The fu—" out of his mouth before Suzie pounces on him like a hungry bobcat.

Suzie grabs Dash by the shoulders and pushes him back inside. Even though he's inebriated, Dash still has enough upper body strength and wits to keep on his feet. He stumbles backward and breaks away from her grasp, and Suzie goes face-first into the dirt.

"Suzie!? How…" Dash trails off as the girl climbs back to her feet like the full-force faceplant wasn't anything. Suzie places her palm against the window of the Deuce as she regains her balance and steps forwards, leaving behind a handprint of blood and dirt.

"No. No way. You're dead," Dash insists, but the Suzie-thing doesn't agree and takes another step towards him. "I saw you fall," he continues, "there's no way!"

Something in what he says sinks in, beyond the feral instinct and compulsion to feed, to kill. Something that whatever remains of Suzie Palmer knows is plain old bullshit. Anger and a fury born from the spark of a cruel and heartless memory fires up the dead parts of Suzie's mind, and she goes haywire.

Suzie growls and lunges at him, but Dash isn't the King of Woodvale for nothing. His instincts kick in, and he side-steps her with well-trained muscle memory like he was faking-out at third.

"Christ! Suzie…" Dash trails off as he gets a good look at all the blood covering her and knows, from the sheer volume of it, that it can't all be hers. "What've you done!?"

Suzie roars at him. The audacity of what he says furthers the conflict within.

Dash looks around quickly, grabs a wrench, and whacks her across the head. Suzie's knocked to the floor with a heavy metal thump.

"Shit," Dash says, and Suzie, dead on the ground with her neck all wrong, fills him with a sickening déjà vu. "Shit!" he says again, seconds later, as she clambers up on all fours with a snarl. Suzie's neck twists back into place and Dash's pants fill with involuntary, warm wetness.

Dash steps around her and makes for the open door. He passes through it, but Suzie grabs the turned-up cuff of his jeans and pulls him to a stop. Dash tries to wriggle his leg free but can't manage it. He looks down, and Suzie bares her teeth. Dash doesn't hesitate and kicks her square in the head with the heel of his free foot, but even with all the force he puts into it, Suzie still doesn't let go. He kicks her again and again, harder and harder, but it's no use. Suzie sinks her teeth into his ankle, and though his jeans and boot take most of it, Dash can feel the pressure of her jaw, like a Pit Bull, and knows if she gets her teeth in, she's not letting go.

With one last effort, Dash manages to pull his leg free, but the force of doing so causes him to lose his balance. He falls back into the garage instead of outside to safety, and the wrench flies out of his hand.

Suzie climbs back to her feet and blocks the door. Dash fakes a right around his car, and Suzie falls for it, leaving the door exposed. Dash falls back, and he's just about there when his foot lands on one of the discarded beer bottles from earlier. Dash slips and lands hard on his back.

Suzie comes back around the car as Dash kicks away from her, but she gains ground fast and drops on top. She just about has him when Dash grabs her wrists, and despite being compelled to kill, despite wanting to more than anything, Dash is still stronger than her. The two of them struggle on the ground. Dash pushes one of her arms away but comes way too close to her mouth, and Suzie, finally, lands a bite.

Dash howls in pain as Suzie rips away a chunk of flesh and taut elastic tendon that snaps with an audible whip. He lets go of her other hand to grab his wound on impulse, which leaves him wide open. Suzie leans in and sinks right into his neck. Her spluttering snarl is almost euphoric.

Dash yells and beats at her with his good hand, manages to get leverage, and pushes her up—she comes away with a full, wet mouthful of him. With a final, desperate shove, Dash pushes Suzie to the side and crawls away from her.

Dash uses his uninjured arm to climb to his feet and catches his breath. With one arm mangled, it hangs limp as even the slightest tension drives the pain home; he has to come to terms with two facts fast. He's never playing ball again, and getting out of this means ending her. After what she did to his throwing arm, he doesn't feel a shred of guilt.

Suzie stands up as she chews on Dash's flesh, almost like she's taunting him. Like she enjoys it.

"What the hell are you!" Dash screams. It'll be easier for him if he thinks of her as a thing.

Dash searches around for another weapon, anything he can use to fight her off.

Most of the tools are at the far side of the garage, but there, on top of the beer fridge—that stupid pen he took from that nerdy bird dog, Buddy. That'll do, he says to himself, and then he curses hard. Right next to the pen are the keys to the Deuce.

The hell was he thinking, trying to run—he could have shut himself in the car and burned rubber out of there. Sure he'd mess up the paintwork, but that'd be a hell of a lot easier to fix than say, a gaping neck wound. His dad once told him that when shit hits the fan, you don't always think right, and it's much easier for folk to make judgments after than to do the right thing in the moment. His old man was right. So, Dash pockets his keys and grabs the pen, holds it like a knife, and charges at Suzie like he's going over the top.

Dash stabs and thrusts the pen deep into Suzie's stomach. The worst place to get stuck, another piece of wisdom imparted by his father, except it doesn't do any good. She doesn't react at all, and now there's no distance between them. Dash barely has time to register what a major mistake this was before Suzie pounces.

Dash, though, is still full of fight and swings a punch at her. "Bitch!" he screams as Suzie falls onto the Deuce from the force of the blow. She lifts herself back up. "Shit," Dash says and punches her again, knocking her back down.

Suzie stirs, as though to sit back up, and Dash just lays into her, hits her over and over. He keeps beating her, but with the blood loss and the booze, he's not got much steam. He grows tired, his punches slow, and he loses his strength. Exhausted, his knuckles red and raw, Dash backs away.

Suzie sits up like it was nothing at all.

Dash, out of breath and out of options, laughs. "No! No goddamn way!" His back hits the wall, and he slides to the ground.

Suzie falls off the hood of the Deuce and staggers forward. She closes in, and from outside the garage, the maniacal laughter of a dying man driven insane by his fate merges with his screams.

As Suzie chews listlessly on a piece of Dash, the presence inside her quietens, satisfied for the moment; it waits for the new connection to form. For its young to hatch within the new host.

At that moment, in that relapse of control, another shred of Suzie lights up. Triggered by the sight of Dash's corpse, fueled by her final, traumatic memory. She feels something deep inside her flare up. Rage. The anger of being grabbed too hard, of being pushed around and falling, and something else. Something not remembered, but real. The sharp object lodged in her abdomen.

The meat falls from her open jaw, and Suzie's hand trembles as it finds its way to the pen jutting out of her stomach. Her fingers twitch as though remembering how to take hold of this object. Suzie manages to form a grip and slides the fountain top out of her—a spurt of blood turned black with ink follows.

She holds it up and looks it over. Something familiar about it begins to light her up. Suzie's eyes start to change, her pupils dilate. The cloudy gray swirls and slowly gives way to the true blue within. Suzie blinks as she finally wakes up.

Her eyes lock onto the pen, and a single word begins to form in her mind.

Too late, the complacent presence within notices what has begun. It tries, in vain, to reassert dominion.

FEED!

NO!

KILL!

Then that word, a word that comes purely from Suzie Palmer. From the happiest of memories buried deep within her.

BUDDY!

HIGHWAY TO HELL

(THE ALL-NIGHT DINER MASSACRE, PART 2)

Despite how it went down, the noise from the Domico house doesn't carry all that far.

Fade to a few miles down the highway, where the only screams that can be heard are coming out of Gordy's car radio. Fresh out of the shop and back on the road, just in time to help Gordy put some distance between himself and what he's done.

Aaaooooooo! Wasn't that a great one, kids? Rockin' Hill Billy don't play nothing' but the best here on WVRK Radio, but folks I gots to be real with ya'll for a minute and ask for a moment of silence to re—

Gordy flips the station, and it turns it to Dale Hawkins singing about Suzie Q. He doesn't find it in good taste, so he shuts the whole thing off. Gordy's been trying hard to stay away from Dash, even sinking as low as hanging out with two of the gearheads who also work at Sam's. Since Betty's been giving him the cold shoulder, he's been seeing the chick sitting in the front seat. He's not that into her and forgets her name half the time. Stacy, right? It's just to keep on keeping on, so he doesn't start to eat himself up for knowing what he knows.

Stu and Chuck stand over near the exposed engine of another car, a cherry-red Buick Roadmaster. The two gearheads have tinkered with it so much; it probably isn't street legal anymore. While the two of them pet at the hopped-up bent eight like it's a puppy, Stu's girlfriend, Bella, sits in the back, working on a pack of gum. She blows some pretty impressive bubbles.

"Come on!" Gordy shouts as he leans out his window. "We gonna race or what?" Stu looks over at Gordy like it's nothing. Gordy taps a make-believe watch and tells them to get a move-on. All this sitting still's driving him stir-crazy.

"We're fixing it, we're fixing it!" Stu shouts over.

Gordy sits back down and wonders, not for the first time, how two guys who talk nothing but cars can't seem to keep their Frankenstein's monster of a Roadmaster running.

"Jeez Gordy, you got ants in your pants or what?" Stacy asks, and the sound of her voice irritates him. Stacy puts the radio back on when he doesn't answer her, and Gordy flips it back off instantly.

"Leave it," he says. "It's killing me."

"What's the matter, hon?" Stacy says and tries to play with a curl of Gordy's hair. He shrugs her off. "What's eatin' you?" she asks.

"You writin' a book or somethin'?" Gordy lashes out, and Stacy takes the hint. They both watch the two morons with the Roadmaster monkey around some more.

"Okay, try it," Chuck says.

Stu jumps around, bangs a beat on the side of their car, and climbs into the driver's seat. He turns the key; the engine chokes but nothing.

"Come on, baby, come on," Stu begs the car to start, and she shows him some mercy by sputtering to life. Chuck cheers and slams down the hood. He runs around the car, hops into the passenger seat, and then slaps his hand against the door with a whoop.

"Let's go!" Chuck yells, and Gordy thinks it's about damn time. Stu drives the Roadmaster onto the highway first, then Gordy pulls his car up alongside them.

Stu leans out the window of his car and shouts to Gordy, "On my count. First to the diner. Got it?"

Gordy revs his engine in response. "Just get countin'!"

"Three…" Stu starts with a grin.

"Say, Gordy, what'd you say happened to your car before?" Stacy asks as the mighty rumble of the engine and rattling starts to make her feel uneasy.

"Two…" yells Stu.

"Wrecked it racin'," Gordy answers, and Stacy's eyes go wide.

"One—go!" finishes Stu, and both cars peel off down the highway in a screeching riot of black fumes and burning rubber.

"Woo!" Gordy screams. "Yeah, baby!" His date doesn't look even half as pleased.

Chuck drums his hands on the dashboard in time to the radio. "Come on, man! Burn rubber!"

Both cars race pretty even along the highway till Gordy starts to get reckless. He takes a corner way too fast, almost going on two wheels, but it pays off, and he takes the lead. Gordy smirks and waves out the window as he passes.

In the other car, Stu's in the zone, full focus on the road, but Gordy pulls further ahead.

"Come on, man!" Chuck says. "Can't this heap go any faster?"

"Don't bug me, man," Stu says, switching gears. He floors it hard, and the Roadmaster kicks ahead with a jerk that sends Chuck and Bella flying back. Bella accidentally swallows her gum and just about chokes.

"Now we're cookin'!" Chuck cheers. "Woo!"

The Roadmaster takes the lead as it goes through another turn, and the All-Night Diner's roadside neon sign looms high above the trees just ahead.

Chuck leans out the Roadmaster's window and flips Gordy the bird. He celebrates early, too early, and Gordy rises to the challenge.

He revs his engine, picks up speed, and Chuck, still half out the window, watches helplessly as Gordy catches up. He keeps pace, stays alongside them long enough to show Chuck the bird himself, and then pulls ahead.

Just as they pass a billboard advertising the new Fiddler's Green housing estate, blue and red lights come to life behind it. A few seconds later, Sheriff Keyes' car joins the race.

Neither Gordy nor Stu notices the heat on their tails, and they push up on each other. Both cars skid into the empty parking lot in a cloud of dust, but as it settles, it's clear Gordy got there first. He kills his engine and looks over at the others triumphantly.

"Aw, come on! That wasn't fair!" Stu complains as he gets out of his car and walks over to Gordy, his arms held out. "I had to haul these two lard asses too!" Bella comes up on Stu and hooks him one for that while Gordy climbs out of his car.

"Bet's a bet," Gordy says. "Now get your ass in there and get me a Coke and the juiciest, fattest burger Rick's got. Go on, get!"

"I'll have one too," Stacy rasps from inside Gordy's car. Even though the vehicle has come to a stop, the rattling in her head hasn't, and she still grips the dashboard with broken nails.

"You heard her," Gordy laughs. "Shake it!" Man, does the euphoria of just about dying, then coming out on top feel right. It's just about the only thing that's been able to break him out of his funk: the adrenaline rush, that sweet surge, and the high of a well-fought victory. For the first time in a week, Gordy forgets that he's an accessory to murder, and God knows what else...

Stu moans, but, as Gordy said, a bet is a bet, so he slumps his shoulders and heads on into the All-Night. A beat later, the Sheriff's car pulls into the parking lot and blocks the road.

"Goddamnit," Gordy curses, and all those good feelings just up and vanish.

"I'll handle it, baby," Stacy says as she slips out of the car and undoes the top few buttons of her shirt. She blows Gordy a kiss and then swings her hips on her way over to the Sheriff. It's all too try-hard, Gordy thinks. Yeah, Stacy's a looker, especially in those capri pants that might as well be painted on, but it's all effort. Not like with Betty—she was a natural. Stacy's just...she's just not Betty.

"Hi there," Stacy says to the Sheriff as he steps out of his car and puts his hat on.

"Evenin' Miss," Keyes says, and he's not for having his apple buttered, not one bit. He motions Gordy and the others to join him. "Outta the cars, folks," and the rest of the kids begrudgingly oblige. They drag their feet and wear hangdog expressions, but they all do as the Sheriff says. "Okay, kids. Mind telling me where's the fire?"

Stacy lays it on all sweet with, "Aw come on, Sheriff." She moves close to him and plays with his badge with her finger. "Don't tell me that Clear Lake County's finest-

finest has got nothin' better to do than pull up some kids for a harmless little old chariot race?"

Keyes casts a mean eye around like he's about to lay down the law when a scream from the diner cuts him off. Everyone turns to see Stu as he bursts out the front door, falls forward, and crawls towards the others.

"Holyshit-holyshit-holyshit-holyshit—" he says without a breath between words as he runs right into Keyes' barrel of a chest.

Keyes grabs the kid by the shoulder and holds him out at arm's length to get a good look at him. Stu's gone so pale that the only color left on his face are the freckles and half-grown mockery of a ginger mustache. "Hey now—"

"They're dead!" Stu interrupts the Sheriff. "Dead! Holy shit, they're all dead!"

Keyes doesn't know what the kid could mean, but ever since finding the body of Susan Palmer like they did, he's been on edge, and he's taking no chances. There hasn't been a murder in Woodvale since he was a rookie, but something changed the day the Rock 'n' Roll Queen died. Keyes hands Stu over to Chuck and Bella, who help sit the rattled kid down on the Sheriff's car. He unholsters his gun and cocks the hammer. "Stay here. All of you," he says, and none of them feel the need to rebel at this particular moment.

Keyes approaches the diner and pushes the door open slowly as he enters with his gun raised. The floor, tables, and counter are splattered with so much blood; it looks more like a butcher shop.

Keyes is hit with an overwhelming pang of sadness at the sight of young Connie Grayson, wedged up against the window of a booth with her skirt hiked up over her knees and abdomen hanging out in shreds. The indignity

96

of it makes it all the worse. If it wasn't for the sloppy sounds of chewing coming from somewhere concealed by the countertop, Keyes would be the kind of man who'd go over there and fix her skirt, crime scene be damned.

He shakes it off and follows the sound to the sight of his old pal, Rick Gardner, on the floor while a teenage girl with a head full of black curls scoops heaps of mush from his open gut right into her mouth. He has just enough time to recognize the ghoul as Betty Blacker before he heaves right there on the floor.

The sound of the Sheriff retching draws Betty's attention. The lifeless eyes of the former runaround girl turn up. The slop of Rick-meat slides out of her jaw and slaps onto the floor though she keeps chewing anyway as she rises.

"Jesus wept..." Keyes whispers as he meets her cloudy, gray eyes. How in the hell can eyes look so dead and so damn hungry at the same time? She isn't blinking either; something about that unsettles him even more than all the rest. Even more than the way she moves, like a puppet with no strings. Like all the parts of her body are just now figuring out how to work together. Like a baby taking its first steps. Keyes knows the girl isn't what you'd call a ballerina, but he's seen her shaking papers at enough home team games to know she's got way more grace and coordination than this.

Keyes has no idea who he's looking at, but this can't possibly be Betty Blacker. So as the girl shuffles towards him, he raises his gun. "Stay back, Miss!" he orders.

The Betty-thing turns her head like she takes in the sound of what the Sheriff says but doesn't comprehend, and makes her way across the diner towards him.

Keyes isn't quite ready to open fire on a girl not much older than his own daughter, even if she is covered in his friend's viscera. Even if she is missing so much flesh around her neck, there's no way on earth she should be alive, never mind closing in on him. Keyes backs up as Betty advances on him and doesn't notice the splayed out girl in the booth behind him twist and claw her way forward. Keyes backs right up close enough for Connie, freshly re-animated, to clamber onto his back.

Keyes is fast, he's a big guy, and Connie doesn't weigh all that much, so he hurls her over his shoulder before she can sink her teeth in. The tussle causes him to drop his gun, though. Connie collides with Betty, and the two of them fall together into a mess of bloody limbs and snarling teeth.

By the time Keyes finds his gun and turns it on them, both girls are back on their feet. He aims it at Betty, center mass. "Miss! I'm warning you. Both of you. Stop!"

Outside the diner, the kids circle Stu, trying to get him to say what he saw, and whip their heads around at the thunder of the gunshot.

They all freeze except for Gordy, who only pauses for a moment before running headfirst towards the sound.

"Gordy, where the hell you going, man!" Chuck calls after him, but Gordy doesn't answer. A second later, Stacy follows. "Shit," Chuck says. "Stay with Stu," he tells Bella, then runs after the other two.

Bella holds Stu close, wondering what the hell is going on. She's so focused, and Stu's so shaken up, neither of them notices a blood-covered Teddy falling around the back corner of the diner.

Gordy barges in through the front door, and what greets him brings him to a halt. Stacy crashes into his back, and a second later, Chuck does the same.

Keyes, gun still raised, points the smoking barrel at two girls so covered in blood and so messed up, none of the kids recognize the pair right away. Stacy screams, and the sound draws the attention of the two bloody girls.

Her eyes are all wrong, but that hair, and those lips, Gordy would know them anywhere. The chunk missing from her neck, a bullet wound in the chest—the sight of what's happened to the girl he loves makes Gordy's whole world fall away. If it wasn't for the two people at his back, he'd probably faint flat on his ass.

"Holy shit!" Chuck shouts.

"Get the hell outta here!" Keyes commands.

The kids are enough of a distraction for Connie to close the distance on the Sheriff. Keyes catches her just in time. The raw, ferocious strength of the girl surprises him; seconds ago, he threw her like a ragdoll, but now Keyes struggles to keep her at arm's length. The hell's gotten into her, he says to himself, and will never know just how literal that thought is.

Gordy's frozen to the spot, and Stacy hides behind him, but Chuck decides to step up. He pushes through, grabs Connie by the back of her shoulders, and tries to pull the girl off the Sheriff. "Give me a hand here!" he shouts. Stacy snaps out of it, runs over, and together she and Chuck manage to pull Connie away. The two of them drag her towards the back of the diner, still clawing at the Sheriff.

Keyes turns his gun on Betty as she moves in on him. "Final warning!" he shouts.

Spurred to action by the sight of the Sheriff aiming at Betty, Gordy yells as he dives towards the lawman. He reaches him just in time to knock his gun aside and save the walking corpse of the girl he loves from a bullet to the head. The Sheriff's aim goes wild as he squeezes the trigger. Instead of putting down the hungry creature in front of him, the bullet goes through Stacy's shoulder on the other side of the diner.

Stacy screams and spins away, clutching her wound. Without her help, Chuck can't hold Connie back, and she falls into him. Connie sinks her teeth into his cheek, and Chuck wails as Stacy falls against the wall and slides to the floor.

Keyes freezes, distracted by accidentally shooting the girl, and Betty grabs hold of his arm. She bites down hard before he can react. He drops his gun; it falls to the ground and slides through a puddle of blood till it comes to a rest at Gordy's feet.

Chuck pushes Connie away, but she takes half his cheek with her. The agony of it drives Chuck mad with rage, and he slams her hard against the wall then delivers a wild right hook that sends the girl to the floor. He backs away, clutching his hand to his face, and laughs nervously as the moment of safety lets a stress-induced hysteria set in. That's all cut short half a second later as the kitchen door swings open, and a bloody, blonde waitress that used to be Christina Cole drags him through before the door can swing closed again.

Slumped against the wall, Stacy winces and sobs as Chuck screams from the kitchen, and a pool of blood leaks out from under the door. The sight of Connie crawling towards her doesn't help much either.

Gordy fumbles with the Sheriff's gun, slick with blood as it is, but he manages to get a grip. His hands tremble as he takes aim with it. Keyes calls out for help as Betty chews on his arm, "Shoot her! Goddamnit!" But he can't—Gordy can't possibly shoot Betty Blacker. No matter what, no matter that she was Teddy's girl and she always told him they were just having fun, no matter that she was never gonna be his, he still loves her. So Gordy does nothing while Betty forces the Sheriff to the ground and looks away, though there's little he can do to shut out the Sheriff's pleas for help and dying screams.

Gordy does nothing while Connie climbs on top of Stacy and tears into her. Stacy, too weak to fight, just reaches out her hand for help and pleads with nothing but desperate eyes.

Gordy does nothing but think about using the gun on himself. In the end, he's too much of a coward even for that. So Gordy does what he does best. Run.

He is out of the diner in seconds and sprints past his car as his old buddy, Teddy, chows down on the bloody, splayed out body of Stu. The kid must have made it to the driver's seat, but he was trapped since he didn't know the trick to start it. Bella's smeared across the Sheriff's cruiser windshield, so Gordy runs straight past and hops into the Roadmaster. He thanks God that the keys are still in the ignition and then burns rubber once more as he races away from the bloodbath at Rick's All-Night Diner.

THE NIGHT BUDDY STOOD STILL

As Gordy races back to town, fade from the starry night sky to the Day house, where Mrs. Day yells, "Buddy! I hope you're not forgetting it's your turn to take out the trash!" She doesn't care about the chores; she just doesn't think wallowing in self-pity is good for the boy. "Young man, I expect to see you down here in five minutes!" She stands at the stairs with her arms crossed, brows furrowed in frustrated concern.

"Leave the boy be," says Mr. Day from the kitchen table. The big man nurses a slice of lemon pie. "C'mon, sit with me."

Mrs. Day does what her husband suggests, but it does nothing to calm her tension. "It's no good for him. Just sulking around like that."

"Well, the boy was sweet on that girl," Mr. Day says as he takes another bite.

"That was never gonna end well," Mrs. Day says and, not for the first time, wonders how her husband can be so cavalier about these things.

"You mean worse than this?" Mr. Day asks.

"You know what I mean," Mrs. Day snaps.

"Yeah, I do," Mr. Day says. "And I also know things ain't going to get any better unless we try."

"It's that easy, huh? You think folks would still read your articles if they knew the color of the man who wrote them?"

"Not saying it's gonna be easy, but listen to him. Listen outside his room at night," Mr. Day raises his voice and then brings it back to a hush. "Listen to the boy cry. We can't spare him the pain of this world. All we can do is show him how to find joy amongst it all."

"You know what people would say. What kind of life is that for anyone?"

"I know your mom and pop didn't care what people said." Mr. Day reaches out and takes his wife's hand. "And I'm glad they didn't."

Mrs. Day pulls her hand away. "And they had to keep moving every damn time someone figured out she wasn't just working for him. Every time some nosy peckerwood saw them hug or kiss. Always on the move. You know what that life is like for a child!?"

"Sometimes it's worth it," Mr. Day says. "A great man once said that to die for love is better than to live without."

"That's stupid," Mrs. Day says. "You're stupid. Who said that?" Her husband answers with a wink. "You quoting yourself now!? Nope, you stole that—"

The sound of Buddy coming down the stairs puts a stop to the argument. Both parents watch as their son comes into the kitchen without a word, his eyes raw and sleeves damp. He seems so fragile that neither of them wants to say a thing out of fear of breaking him.

Buddy pulls the trash bag out and drags it through the back door. The pitiful sight of him makes both Mrs. and Mr. Day realize their argument is pointless.

"What are we gonna do about him?" Mrs. Day asks, wistful with worry.

"Not much we can do," Mr. Day answers, and he retakes his wife's hand. This time she lets him and slips her fingers between his. "A man loves what he loves." His kind smile is infectious.

Mrs. Day raises a brow and lowers her eyes down to the now empty plate in front of her husband. "You mean me or the pie?"

Mr. Day leans over and kisses her. "Why can't it be both?"

Jump-cut outside to the backyard. Blissfully quiet, save for the crickets that chirp in sheer ignorance of the hell coming for this suburban pastoral. The house sits on the edge of town, which means it's pretty dark out. The porch light comes on, but the damn thing just loves to flicker on and off for a good few minutes despite Mr. Day's claim that he fixed it.

A gentle summer night's wind stirs the shrubs.

The back door opens, and Buddy steps outside. On any ordinary night, Buddy would wait for the light to stay steady before going around to the bins, but he just wants to get back into his room and shut the world away.

He struggles down the back steps with the trash and dumps it on the ground next to a metal trash can at the corner of his house. Buddy lifts the lid and pushes the bag inside it, though it doesn't quite fit.

"Oh, come on!" he moans, and he tries to push the bag down to little effect. He shoves it a little harder, but it still won't fit, and it breaks the dam inside him: so much anger and frustration races to the surface.

Buddy pounds on the trash and smashes down on it. He lets the fury flow. "Goddamn piece of shit!" he yells as he turns the garbage into a punching bag to the staccato beat of the flickering porch light. He needs this, needs to let it out, and boy, does it feel good to smash something.

104

When he's done, Buddy stands over a mess of ripped plastic and discarded trash, out of breath and elated. He feels infinitely better, though knows it won't last.

Buddy cleans up the mess, and it's only after he puts the lid back on that he notices he's covered in gunk. He wipes the filth on his shirt to his immediate regret. His mom really isn't going to like that, and the thought brings him back down.

A rustle in the bushes distracts him. It's something more substantial than the wind, and it stops Buddy in his tracks. He watches the shadows with suspicion. Something cracks, and Buddy just about jumps out of his skin.

Then nothing.

The silence that follows almost convinces Buddy that he's alone. Except he's unwilling to take the chance, so he keeps still and watches as the bush rustles. Even as the wind dies down and all else is still, Buddy can feel something in there, watching him.

Another crack. There's no denying it now—something's in there, and Buddy knows he's going to have to deal with it. Living on the outskirts means it could be anything from a badger to a bobcat.

It's something much worse.

Buddy approaches and pulls aside some branches…nothing, except maybe…the flickering porch light doesn't help at all either.

Maybe it was a mouse or something, Buddy says to himself as he peers closer and still finds nothing.

YEOW!

The Fredericksons' cat yowls as it leaps out of the shadows and lands a claw across his cheek on the way. Buddy yells as he falls flat on his backside, and the mean-spirited beast hisses at him in indignation as it struts away.

"Damn cat," Buddy complains as he climbs to his feet and dusts himself off. He turns to head back inside just as the porch bulb finally quits flickering, and as the light burns bright and steady, Buddy sees what stands by the back door of his house.

For a second, he thinks it's his imagination. It can't possibly be Suzie Palmer standing there in the furthest reaches of the porch light. Except he can only really make out her face, her messy yet unmistakable pageboy cut, and those perfect baby blue eyes. The rest of her is covered in so much dark blood and filth, she blends in with the shadows.

Logic, reason, every scientific bone in his body says it can't be her; there's no way, and yet Buddy doesn't even question it.

Suzie sways like she's sleepwalking. She lifts one arm, her fingers twitch independently of each other, and thick droplets of blood drip from each of them. Her mouth twitches, somewhere between a snarl and a cough.

"Bu-bu-lp-he-u-ck," comes out from between her lips, and even from a distance, Buddy can smell the fetid stench of decay and fresh blood. It doesn't offend him though—as unpleasant as it is, it's proof that she's really there.

Suzie coughs, chokes, then words form. Real, human, living words. "He-h-he-help. Help. He-help m-me. Bu-u-ddy. H-help me B-Buddy." And she faints forwards.

Buddy races in and catches her. She feels unbelievably light in his arms. As she passes out, her hand relaxes, and something falls from her clenched fist—a black, monogrammed fountain pen. The very one Dash stole from him a week ago. The very one Suzie gave him for

106

his birthday years ago when he said he wanted to be a sci-fi comic book writer.

"You better write one about me! Zoozie, the Space Pirate," her words echo from his memories, and he remembers the way she stood on the edge of his sofa like it was the bow of a ship. The way she whacked him with a wooden spoon when he tried to tell her that girls can't be space pirates.

He looks around, confused, then down at Suzie's face. Even covered in filth, even with her blonde curls stained and clotted with gore, she's the most beautiful girl in the world to him. It doesn't matter how messed up this is, that she's supposed to be dead, that she's covered in so much blood it can't possibly be all hers. It doesn't matter—Suzie Palmer is back, and she needs his help. So Buddy checks that the coast is clear before he lifts her up in his arms and carries her over to the door.

When he gets there, Buddy gently lays her body to rest and creeps the back door open while praying his dad did a better job fixing the door squeal than he did the porch light. The door opens without so much as a squeak. Buddy takes a few quietly careful steps through the kitchen, now empty, and passes the door down to the basement where he intends to sneak Suzie. First, though, he needs to make sure his parents aren't going to come into the kitchen and catch him holding a dead girl's body. That would just look all kinds of wrong.

As Buddy slinks into the hall, he takes extra care not to step too hard and make any of the loose boards creak. This whole escapade makes him painfully aware of his father's lackluster and scattergun attitude to home repair.

He cracks the living room door open, and a quick peek inside lets Buddy see his folks all snuggled up together watching the opening credits for I Love Lucy.

That's a relief; they'll make so much noise laughing their asses off soon enough that they wouldn't hear him even if he threw Suzie down the stairs and she landed on a marching band.

With the coast clear, Buddy returns to Suzie and wedges the back door open. Just as he stoops down to take Suzie up in his arms, a hissing ball of nightmares and fury that is the Fredericksons' cat jumps up to the back door and blocks his way back in.

Buddy tries to shoo it away, and the cat just hisses at him. When Buddy gets a little bold and swings his arm at it, the cat slashes back. It manages to land a pretty nasty cut across his forearm, and he recoils in pain. The cat yams loudly at him, daring him to do it again. Buddy has had enough and charges at it. The cat, never having seen Buddy act so bold, skitters away in shock. It skulks into the shadows to lick the blood from its claws and plan its revenge.

Buddy stops for a moment and casts a cautious eye around to check that no one is coming to investigate the screeching. When he's satisfied he's still good, he lifts Suzie and carries her into the house.

Halfway through the kitchen, Buddy can see down the hall to the back of his parents' heads, bathed in the glow from the TV. Canned laughter blends with the real stuff. He's just about at the door down to the basement when his dad calls on him from the living room.

"Buddy?"

Buddy freezes. "Y-yeah, dad?"

"Don't stay up too late, you hear?" he calls back.

"S-sure thing dad," Buddy says and tiptoes the rest of the way.

The basement of the Day house, half-den and half-workshop, hasn't seen much traffic in recent years. Not since Buddy and Suzie stopped building dens and forts out of bedsheets and pillows. Not since Buddy's dad gave up on being "handy." Most of the tools were long since packed up and stashed in the backyard shed, the worktables taken over by the Handy Andy Precision Microscope and Lab sets Buddy got last Christmas.

Buddy carefully continues down the stairs, and even though Suzie doesn't weigh all that much, it's enough to put him off balance, and he slips. Luckily, though he makes a lot of noise, he manages to keep hold of Suzie, and the noise from the upstairs TV covers him.

At the bottom, Buddy carries Suzie over to the old sofa by a useless, uneven pool table and moldy recliner. She'll be safe enough there; his parents don't come down here all that much anymore, but he's going to need to get her some clean clothes at the very least. That means going back upstairs and right past the two of them.

Luck is on his side once again, though, and neither his mom nor his dad notices him as he creeps past them—Lucille Ball is, and always will be, the perfect distraction.

Upstairs, he grabs a few towels from the bathroom first so that he can put off sneaking into his parents' room as long as possible. There are just some places a teenage boy doesn't want to go, and one of them is his mom's underwear drawer.

Buddy doesn't want to think about this too much, but his mom and Suzie don't exactly have the same…figure. He grabs her a loose looking chemise and tries hard not to look at the black lace things tucked away at the back of the drawer, then hunts for some clothes in the closet. He remembers his mom complaining about dresses and things she bought that were too tight to wear, but he also knows she's not the type to throw them out. That'd be giving up, and Buddy knows all too well that Mrs. Day does not back down from anything. Even the mail-order capri pants suit that she couldn't even get past her thighs. Buddy still remembers how his mom made them all eat nothing but salad for a whole week after that episode. There's no way she'd send it back and ask for a bigger size, though, so it, like many other items, found their way to the back of the closet. Sure, it doesn't fit his mom, but Buddy reckons it should fit Suzie just right.

As Buddy rummages through the closet, he knocks open an old photo album onto a photo of his parents standing outside the house. It still has a SOLD sign in the yard, and from the size of his mom's stomach, Buddy guesses the photo must have been taken just before he was born. They both look so happy, and it reminds Buddy that Suzie's parents are still out there, thinking their daughter lost to them. He wonders if he should call and let them know she's here. How, though? They'd never believe for a second she was back from the dead; Buddy's having a hard enough time wrapping his head around that one, so how could he expect them to accept it over the phone? They'd think it a prank and hang up, or worse, call the Sheriff on him. One thing at a time, Buddy tells himself. Get Suzie on her feet first, and then he can take her home himself.

He flips through the photo album and lands on some old photos of his grandparents. He didn't know them all that well; both died when he was little. His grandfather was a thin man. Tall, rakish, with thick, untamable hair. Buddy guesses that's where he gets that from since the only real difference between the two, physically, are Buddy's darker skin and the black-rimmed glasses he wears. He wishes he had the devil-may-care attitude his grandfather exudes, though. Buddy's heard about how hard life was for the two of them, but he can't picture it. Every other page, they're in a new apartment, and he sees his mom grow up in dozens of different places. Buddy can't even imagine. He's barely been out of Woodvale, after all.

His grandparents weren't allowed to marry. He was white, and she was black, but despite it all, they loved each other. They made it work. Buddy wonders, for a moment, that if his grandparents could, then maybe—

"Buddy!" his mom calls from the bottom of the stairs, on her way up.

Buddy quickly tucks the clothes inside the towels and checks to make sure he's left the room just as he found it, and runs back out into the hall.

On his way back down the stairs, Buddy comes face to face with his mom. He gulps.

"Buddy, where are you going with all those towels?" she asks, and Buddy presses his haul tight against his chest to hide the stolen clothes.

"Um," he tries, "I kinda messed up a science…thing. It's a mess." When his mom's eyes go wide, he leans in. "A real mess. I'll clean up! Don't worry, mom, but you really don't want to go down there."

Mrs. Day squints at her son. "What's that smell?" she asks, and Buddy realizes his shirt stinks with all the blood and filth that rubbed off on him as he carried Suzie.

"It's the experiment. I made a mistake, and I'm probably gonna need at least five baths to get rid of it, so…"

His mother throws her arms in the air and shakes her head as she walks past her son.

A few minutes later, Buddy's back in the basement and hopes to hell his cover story holds. He takes a towel and wets it at the rusty old sink in the corner, and starts to clean up Suzie's face. As all the grime and gore come away, his heart breaks at what's been done to her. Somebody's worked her over but good, and the rage that builds inside Buddy is almost enough to have him rip the towel in two. It's the peace and grace underneath that cools his heels, though. Despite it all, she still glows. He'd forgotten how beautiful she was. Or, perhaps, he made himself forget?

Especially the way she sleeps, all poised yet peaceful with her lips parted just slightly. No air slips from between those lips, but Buddy doesn't question it. She's back, and that's all that matters. As Buddy cleans the blood smears from her lips, he finds his finger lingering on them. They're so soft, so sweet, so...Suzie.

Her eyes jerk open, and Buddy yanks his hand away.

"I—" Buddy tries to say, but Suzie interrupts as she leans over the couch and spews up all the vile stuff inside her over the edge. Buddy moves back, gives her some room as she goes again, and a black, bilious foul goo pours out of her.

She looks up when she's done. Vomit runs down from her mouth. "Thanks, Buddy," Suzie says. "Sorry for blowing chunks all over the place." And she passes out again.

Buddy wipes away the spit and puke, thinking that when his folks are out tomorrow, he can sneak her upstairs to the shower.

He fishes out some sleeping bags from the camping gear stashed in a beat-up old wardrobe, and it brings back memories from a hundred years ago when he and Suzie used to lie on them out back and watch the stars.

Despite being ice-cold, Suzie doesn't shiver, but Buddy still covers her up anyway and leaves a bucket by her side just in case. He takes the other sleeping bag over to an old, duct-taped recliner and curls up like he does most nights, though this time, Buddy drifts off without tears or screaming into his pillow.

When Buddy finally falls asleep, it's with a smile on his face. The first in a very long time.

NECKING AT THE DRIVE-IN

Buddy isn't the only one cozying up next to a sweetheart this fateful evening.

Cut to: the Paradiso Drive-In Theatre, just over the town line between Woodvale and Cherry Lake. Cut to: the eternally deluded optimist Johnny Freemantle, who sits in his cousin's car with the equally eternally sour-faced Sally Perkins. It would be fair to say she doesn't look all that keen to be there. It beats sitting at home alone all night, or so she thought, though if Johnny tries to get his arm around her one more time, she's liable to break it.

Like most Saturday nights, the Paradiso is jammed full of cars with kids either snuggling up with their dates or fooling around with their buddies. On the screen, pink jelly slops all over a diner. The movie's about the only decent thing to come out of the night, Sally reckons. That Steve McQueen too, she smiles, and at least the smell of butter and popcorn helps cover up the aroma of stale farts and burger wrappers that's soaked into the seats of Johnny's cousin's car. Sally wonders if it was this dirty before Johnny's cousin loaned him the jalopy, though if she were a betting gal, she wouldn't put money on it.

Johnny mistakes the way Sally sits with her arms folded, eyes fixed fast on the movie as intent focus, and not a concentrated effort to ignore him. Perfect, it's showtime, he thinks, and fakes a yawn just for Sally to say, "Don't even try it, Johnathan Freemantle."

Johnny stops mid-maneuver and slumps down. Disappointed, he sighs. "Why she gotta use my full name," he says to himself. It makes him feel like a kid in trouble.

"At least we've got it stopped!" comes through the drive-in speaker clipped inside the car's window. "Yeah, as long as the Arctic stays cold," another, more rebellious voice says back.

"Just send it here," Johnny says under his breath and snorts a laugh as he casts a dirty glance at Sally.

She snaps her head towards him, no idea what's so funny but sure she's being insulted, and Johnny tries to deflect with a cheesy smile. He reaches around for an excuse, comes up with a half-empty popcorn tub, and tosses the rest into the back seat.

"Popcorn?" Johnny asks. "We're outta popcorn! Gonna get some more. Want some—I'll get you some!"

Sally shakes her head at him and turns back to the movie. Johnny shrugs and climbs out of the car, and Sally thinks maybe she's too rash. "Johnny," she leans out the window and shouts to him, "get me a Coke?"

Johnny, who will take whatever victory he can, smiles. "You got it," he says, overjoyed she'll let him buy her something without really thinking too hard on what that says about him as he struts over to the Snack Stand. Johnny waves the empty tub of popcorn around as he walks and rehearses the conversation he fully intends to have with Buddy the next day. "Hey man, how'd last night go? Oh, you know, not too bad. Necked with Sally Perkins. What, seriously? Yeah, sincerely. Way to go, man, way to go! Thanks man, she is stacked! Tell me about it…"

Johnny reaches the Snack Stand and dumps the empty popcorn tub into the trash. He sighs as he comes back down to Earth. "Yeah, right," he says. "This night can't get any worse." He walks inside.

The place is empty—no sign of anyone, not even the perpetually bored bubblegum-blowing champion behind the counter. The one who somehow manages to make pouring soda an act of aggression. Johnny walks up to the bar and sees no one there either. He wonders if he'll get away with pinching an unused poster or two, thinking how a few sci-fi ones might help cheer Buddy up. Maybe grab that racy *Teenage Monster* one and some Hot Tamales for his good self while he's at it.

His better angel wins out, though, and Johnny drums loudly on the countertop for attention instead. "Hey!" Johnny calls out. "Anyone here?"

There's no reply, but Johnny can hear something over the hum of refrigerators and air conditioning. He leans over the counter, and there's nothing, except that noise is a little louder—something like a dog gnawing at a messy bone. He walks around the side of the counter and right into a scene from a horror movie. The concession girl is on the floor with her smock ripped open and most of her face too. All bloodied up, another girl leans over the body and mindlessly picks at the corpse as though it was a snack bowl. Johnny doesn't recognize it's Connie Grayson till she slowly turns, sensing something warm and alive behind her.

The thing that used to be Connie looks up, and a mushy glob of torn flesh and stringy, bright blue, twice chewed bubblegum slips from her snarling, bared teeth.

Johnny's seen a lot of horror movies. Nothing like this, though, and for once, Johnny Freemantle doesn't have anything to say. There's no dramatic music, just the mechanical whirl of the soda machines, the wet slaps of hands sticky with fresh blood, and snapping teeth as Connie crawls towards him. She uses a candy rack to climb up, only to pull it over and have it pin her down.

Johnny backs up and right into the cold dead bulk of Sheriff Keyes as he stumbles through the back door. Keyes has trouble coordinating his big arms, and by the time he moves to grab hold of Johnny, the kid manages to squirrel away with the kind of agility you wouldn't associate with someone of his build.

Seconds later, Johnny skids out of the Snack Stand with his head turned so far around he runs smack into a bunch of jocks wearing Cherry Lake High letterman jackets. One of them grabs Johnny by the shirt, pulls him up, then throws him to the ground. "Watch where—" the jock doesn't get to finish his threat as Johnny picks himself up and takes off at warp speed.

"What a weirdo," another one of them says, and the three of them laugh while watching Johnny peel away across the drive-in.

"Yeah, run, lard ass, run!" the third one shouts, and the three of them swap high-fives. Not looking where he's going himself, the jock turns and whams right into Connie, though he's not as fussed on account of her potentially being a cutie.

"Woah, babe," he laughs and looks back at his friends who join in again. He takes her by the shoulder and holds her out to get a good look, and his face turns sour at how filthy she is. It's like some wild cat whose fur is all matted with mud; she smiles like she's all gum, and what the hell is that stuck in her teeth? As the jock's face drops, Connie opens her mouth, rolls her head back, and swings her snarling teeth into the bottom of his neck. He screams and grabs hold of her but can't get her loose.

The others panic and run off, though Keyes emerges from the Snack Stand and grabs one of them as he whips past. The jock is lifted off his feet like he was nothing. The last one scatters, races to the exit, and then skids to a halt. More of those things emerge from the darkness at the edge of the drive-in.

Johnny runs past two parked cars and glances behind him just as the first jock is forced down with Connie on top of him, and Keyes bites down on the second one's head like it was an apple. Even over the thunder of his own heartbeat, Johnny swears he can hear the crunch.

"Damn…damn," Johnny pants, and then "Damn!" as he comes to a hard stop. Two more of them, those bug-eyed things, except he recognizes them. Teddy Duchamp and Betty Blacker, or at least they used to be, and they're just about to close in on a convertible from both sides. The kids in the car are so busy swapping saliva they don't see Teddy and Betty coming.

Both of them lean inside, almost in tandem, and pull then tear the screaming couple apart.

"Damn," Johnny says, and he draws the attention of Betty, who drops the teen girl at the sound, and Johnny adds another "Damn!" just for good measure. The girl in the car isn't dead, but from the force of the spray coming from her neck and the way it washes the windshield red, it won't be long before she is. Her boyfriend's a goner for sure. Teddy is right on top of him, and he's not struggling anymore. Betty, though, she's got eyes for Johnny now, and she's on the move.

Johnny breaks for it again and promises himself that if he makes it out of this, no more junk food. He's gonna run the track every morning before school and get in shape. Every part of him chafes, but he reckons that's nothing compared to what those things have done to

118

those two in the convertible, what they'll do to him if they catch him.

So Johnny runs like he's never run before. Runs past another car—the door opens, and a teenager falls out with Chuck from the Stop-n-Go on top of him. Johnny just sidesteps and keeps on running as Chuck silences the screaming kid by ripping out his throat with one full-mouthed bite.

Jump-cut to: Johnny's cousin's car. A girl screams over the drive-in speaker, though it kinda sounds to Sally like it came from further away than that. She doesn't think too hard about that as she sits with her arms crossed and nibbles on her nails while wondering just what in the hell is taking Johnny so damn long. The driver's side door is yanked open, and Johnny throws himself inside the car, giving Sally a hell of a fright. "Jesus, Johnny!" she shouts. Johnny ignores her and tries to start the engine. "What the hell, Johnny?" she asks, then seeing as he's empty-handed, "Where's my Coke?"

The car starts, and Johnny throws it into reverse. He pulls away hard, rips the drive-in speaker cord, and floors it as fast as it can go backward. "Johnny, what the hell are you doing?" Sally demands to know. "You're gonna have to pay for that!" But Johnny's way past listening, and he's full-on for getting his ass out of there.

Trouble is, so are most of the other cars that aren't currently under siege from bug-eyed teenage monsters. All over the drive-in, cars start up and make for the exit, except all they do is jam each other up and block the road for kids on foot fleeing more of the things.

Johnny drives with the ferocity of a bootlegger, with Sally plastered to her seat. "Johnny Freemantle, you stop this car right now!" she demands, and when he doesn't, she grabs hold of his arm and forces him to look at her.

Sally sees a look in Johnny's eyes that she's never seen before, a hard and focused intensity that turns his goofball awkwardness into something sincere. Sally doesn't know what's happening, but she knows it's serious, and she breaks eye contact just in time.

"Look out!" she screams, and Johnny turns back to the road just in time to see the car run over somebody. He hits the brake, and the car skids to a halt as whoever it was thuds and bounces over the roof. Johnny and Sally turn in unison and look out the rear window to see a bug-eyed thing with the unmistakable black curls of Betty Blacker sitting up like being run over wasn't even a thing. They watch as her twisted limbs click back into place, almost like the whole incident was happening in reverse.

Another car squeals around them, taking the sudden curve hard but well. It's missing a door, and there's a severed arm clinging onto the back bumper.

Johnny and Sally turn to each other before peeling off and leaving Betty to climb to her feet in their dust.

The car in front races towards the exit, right as a blood-splattered blonde waitress stumbles out of the entrance kiosk, leaving behind a half-eaten attendant, and stands in the middle of the road. The convertible spins out as it tries to avoid hitting Christina. Whoever's driving loses control and skids to a sideways halt right in the middle of the exit—blocking the road. A second later, another car crashes into them. Then another. And another. Just like that, there's a multi-car pile-up sealing off the only way in or out of the Paradiso.

Johnny sees the whole thing happen, almost in slow-motion, and he slams on the brakes, bringing his cousin's car to a halt before it could become part of that mountain of twisted metal and broken glass.

Sally sighs with relief and thinks, "Thank God for Johnny." He's saved her twice tonight, and she swears she's going to treat him nicer after this. She always thought he was a candy ass, but after this, not anymore. Sally unlocks her seatbelt to lean over and plant a big kiss on him, and just as she makes her move, another car crashes full speed into the back of them. The impact sends Johnny's head into the steering wheel, knocks him out cold, and Sally right through the windshield.

Johnny wakes up to a powerful ringing in his ears shutting out all the screams; more cars have rammed into the pile-up. Whatever survivors there are struggle to climb out of the wreckage while flesh-hungry goons grab at them.

One of the ghouls pulls a girl free from the carnage and saves her from burning to death, only to sink his teeth into her.

Johnny watches as his date is dragged from the roof of a pickup by what looks like old Rick from the All-Night Diner. "Oh Jesus, God no!" he cries as he fumbles with his belt and tries to open his door. It's jammed, and there's nothing he can do to stop the cook from having a bite to eat.

Johnny forces the door open, and the momentum flops him to the ground. Worse still, he can't get his legs to cooperate enough to stand up, so all he can do is shuffle away from the wreckage on his backside. Johnny crawls backward till he bumps up against something, up against the legs of Betty Blacker. He stares up at her, and even though Johnny once said he'd die a happy man if he ever got between Betty's legs at the Paradiso, he screams, "NO!" as she snarls and pounces on him.

Above the screams and chaos at the Paradiso, we pull up, as "The End" hangs on a screen pocked with magnified blood splatter and framed with thick, black smoke. It catches fire and burns like the rest of the passion pit.

ATTACK OF THE
TEENAGE ZOMBIE

The singed, orange hue of the acrid sky over the drive-in fades to the harmonious, golden sunlight of a beautiful morning.

Ignorant of the horrors from the previous night, the town of Woodvale rises like any other day. Men in slippers and robes, cradling cups of coffee, wave politely to one another as they fetch newspapers from their mailboxes. Dogs take up their porch vigils, basking in the morning light, and the Fredericksons' cat returns home to sleep in the shade, still bitter from the audacity of the Day boy.

Cut to: Buddy as he wakes up, only he's a kid again. Comics, toys, and candy wrappers are scattered all over the floor. Buddy's hair is flat on one side, and his glasses sit at a weird angle. He gives them a quick check to make sure he's not broken another pair; his mother had warned him on many occasions not to fall asleep with them on for that very reason.

There's an empty sleeping bag across the room, and right behind Buddy, cuddled up in a ball of blonde curls and bobby socks, there's Suzie. They must have fallen asleep as they shared the latest *Weird Fantasy* comic. She snores, ever so slightly, and it's more like a gentle hum than anything abrasive. Buddy doesn't want to wake her up, but he has to. She really shouldn't be here. When she came over last night with a bag of chips and the new issue she bought from Greene's, what was Buddy supposed to do besides sneak her into the basement?

Suzie told him that her mom thought she was at a sleepover at Christina Cole's house, but since Christina's kind of nasty, Suzie decided she'd rather hang out with Buddy. He's amazed that she managed to stay all night without getting caught, and though they're probably safe enough, he doesn't want to push his luck further. They'd be in big trouble if her folks knew she was there.

"Suzie, wake up," Buddy whispers. He nudges her a little.

Suzie bats at him with a sleepy hand, still coated in a fine layer of chip dust.

"Come on," Buddy shoves her again. "Wake up, please, Suzie."

Suzie mumbles something incoherent and then turns her back to Buddy.

"Suzie." Buddy puts his hand on her shoulder and pulls her over to him. "We're gonna be in trouble if you—"

Suzie turns, and her eyes are wide open, clouded, and lifeless. Her mouth is smeared with blood, and when it opens, a skittering mass of black, chittering ants flood out. They cover Buddy so fast he doesn't even have a chance to scream—

Buddy wakes up for real, gasping for breath. His forehead is slick with sweat and he can still feel the pinprick tickling sensation of those ants crawling through his open mouth. He slaps both sides of his face and spits, though nothing but morning breath scented drool comes out.

Wide awake now, Buddy picks up his glasses and fixes them on his face. He glances at the sofa, and it's empty.

At some point during the night, Suzie must have come over and curled up next to him. Maybe it's the fresh morning light, but she doesn't look half as banged up as she did last night.

Suzie's grown some, for sure, but she looks like a kid again for just a second as she sleeps next to him, though she doesn't snore like how Buddy remembers. As Buddy watches her sleep, he's not sure Suzie's even breathing. Even wrapped up and snuggled into him, she's cold. Not just cold, but devoid of all warmth. Buddy wants to put his arm around her, rub some heat back into her, but would that be right? Did she come on over and climb onto the recliner with him on account of how cold she was? He reaches out, shakily, to stroke her hair by way of a compromise, and her eyes open just as he's about to. Buddy stops but doesn't pull his hand back.

"H-hi," Buddy says because he can't think of what else to say to a dead girl who's just woken up beside him.

Suzie smiles at him. "Hi Buddy," she says, and then her smile falls away as she trembles and sobs. Buddy doesn't know what to do, so he just holds there as Suzie opens up. "I've done bad things, Buddy," she cries and leans into his chest.

"Suzie," Buddy ventures. "W-what happened to you?" But that doesn't help one bit.

"I don't know!" Suzie wails, the sound muffled by Buddy's shirt.

Buddy doesn't know what to say or if he should say anything at all. He works up the courage to put his arm around her. Buddy holds her close, and Suzie lets it all out. After a few minutes, she regains some composure. Suzie looks up at Buddy and tries to put it all together. "I fell, I think, and then…then it was like I was in this dream." She wipes a tear away. "And in the dream, I was doing all these bad things, and I couldn't stop myself even though I wanted to. There was this thing, it sounded like a lot of things all at once, whispering to me, telling me to do more and more, telling me to bite people, to eat them, Buddy! *Eat* them! Then I woke up, and all the bad stuff was real!"

Suzie bursts into tears again, and Buddy holds her tighter. "It's okay—"

"And, and when I woke…all I could think of was you, Buddy," Suzie interrupts him. "I think it was remembering you that woke me up. I know that doesn't make sense, but you're the only guy I know I can trust."

"Suzie—"

"Please, Buddy," Suzie asks. "Please help me figure this out?"

Buddy holds her chin gently and tilts her face to his to meet her eyes. "We're gonna fix this," he says with confidence he never knew he had. "Whatever this is. Whatever happened to you, we're gonna fix this."

Suzie has never seen this side of Buddy before, but to be fair, no one has. He doesn't look like the boy she used to put pots on her head with and pretend to be robots from Mars. There comes a time in a person's life when something happens that snaps them out of who they are and turns them into who they need to be. For Buddy Peter Day, it's his childhood best friend Suzie Palmer, in deep trouble and no one to turn to but him.

"You're not scared?" Suzie asks.

"Why'd I be scared?" Buddy answers.

Suzie pulls away just a little, not wanting to tell Buddy the full details of what she's done. Frightened she might lose it and do to him what she did to Dash and Teddy and…Betty…

"There's somethin' wrong with me, Buddy," she tries to warn him. "Somethin'…somethin' bad."

"It's okay," Buddy says. "You're…Suzie; you're a lotta things. Bad ain't one of them. It's gonna be okay. Promise."

Suzie smiles, and for the first time since she woke up in that casket, she feels almost human. She leans back into his chest. "Thanks," she says. "Thank you, Buddy."

So Buddy works out a plan, or at least the start of one, and it begins with pouring Suzie a bucket of hot water and finding her some soap. It's not much, pretty undignified, but she'll be able to clean up a little. It'll also give her something to do while he heads upstairs and tries to figure out what the hell he's gonna do to take care of this.

Up in the kitchen, a coffee pot steams on the countertop, the rest of the Day house just coming to life. The pot boils, but his folks are nowhere to be found, which isn't like them. Usually, there's a race on to be the first to pour some of that jet-black, steaming liquid.

The TV carries through into the kitchen, though it's not clear enough to discern. Buddy follows it and finds his folks as they stand together, blocking the screen from view. He creeps in close enough to listen to them as his dad says, "We should tell him."

"No," his mom says. "No, it's too…ghastly."

"He's got a right," his dad says. "He can handle—"

Buddy butts in, "Handle what?" and he walks into the room. When neither of his parents answers him, he asks again. "Handle what?"

"Buddy…" his mom starts but trails off as she breaks eye contact.

Buddy turns from his mother to his father for answers instead. "What is it, dad?"

"Buddy," his dad starts. "It's—"

"It's on again!" Mrs. Day interrupts, and she turns to the TV. "Shut it off!"

"No," Mr. Day insists. "He's a right to know."

The three of them stare at the TV as a newscaster speaks: "It is indeed a sad day for all of Clear Lake County as a tragic pile-up, and the resulting fires at the Paradiso Drive-In Theatre in Cherry Lake have claimed the lives of a yet unknown number of people. Authorities are still to report in on the death toll as reports suggest they're having trouble identifying the dead. Meanwhile, yesterday the town of Woodvale mourned the loss of one of its brightest stars. Young Susan Palmer, who was to be buried this afternoon. A few hours ago, her body was reported stolen from the Eternal Gardens Funeral Parlor. Clear Lake County Sheriff's Department suspects the theft is part of a CLU student fraternity prank; however, Sheriff Keyes cannot be reached for comment regarding either incident. The Palmers…"

While Buddy and his folks listen to the news, cut over to the Domico house where Danny "Dash" Domico has just woken up, and boy is he hungry. All he can think to do is:

FEED.

Dash rises to his feet, uses the Deuce to get all the way upright, and pauses. There's something about the car that, for the slightest of moments, causes him to twitch.

128

A flicker of something important, the ghost of a memory, and then:

FEED.

Dash staggers past the car and out through the open doors of the garage. His bulging, gray cataract-scarred eyes fix on the house at the top of the hill, and he bares his teeth in a ravenous snarl.

Inside the house, little Jessie Domico lies in bed asleep. She doesn't hear the door to her room creak open. Nor does she see the thing that was once her big brother as he stands in the doorway. Dash watches her as she gently snores. Maybe a part of him fights against what the hunger wants him to do, remembers that this sleeping child shares some of the same blood as him. He hesitates and lingers on the threshold, drool spilling over his inhumanly curled lips.

Jessie stirs, turns around, and sighs. Whatever she dreams of brings an adorable pout to her face.

FEED.

Dash's eyes narrow, and he moves into the room. His steps are awkward and jilted. Toys clatter, yet the racket does not wake little Jessie as Dash approaches the bed and towers over her—

"Jessie, darling!" Mrs. Domico shouts from down the hall. The sound draws Dash's attention, and his head turns as Mrs. Domico's footfalls pad closer on the wooden floor outside Jessie's room. "Time to wake up," she says from the other side of the door, and then she walks in, hair loose and messy, wrapped in a purple bathrobe and still wet from a shower.

She's taken aback by Dash's presence and doesn't immediately notice the blood, the cold, pale skin lined with dark veins, or the lifeless, cloudy eyes. "Daniel?" she says before any of that can sink in.

Jessie sits up at all the noise and yawns, and when she sees her big brother, she's elated. "Danny!" Jessie calls out.

Dash turns back to her at the sound, and she giggles. "Your eyes are all funny. You look like a bug!" she says, and then her big brother grabs her head. Before she can scream, Dash stretches his mouth wide enough to cover her face from ear to ear and takes her little head in his mouth. With a sickening crunch, Dash cracks her skull with the pressure from his jaw alone.

"Daniel!" Mrs. Domico screams as the vertigo of her world, falling away, hits her. She runs into the room and attempts to pull Dash off Jessie, but she's not strong enough. Jessie can't scream, but her little arms and legs thrashing says enough. Her mother pulls and pulls, and, with monumental effort, she yanks Dash away, though the momentum sends her across the room. She falls back, lands on the floor, and whacks her head hard against a dresser.

A music box falls open, and Dash turns around, almost in sync with the slow, out of tune calliope music. As Mrs. Domico's vision comes back into focus, she sees Dash with most of his little sister's face still clasped between gritted teeth.

Jessie, somehow still alive, tries to climb out of her bed. She falls onto the floor. Dash clambers over after her and grabs her hair before she can escape. He lifts her like a rabbit and Mrs. Domico can't do anything but watch as Dash takes another bite out of her.

"No!" Mrs. Domico hollers.

Dash discards Jessie, tosses the child face down onto the floor, and this time the little girl lies still.

"You bastard!" Mrs. Domico curses as she claws at her eyes. "You goddamn bastard!" She charges him with her daughter's silver gymnastics trophy in hand and smashes it against Dash's head. The impact sends the monster backward, over the bed, pulling a bedside table down with him.

Mrs. Domico stands with the trophy, primed for another attack, but Dash is out cold. She drops the weapon and kneels beside her daughter. She takes the limp body in her arms and weeps as she brushes Jessie's gore-matted hair away from what used to be her face.

"My baby, oh god, my baby!" she cries, and she doesn't notice as Dash sits up. He snarls, which draws her attention and the ferocious, unbridled rage of a parent who's lost the only thing in this world that matters. "You bastard!" she curses.

Dash growls in response.

Before she can get to her feet, before she can reach out and grab the trophy to defend herself with, Dash leaps over the bed like a savage, wounded wolf determined to bring a foe with it. Mrs. Domico scatters backward and avoids his swipes. She gets to her feet and staggers out of the room as Dash stands up and follows.

Mrs. Domico backs away through the hall and knocks over a nearby table. She keeps going and shuffles back until she's against the wall by the stairs.

Dash stumbles after her with alarming speed for someone, or something, with his injuries. Immune to the pain, Dash comes after his stepmother as she backs down the stairs. She slips, falls, and bounces down them—landing on the floor with a crack and writhing in pain.

It's not fair, she thinks. This can't be real.

Dash descends the stairs one at a time. Each thud tells her that this is all very real, and if she wants to survive, if she wants payback, she has to move now!

She uses the wall to get to her feet and leans against it as she heads into the kitchen. Mrs. Domico stumbles through the kitchen door, barely able to keep her balance. She uses a countertop to steady herself and pushes along to the far side, just as Dash enters.

To one side, there's the back door—she could probably make it, and once outside, she knows she could outrun this bug-eyed thing. Whatever has happened to Dash has messed him up but good, and if not for the single-minded focus, she'd swear he was drunk. She doesn't want that, though; Mrs. Domico wants revenge. So she turns to the other side, to where she keeps the kitchen knives.

Mrs. Domico grabs a meat cleaver just as Dash comes around the table to face her.

"You never cared one bit about this family," she says as she swings the cleaver. "Just your drunk loser of a father!" The knife, like her words, has a satisfying heft.

Dash growls; that insult triggers something within, but since the rage serves the thing that commands him, it does not intervene. It allows Dash to feel something real for just a moment, and it pushes him forward with unexpected fury.

Mrs. Domico screams and slams the knife down hard. She aims for his neck and instead embeds it in his collarbone. As triumphant as it feels, the attack does nothing to slow Dash, and he's on her a second later. She screams again, this time in frustrated agony, as Dash bites into her neck.

Dash pushes his stepmother onto the floor. He tears into her as her blood spills over the clean, white tiles.

Cut back to the Day house, where red pasta sauce splashes from a broken jar all over the floor. Mrs. Day enters, summoned by the sound, and takes in both the mess and her husband, who sits at the kitchen table with his newspaper. "Buddy!" she complains.

"I'm cleanin' it up! It was an accident!" Except it wasn't. Buddy knows his dad will leave the house for work soon, but he couldn't be sure his mom would go out, so he figures ruining her dinner plans might prompt her to head on out to the store, giving him and Suzie the house to themselves.

Mr. Day laughs, and Mrs. Day hits him playfully with a tea towel. "Laugh it up, Chuckles," she says. "There goes dinner."

Buddy drops to his knees and picks up the shards of glass. He cuts his thumb on an unassumingly sharp piece and winces.

"Let me see that," his mom says, and Buddy stands and holds his thumb out to her.

Mr. Day leans over from his paper, has a look, and whistles. "Gee that looks bad, kiddo." He turns back to his paper. "A little deeper, and you'd have lost it," he jokes.

Mrs. Day pushes her son's wounded hand back to him. "You'll live," she says. "Go clean it up. After you're all patched up, you can take your bike over to the store and pick up some more."

Damn, Buddy thinks. His plan backfired and fell apart just like that. He wanted his mom out of the house. Now

Suzie's going to be left alone down there while he's out. Still…maybe this can work, he thinks. Perhaps he can use this as an opportunity to get some other things he might need without having to make an excuse. "Sure, mom," Buddy agrees. "No problem."

Mr. Day chuckles, and Mrs. Day gives him another whack with the towel.

"Ouch!" he says. "What's that for?"

"Get a brush and get this cleaned up."

"Hey! What'd I do?"

"You said I do," Mrs. Day answers. "Now get that brush."

He puts his paper down and grumbles. "Starting to regret those words…" His wife playfully whips him with the tea towel again as he heads over to the closet.

Buddy comes back into the kitchen and holds out his bandaged thumb for his mother to inspect while his father gets to work with the brush and the glass. Buddy goes to take up the mop after, and his mother stops him. "That's okay," she says, "your father's cleaning it up."

"You know, some wives show their husbands respect," Mr. Day mumbles.

"And some wives sleep in separate beds…" Mrs. Day threatens.

"Good point," Mr. Day concedes and then turns to his son. "Bit of advice, kiddo. Women are like an occupying force. You shut up, do what they say, and hope to make it through the day."

Mrs. Day whips him with the towel again, hard enough to hear it crack, and Buddy laughs. "I'll keep that in mind, dad."

"Don't listen to him, honey," Mrs. Day says. "What does he know? You meet a nice girl, treat her sweet, and she'll take care of you. Act like a jackass, and you'll get more of this!" She threatens her husband with another whack of the towel.

Buddy, embarrassed by all the love on display from his folks, takes an out from the awkwardness. "I'm gonna go get that stuff from the store now…" He slinks away, though not before another thought occurs to him. "Can I take something to eat with me? I might go for a long ride to clear my head. Is that okay?" Buddy knows that if he acts vulnerable, it's more likely to elicit sympathy and trust. Right now, he needs that trust as much as he doesn't like having to betray it.

Mrs. Day ruffles her son's hair. "Sure thing," she says with a smile. "Maybe get a haircut while you're at it," she adds and starts on preparing him some lunch. Buddy goes up to his room to empty his backpack.

"It's great to see him starting to bounce back," Mrs. Day says after her son has left. She watches him mount up on his bike from the kitchen window.

"That's our son," agrees Mr. Day.

"We're fortunate," she adds.

"Honest, hard-working. Chip off the old block, really—ouch!" Mr. Day cuts his finger on the same piece of broken glass as his son.

Mrs. Day doesn't notice. "Not like some of these other kids his age," she says. "Getting drunk, drag racing, sneaking girls into their rooms…"

THIS ISN'T SCIENCE
FICTION THEATRE

Buddy heads out with some cash in his pocket, a lunch bag in hand, and an empty backpack slung over his shoulder. He walks his bike down the path to the sidewalk and then turns towards town. Once he's out of sight of his house, he doubles back towards his garden. He ditches his bike behind some bushes and creeps over to one of the basement windows with his back low, and the brown paper bag clutched tight.

Buddy raps on the window, gentle enough to not alert his parents, but loud enough to draw Suzie over.

Suzie cracks the window, surprised to see Buddy outside. He was supposed to come right back down after he got his parents out of the house. "What's going on?" she asks.

"Change of plans—don't worry, it's gonna be fine though," Buddy says as he passes her the lunch bag. "Here's some food that'll last you till I get back."

Suzie takes the bag from him, still confused. "Where are you going?"

"My mom's making me go out to get something, but I'm gonna sneak into the school and see if I can get some stuff to help us figure this out. Can you keep quiet and hide down there till I get back?"

Suzie really doesn't like this idea, and really doesn't want to be left alone, but she can't see any other option

136

that doesn't lead to even more trouble, so she agrees. "Okay, Buddy. Just hurry, though?"

"Sure thing," Buddy says. "I'll be back in no time." He crawls back over to his bike, Suzie puts her palm up against the glass. She watches as Buddy rides off down the street.

Buddy whips through the quiet little streets on his bike, and with his eyes on the road ahead, he doesn't see the bug-eyed girl on top of a neighbor. Just some kid from school whose name he's probably never heard, who last night was at the drive-in with her boyfriend and now tears into the soft, flabby flesh of a middle-aged accountant. From the discarded slipper, and the newspaper clutched in his hand, he went out to get the paper from his mailbox and ended up breakfast for a flesh-hungry teenybopper. The sound of the bike draws her attention, but it's gone too fast to pull her away from the suburban dad-guts she's got snagged between her teeth like lumpy links of sausage.

Cut back to the basement of Buddy's house, where Suzie also feels an overpowering hunger. She casts a hungry eye down at the brown paper bag. Suzie opens it and takes out the contents: a sandwich, an apple, a candy bar, and a juice carton. She unwraps the sandwich slowly and sifts through it. It doesn't smell right to her; sure it looks freshly made, but it just doesn't feel like food. Still, she's hungry as all hell, so she takes a small bite and chews slowly, but it just doesn't feel right in her mouth.

A beat later, Suzie hurls the sandwich into the bin and spits out the rest. She doesn't know why, but it's like her body rejects it. She picks up the apple and takes a bite; the same deal. It ends up right in the bin too, and she notices, crammed down at the bottom, the towels Buddy used to clean her up last night.

They're dried hard with blood, and she can still taste all those different flavors: the slightly sour taste of Teddy Duchamp, the bittersweet Christina Cole, the rich tang of Betty Blacker. The dried and crusted gore is a thousand times more enticing than the whole lunch bag combined. Suzie reaches down and pulls out one of the soiled towels. Both halves stay fused as it dangles from her fingertips. She stares at the dark brown coagulated clumps. A sharp pain stabs through her head—she drops the towel and grabs her temples as she falls to her knees, then to the floor and doubles over in pain.

FEED.

The words aren't so much spoken as they are formed in her head. In the fractions of seconds before and after, Suzie can detect a vibrating drone, like hundreds of insects moving as one.

"Leave me alone!" she begs as she clutches her head.

NO!

Suzie flashes inside the garage of Sam's Stop-n-Go, only she's not Suzie anymore. The height's all wrong, she's taller, and there's Betty right next to her, holding her sticky hand. Suzie can feel the pressure and the grime as though she was there. She's wearing a blue-sleeved letterman jacket, and suddenly she knows she's Teddy Duchamp, or at least she's seeing through his eyes. There's something else too, a faint hint of fondness—

138

"Hello there!" someone shouts from outside, and she feels Teddy snap awake. His hand slips from Betty's as whatever humanity remained in his hibernation disappears, and the command to feed takes over. Suzie's as powerless to stop this as she is to look away.

Teddy doesn't even blink.

Back in the den, Suzie rolls around on the floor, her back arcs, and she dry heaves.

"Is anyone there?" comes the voice from outside, and its owner, a portly man in a suit, steps into the garage. He comes around the side of a broken-up heap of a pickup. "I'm in a bit of a hurry here if…" he trails off as Teddy lunges out of the shadows with Betty right behind him. The businessman yells as the pair forces him against the car and bites into his neck from both sides like two sugar-rabid kids fighting over a PEZ dispenser.

Cut to: the floor of Buddy's basement. Suzie feels the vital red surge of the businessman's blood even though he's all the way out of town.

The connection between her and Teddy vanishes, and Suzie's left alone, distressed and terrified by her out-of-body experience.

Through the window, Buddy's dad waves goodbye to his wife as he heads to his car. The slam of the door snaps her attention, and Suzie throws herself up against the glass.

From this angle, Suzie can see the bare, exposed skin of Buddy's mom's ankle, and she wants nothing more than to sink her teeth into that golden honey flesh.

 FEED!

Suzie slams against the wall, and her lips form an animalistic snarl. Her teeth bare themselves, and her tongue reaches out, desperate to get as close as possible to that warm meat.

Mrs. Day disappears back into the house, and Suzie can hear the clack of her heels on the wooden floor above her. She knows there's only one thing that will satisfy her hunger, and there's not much she can do to resist.

Cut to: Buddy as he dismounts his bike outside Woodvale High. With the school still closed, and all the quiet chaos steadily spreading through town, he's the only person in sight. Still, Buddy hides his bike in the bushes just to be safe.

Though Buddy's not the type, he knows all about the broken fire exit around the school's west side. Kids have used it to sneak outside to smoke during study hall for years. It takes a bit of effort to open it from the outside, but it's not impossible, and within minutes Buddy walks through the uncomfortably empty corridors. There's something distinctly not right about an empty school; even in broad daylight, it gives him the creeps.

Still, Buddy's on a mission, and he isn't going to let the heebie-jeebies get to him even as he passes the infamous haunted closet where an old janitor hung himself, or so legend has it. Legend also has it that when the school is empty, you can hear the creaking of the rope from outside the closet, but if you open the door, all you'll see is a quickly vanishing shadow. Buddy never bought that story, mainly because if the school had to be empty for it to happen, how could anyone know about it? Regardless, he picks up the pace as he passes that closet on his way to the science department. He also tells himself it's just his imagination that makes the sound of a strained, old rope as he passes.

Buddy finds his classroom and the door unlocked. Trouble is, there's a reason for that. As he opens the door, Buddy hears the steady footsteps of someone coming down the opposite end of the corridor. He slips inside the room and ducks behind the nearest counter.

Just as Buddy hides, cut back to Suzie. She does the same thing when she hears the door at the top of the stairs open. Suzie shuts herself inside the nearest closet, and there's barely enough room for her with all the junk. For some reason, there's a stuffed gopher that appears very bitter about its fate. The mean thing glares at her, an inch from her face, with intense hatred. Suzie keeps the door slightly ajar out of necessity, so she can peer out.

Mrs. Day comes down the stairs, and the scent of her, the heat radiating from her body, makes Suzie drool, but she holds herself back even as the stuffed gopher disapproves. "Nope," Mrs. Day says to herself. "Nope! He can tidy it himself." She walks around the room and over to the side with the windows and cracks them all open. "It stinks in here, hoo boy!"

Suzie has a hell of a lot more going on at the moment to take that personally. She struggles to restrain herself, digs her nails into the wooden door frame, and bares her teeth.

FEED!

The thing inside her head commands her to kill, and she uses every ounce of strength she has to resist.

Through the gap in the door, Suzie watches as Buddy's mother lifts one of those bloodied towels from the wastebasket and holds it out at a full arm's length like it's radioactive.

"Oh my god!" Buddy's mother almost loses her lunch while Suzie almost loses control. "That boy! Nope! He can do it himself," she says and drops the towel back into the wastebasket. She heads back out of the basement with her hands held out, afraid to touch anything till she can get upstairs and sterilize herself.

When Suzie hears the door close, she falls out of the closet onto all fours and growls up at the ceiling above.

Meanwhile, cut to: Woodvale High, where Buddy, also on the floor, pushes his back to the counter and listens. He breathes a quiet sigh of relief as whoever is in the corridor outside passes by. Satisfied that he's safe, Buddy goes about gathering a few things he thinks he might need. Mostly books on all kinds of biology as well as some Petri dishes, samplers, and syringes. Really it's just a grab bag of whatever might be useful. The dead coming back to life isn't something he's read about much outside of *Weird Science*, but he figures since nobody is glowing from radiation, it's got to be something chemical. Like that episode of *Science Fiction Theatre* where the guy tests a new drug that makes him so violent he kills someone. So, Buddy reckons, he needs a good look at what's inside Suzie if he's going to figure anything out.

The problem is, he's so caught up hunting for what he needs that he doesn't hear his science teacher, Mr. Cormac, enter the classroom behind him.

"Can I help you," he says, and it's really more of a statement than a question.

Buddy jumps at the sound and whacks his head good on the top of the cupboard he's half-tucked inside. When he pulls himself out and turns around, Mr. Cormac relaxes, seeing that it's only Buddy. As odd as it is for a student to be in school while it's closed, he knows that Buddy Peter Day isn't here to steal or vandalize. People know a lot of things that don't end up being all that true, though.

Mr. Cormac puts the box he's carrying down on his desk, and there's a telltale clink of bottles hitting each other. From the open shirt collar, necktie that hangs low, and about a week's worth of stubble on his face, Buddy suspects those bottles are not the science experiment kind. "There's no class today, Mr. Day," the teacher says. "Not trying to steal anything, I hope."

Buddy's hit with an involuntary cold dread. He's the kind of kid who sweats it if he forgets his homework, never mind getting caught stealing from the school. Suzie needs him, though, and the longer he leaves her alone, the more likely it is she will be found. He snaps to life. "No! No, I was…I was hoping to b-borrow some things," Buddy explains.

"Uh-huh?" the teacher says, curious about where this is going.

"It's for my project," Buddy insists as he attempts to block the teacher from seeing the half-full backpack. "I swear I'll clean them and bring them all back. I've got a microscope and stuff at home, just not…" Buddy trails off and worries that if he keeps talking, he'll say too much.

"Just what exactly is this…project all about, Mr. Day?" the science teacher asks.

Buddy searches the room for something to help him concoct a half-decent cover story. His eyes settle on the

143

ant farms from the other day. "Ants!" he says and hopes that's enough.

Of course, it's not, and the science teacher asks, "Ants?"

"Yeah," Buddy says. "Uh, see, my dad used poison, and it killed them. Dead. Then…they sort of came back, the dead ones, that is." Buddy amazes himself at the ease at which he lies to an authority figure. He never knew he had this in him; it feels like going no-hands on his bike for the first time, simultaneously freeing and frightening.

"And you're absolutely sure these aren't just different ants, young man?" Mr. Cormac asks. "They do tend to look alike, you know."

"Yeah, I mean no, they're definitely the same ones. I've, uh, isolated them from the queen and been watching as they come back," Buddy lies.

"I'm starting to suspect, young man, that you've been daydreaming in my class," Mr. Cormac says. When the boy gives him nothing but a puzzled look for an answer, he continues. "Last Friday, when we discussed species of worker ants capable of laying eggs, though such offspring are lesser than the progeny of the hive queen?"

"Oh," Buddy says and wonders how he missed that, till a sideways glance lands his eye on Suzie's desk. Was it really just a week ago that Suzie sat with her friends, giggling and messing around with Dash? Buddy was, clearly, too distracted by the sight of Dash pawing all over Suzie to catch the lesson. What he wouldn't give to just go back to dumb, high-school drama and heartbreak like that; if only it meant Suzie would be okay. "Sure, yeah, but these ants are super-aggressive. Like, way more than normal, and they don't seem to care if they die or nothin'."

144

"Such mindless, selfless action is quite common for worker ants. You should know this, Mr. Day."

"Yes Sir, but it's way more than normal. Is there anything that could do that, Mr. Cormac? Like some kind of virus?" Buddy seizes the opportunity to gain some knowledge that can help him and Suzie out without blowing his cover.

The science teacher, who's now somewhat invested in the hypothetical phenomena, rubs his chin. "Well, this is skipping ahead a few weeks, mind you, but you might want to read up on parasitoid reproduction. Our next study topic covers endoparasitic reproduction," he explains. "That's when insects inject their eggs into other organisms who essentially carry their young for them all the while being devoured from within."

"That's horrifying," says Buddy.

"You'll find, young man, that the insect kingdom is far more terrifying than any of your B pictures can imagine," the science teacher says. "Especially when the parasite manipulates the host for its own benefit," he adds with a droll, ghoulish delight. Like if Truman Bradley did a Peter Lorre impression.

"How?" Buddy asks, this sounds like the right line of thought to him.

"Well, suppose you have a parasite whose ideal host is a bird. Capable of carrying its young across vast distances. A bird, however, is not so easy to infect. A caterpillar, though, is slow, docile, so much easier. So the adult insect injects its eggs into a hapless little caterpillar. The growing larvae releases chemicals that manipulate the caterpillar to climb higher and higher until," Mr. Cormac caws like a bird and swoops with his hand, "it gets eaten and the parasite reaches its ideal host. Then again, there's also Ophiocordyceps."

145

"Orphy-what?"

"It's a tropical fungus that hijacks the brain of insects, ants typically, and forces them to behave in such a way as to help the fungus reproduce. Much to the detriment of the ant who dies in the process, though not before spreading the fungal infection to other ants," the science teacher explains.

"Woah," Buddy says. "How does it spread, though? Like through a bite or something? And could this stuff do the same to an animal? Or a human?"

Mr. Cormac laughs. "Yes, though more commonly through spores. Thankfully, though, this isn't *Science Fiction Theatre*, young man, so no, it does not affect humans. Besides, if the Ophiocordyceps ever did make the jump to mammals, that would be the last of us." Buddy doesn't know what to say to that. As fascinating as this is, it doesn't explain what's happening to Suzie. "Anyway, I don't think I can let you take these things home with you, but you're free to use them here as much as you want. I'll be in my office, so the room is yours."

"But…" Buddy tries, but the science teacher gives him a look that says, don't. Buddy gives it a go anyway. "Please. I'll have it all back by tomorrow. I promise."

"Sorry, Mr. Day, but that's school property, and a science class isn't like the baseball team. If we break something or lose it, we don't get a replacement."

"Please?" Buddy tries again.

"Sorry," and Mr. Cormac shuts him down. He puts his hand on the boy's shoulder. "Maybe you should just take the day off," he says and feels a great deal of empathy. He sees in Buddy his younger self, keen to bury his woes in science and study.

Ever since Susan Palmer died, Mr. Cormac and his partner have had to cool things off. They always knew they were walking a tightrope in this town, and with all the scrutiny, all the gossip, and all the press, there's just no way a high-school teacher and a sheriff could keep their romance hidden. Getting found out would cost them both their jobs, but the oaf could still call at least. Cormac hasn't heard from Keyes in over a day, and that just isn't like the man. It's why he's in school today and why there are two bottles of whiskey tucked into that cardboard box along with unmarked projects and workbooks.

Mr. Cormac lets go of Buddy, picks up his box, and turns his back on the kid as he walks towards his office. "I understand what you're going through," he says. "You want to work your way through hard times. It's commendable."

Buddy glances over at Suzie's empty desk.

"Sometimes we need to do things just for ourselves," the teacher says as he disappears inside his office. Sometimes we need to do things for others, Buddy says to himself. "Take my advice, Mr. Day," he calls from behind the door, and Buddy does just that. He won't be leaving here with answers, sure, but he won't be leaving without hope either.

Nobody ever expects Buddy to break the rules. They won't be surprised when he recites pi to three hundred places, or names each constellation in the night sky, but stealing from the school? Before today, Buddy hasn't so much as talked back to a teacher. Suzie needs him, though, and since he couldn't get answers here, he's going to have to find them himself, even if that means breaking the rules. Even if that means stealing. He can't go home empty-handed, it can't be for nothing.

So Buddy grabs his backpack, slings it over his shoulder, and grabs a few more books as he sprints out the room.

"Are you listening to me, Mr. Day?" the teacher asks as he pops his head into an empty classroom.

While Mr. Cormac sighs with disappointment, we cut to: Suzie as she heaves in pain on the basement floor. The pressure in her head is so intense it feels like she's about to explode.

FEED.

FEED.

FEED!

NO!

Suzie refuses, and her head rattles like a kicked hive.

FEED!

NO!

FEED!

NO!

Suzie flashes, and suddenly she's inside the halls of Woodvale High. She sees Buddy as he runs down the corridor and takes a hard corner, almost slipping but righting himself up enough to keep going. Suzie wants to reach out for him, call his name and tell him to wait for her, but her body won't obey.

Of course, it's not her body. She doesn't know who she is right now. The body Suzie's riding along in takes a few shuffled steps forward, but there's no way it's going to be fast enough to keep up with Buddy. Still, it tries, and Suzie sees the bottom tips of a familiar blue skirt and white tennis shoes, stained with blood and burger grease. No, of all people, no, Suzie begs, but there's nothing she can do as she's forced to watch through the unblinking eyes of Christina Cole.

The sound of glass smashing, and a familiar voice cursing, draws Christina's eyes towards the open door of a nearby classroom. Suzie recognizes the room and is forced to watch as Christina carries her through it. Christina walks through stools, knocks them aside, cares nothing for the mess or clatter she makes—only that she:

FEED.

"Conscience got the better of you?" comes a voice from the office that Suzie recognizes as her science teacher Mr. Cormac. She feels Christina's lips pull back and her jaw opens wide in anticipation.

Mr. Cormac is on the floor, gathering up shards of broken glass, when he looks up and sees that it's not Buddy with a change of heart, but Christina Cole instead. "My god, Christina, what in the blazes happened to you?"

Suzie can see Christina's reflection in the glass of a cabinet at the back of the room. She sees what she's done

149

to Christina, and even though she never liked the girl, Suzie is disgusted with herself all the same.

There's a struggle, and then Mr. Cormac pushes her back. He brandishes the head of a broken bottle as a warning, but Christina charges anyway. Suzie can feel the ragged glass scrape against Christina's teeth, flay her flesh, and yet there's no pain. Only the rich taste of iron as Christina forces herself on top of the teacher and rips into his throat.

Suzie's filled with the paradoxical impulses to both throw up and devour at the same time. She begs for the connection to end, to be back in her own body, but it doesn't. As bad as it was watching through Teddy's eyes as he killed that businessman, this is so much more harrowing. She knows Mr. Cormac. Likes him even, and it's abhorrent to her that the sensation of his blood in her mouth, even by proxy, should feel so damn good.

The connection holds even after Christina finishes with the teacher and stands. Suzie can see her reflection, once again, in the glass. The right side of Christina's cheek, gouged and sliced away by the broken bottle, shows bone from her lip all the way to her jowl. It's a cruel, horrific wound that sits on the waitress' face like a wicked, rictus grin, and Suzie can't help but feel that Christina's trying to say something as the connection drops.

Suzie falls to her knees in the basement and fights to keep control of her body. It takes all she has to resist as the thing inside her tries to drag her towards the stairs.

NO-NO-NO-NO!

FEED!

The Fredericksons' cat slips in through one of the open windows while Suzie fights a war with the monster within. It's unconcerned with the girl in agony on the floor and proceeds to scratch the sofa. The sound of fabric being shredded snaps Suzie out of it and draws all of her snarling focus. She needs to:

FEED!

Suzie grabs hold of the cat. It twists in her grip, slashes at her repeatedly, but she doesn't feel any of it. Inside she begs, please don't. Don't make me—

FEED!

NO!

Suzie resists but can't bring herself to let go of the creature. It spits and hisses at her like a viper.

FEED!

It's too much. Suzie can't fight it forever, and she loses control. She bites down on the cat, and, as much as the yowling, pitiful wails horrify her, the release from the droning is pure bliss.

Okay, Maybe This Is
Science Fiction
Theatre

Fade to Main Street, to outside Greene's Groceries, as Buddy pulls up on his bike. His shirt plastered to his back after riding away from school like the Devil was on his tail, Buddy takes a second to catch his breath.

Old Man Greene himself is behind the counter when Buddy walks in. Usually, he'd stop by the magazine rack to see what new issues were in, but all Buddy can think about is getting back to Suzie. So much so that he would have forgotten all about the pasta sauce if he didn't ride right past Greene's.

Greene is a decidedly old-school man and has Buddy wait while he fetches a bottle of Mama's Red from one of the shelves behind the counter. It's not so much that the store has a problem with shoplifters, more that Old Man Greene thinks that a grocery store should be a service. All of his kids insist it'd be easier on the old fool to move the inventory out and let folks find what they need themselves. Hell, they might even pick up more than what they came in for that way, but that doesn't sit right with him. It feels lazy, impersonal, and exploitative. Old Man Greene likes to take his time.

Buddy, though, as he watches the back of Old Man Greene's balding head, really wishes he'd hurry up.

"Here you go, kid," Greene says and puts the jar down, then rings Buddy up. Buddy pays and says thanks, but just as he heads for the door, Greene says, "You're Buddy Day, aren't you, son?"

Buddy nods. He just wants to go, but Buddy knows if he acts out of sorts, he's bound to draw attention, and he's already in enough trouble as it is.

"Yeah, I knew it," Old Man Greene says. "Never forget a face, I don't. You ain't been in here in a while, though. Boy, I remember you and that Suzie Palmer used to be here every Saturday flippin' through the comics like it was a library!" The old grocer's smile fades, and his kind eyes drop as he remembers. "That poor girl, she used to work here on Saturdays, you know. Terrible thing to happen."

"Yeah," Buddy agrees. He dials up the pity with a put-on hangdog expression, hoping that'll put an end to the conversation.

"Tell you what," the grocer says. "You take something from the rack for yourself. On the house, you hear?"

Buddy grabs the first comic that he sees without paying any real attention to it. He thanks Old Man Greene on his way out.

After the boy is gone, the old man kicks himself for putting his foot in his mouth like that. "Poor kid," he says to himself, and the sadness overwhelms him. "It just ain't right, a young'un, dying like that, it just ain't right."

A commotion in the back room pulls him out of it. "Boy," Old Man Greene shouts, "what you up to back there! Quit your foolin' around!" That damn grandson of his, no good for nothing. Flunked out of college, fired from every job he ever worked, so somehow his folks think working with his grandpa is for the best. What can he say though, the kid's family—but if he's smoking any more of that damn reefer back there, he's going to have a few words with him and his folks.

Old Man Greene steps into the back room. "Dear god..." he says as his jaw drops at the sight of his no-good grandson dozing in the corner with a lit joint dangling between his fingers. "Boy, I am gonna whoop your ass, then your daddy's just for letting you turn out like this!"

His grandson doesn't respond, and before Old Man Greene can make good on his word, the wide-open back door catches his eye. "Son of a—I done told you to keep that door shut! The last thing we need is some beatniks helping themselves like they do. Times are hard enough as is, boy..."

Old Man Greene curtails his rant as a hefty man, just about the door frame's size, steps in through it. Greene knows him as Gus, the delivery driver, but something ain't right about him, and it's not just the smell of reefer that wafts off him in confirmation of all Greene's suspicions of where his grandson was getting the stuff. It isn't out of place for Gus to have stains all over his uniform, but not this much. Then there are his eyes. Old Man Greene's only ever seen eyes like that on the bodies of dead soldiers back in Iwo Jima.

"Gus," the grocer says, "what's this all about?" His eyes follow a snail trail of red smears that starts at Gus' feet and winds across the room. He turns his head and follows it back to his grandson, who's now awake. Though he's getting old and forgets things now and then, he's not so damn old that he can't remember the color of his grandson's eyes, and this isn't it. They're just like Gus', all wide, lifeless, and staring at him hard like a hungry cricket.

Before Old Man Greene can grasp what's going on, both the delivery driver and his freshly re-animated grandson grab onto him from either side. It's too late for him to do anything but scream.

Cut to: Buddy's house as he walks in through the back door. "Got the sauce, mom!" he shouts and drops it on the kitchen table so fast it wobbles as he makes a line right for the basement.

"Buddy!" Mrs. Day shouts from somewhere else in the house, and it pulls him to a stop.

"Yeah, mom?" he calls back and hopes she stays where she is.

"Clean that damn den of yours! It's a disgrace!" Mrs. Day shouts.

Buddy rolls his eyes, more with relief than anything else. "Okay, mom," he shouts back and heads on down. He's no sooner at the bottom of the stairs when the wind gets knocked right out of him as Suzie lunges. She forces him down and thrusts her face into his chest.

Suzie's whole body trembles. Buddy, after a moment, wraps his arms around her. It seems to work, and she's able to pull herself together enough to talk.

"I've done a bad thing," Suzie says between sobs. "A real bad thing!"

Buddy takes her by the shoulders, and she sits up enough for him to look into her sad, blue eyes. "What's the matter?" Buddy asks. "What happened?"

Suzie looks away and points over to the wastebasket. Buddy lets go of her and moves over to the bin. Suzie tenses up, and Buddy prepares himself for whatever he might find. He looks down inside and sees what's left of the Fredericksons' cat. Buddy turns back to Suzie for an explanation, but she won't meet his eyes.

"Suzie?" Buddy asks, and she turns her back to him. He knows what she's done is wrong; the sheer understatement of that and its implications escapes him because right now, all Buddy can think about is that Suzie needs him.

He walks to her, pauses, then puts his hands on her shoulders. Buddy turns her around and pulls her into his arms. "It's okay, Suzie," he says.

"I—" she tries.

"I know," Buddy comforts her. "I know."

"There's something wrong with me, Buddy," Suzie says. "I killed a cat…"

Buddy flashes back to something, a conversation between two kids in a backyard on a starry summer's night, like the words themselves are trying to find their way to him. "Pretty sure that cat was evil," he says.

Suzie looks up at him, and for a second, she doesn't see the awkward teenage boy badly in need of a haircut. She sees the goofy kid who was her best friend a million years ago. The kid who used to make her laugh so hard she snorted at least twice a day.

"Like, from outer space evil," Buddy finishes, and it brings a genuine, heartfelt smile to Suzie's face.

The comfort only lasts for a second, though, and the horror hits her again. "I-I couldn't stop myself," she tries to explain. "I was so hungry." She points to the wastebasket. "This thing inside me wanted me to do that to your mom!"

Buddy falls into shock at what Suzie says.

"It wants me to bite people, to kill them." It's been a dream since Suzie came back, but this is a stone-cold reminder that this is serious. "I was gonna, your mom, I—"

"But you didn't," Buddy tells her. Tells himself.

"But I nearly—"

"But you didn't," Buddy insists as he pulls her close. "That's all that matters."

They both hold each other and wish, with all their hearts, that they could stay like this forever. Live in this sweet little moment for the rest of time. They can't, though, and Buddy breaks the hug first. He sits Suzie on the edge of the sofa.

"I've done other…stuff," Suzie confesses. "Real bad. I…I think I've hurt people, Buddy. I think I've—"

"Suzie?" Buddy cuts in. "I don't care." And he tears up. "When I saw you in that casket, I knew that I'd lost the best damn friend I ever had, and all I could think about was how stupid I was. I never should have listened to…I'm sorry, Suzie. I'm sorry for not being as good a friend as I should've. Maybe…maybe none of this would've happened if—"

Suzie jumps to her feet. "Don't you say that, Buddy Peter Day! Don't you dare!" She grabs hold of him. "You're the one guy…the one person I know I can count on! Don't you dare!"

"Suzie…" Buddy says as she hugs him and punches his chest at the same time.

"Goddamnit, Buddy, you're such a goof. Here I am tellin' you I might've killed people, and you're blaming yourself."

Buddy wipes away a tear. "Still, I'm sorry for letting us get like this," he adds as they calm down. "I could have—"

"And I could have too, that's just life, Buddy. People, I guess they just drift apart, but if they're meant to be, they find each other again…" Suzie trails off as they look each other in the eye.

Buddy very much wants to kiss her right now, but instead, he just says, "Thanks."

"For?" Suzie asks.

"We'd better get moving," Buddy says as he ignores her and changes the subject, because if she keeps being sweet to him, he's not gonna be able to hide how he feels, and this isn't the time for that. Suzie needs his smarts and his support right now more than anything.

"Huh?" Suzie says as Buddy empties his backpack onto a workbench next to all his science stuff.

"I have an idea," Buddy explains. "I saw Mr. Cormac today, and he told me about how these parasites, and this fungus, makes bugs do stuff even if it kills them."

"A fungus?" Suzie raises an eyebrow. "Like a mushroom?"

"Sort of," Buddy says. "But what you said earlier about biting people—can I get some spit?"

"Spit?" Suzie asks, both weirded out and amused by Buddy as he goes full mad scientist on her.

"Yeah, with stuff like this, it's either in the blood or saliva," Buddy says as he hands her a slide to spit on.

Suzie wets her mouth and drools a little onto the glass slide. "What about blood?" she asks as she hands it back, and Buddy doesn't answer. He takes the Band-Aid off his wounded hand and pinches the skin hard enough above the cut to make it bleed fresh without even wincing at the pain. She thinks back to the same kid who made such a big deal out of cutting his hand way back. It reminds her of the time she and Buddy carved their initials into the support beam, and she goes over to see if it's still there.

It is, though the blood has long since faded away, the letters remain. Suzie glances over at Buddy, fully absorbed with his head darting between the microscope and a book he's wedged open. When she was a kid, and they carved their initials into the wood, Suzie wanted to cut a heart around it all, but she was scared. Afraid it'd gross Buddy out, or he'd think it was silly. As she watches him obsess over finding a way to help her, she traces a heart on the wood with her finger instead. A flicker of a smile twitches across her face.

"Huh?" Buddy says.

"What is it?" Suzie runs over to him. "Is it bad? It's bad, right?" Buddy doesn't answer her, and that just causes more worry.

Under the scope, the saliva cells look like ordinary globules. Except inside, they teem with what looks like myopic translucent beans, each with a solid black dot at the core. Buddy's never seen anything like it though; to be fair, nobody on Earth has. The closest match Buddy can find in any of the books are ant eggs, but he can't imagine how they got inside the saliva cells.

Buddy takes the sample of his blood and introduces it to the saliva, and like a piranha feeding frenzy, all of Suzie's cells swarm his. They force their way through the membrane, and Buddy watches as the egg things swell once they've penetrated the blood. One of them grows fatter and begins to pulsate as it absorbs the others.

"Endoparasitic reproduction," Buddy says under his breath.

"What-repo-what now?" Suzie needs to know.

"It's using us to carry its young," Buddy explains.

"That's disgusting," Suzie says and tries not to throw up.

"Oddly enough, you're not the first person to say that this week." Buddy recalls Johnny's horror at how seeds work and realizes that he misses the doofus. Suzie gives Buddy a look, and he says, "Never mind."

"Can you, is it okay if we look at your blood?" Buddy asks, and he dives back into the real-life *Weird Science* scenario he's beginning to piece together in his head.

Suzie takes a pair of scissors from the worktop and cuts herself like she doesn't even feel it, then holds the wound out for Buddy. Impressed, he takes some blood from her and puts it under the scope. Then Buddy goes deathly quiet.

"What's the tale nightingale?" Suzie asks.

"Huh?"

"My mom…my mom says…used…she says that," Suzie says. "Clue me in, how do I look?" she asks and nods to the microscope.

"Fine, absolutely fine," Buddy says, and Suzie raises an eyebrow.

"I mean the blood sample, poindexter," Suzie smirks.

"Yeah, that's what I meant," Buddy says, though the blush of his cheeks doesn't agree. "I mean, it's oxygen-starved, but then again, I don't think you're actually breathing, so I guess that makes sense, but normal, it seems. No eggs."

"What eggs?" Suzie asks, and Buddy realizes his mind's been racing miles ahead without letting Suzie know what he's thinking.

"In your spit, there are these eggs, impossibly tiny, and they sort of…invade the blood cells, feed off them, and grow. But they're not in your blood, so…"

"So…" Suzie asks with wide eyes.

"So, I think they might have been, but it's gone now," Buddy thinks aloud. He checks his blood sample, and it's almost oxygen-starved too. The egg ruptures and Buddy jumps out of his skin as something with mandibles stabs at the slide and cracks the glass. "Woah!" he yells and nearly falls off his chair.

160

"What? What is it?!" Suzie asks.

"Maybe this is *Science Fiction Theatre* after all..." Buddy says.

"Huh—" Suzie says, and she's interrupted by an ungodly yowl as the remains of the Fredericksons' cat glares at them from the sofa. The broken, ragged bag of fur launches across her, and it latches onto Buddy's shoulder.

Buddy spins in circles and tries to get the cat off. Suzie grabs it and yanks it hard enough to rip Buddy's shirt and leave him with a few new cuts. The cat writhes in Suzie's grip but ignores her entirely, even though the skin of her arms is within biting reach—its bugged out, gray eyes only have room for Buddy.

The cat can't go anywhere; Suzie's grip is like a vice, but that doesn't stop the thing from hissing and swiping at Buddy with a singular, possessed fury.

Buddy can't believe what he's seeing. There's no way this cat should be up and on the attack like this. It's all but hollowed out and eviscerated beyond recognition. One of its legs is nothing but bone and a single shred of loose, flappy fur.

"Do something!" Suzie shouts, and Buddy has an idea. He quickly ferrets an old hamster cage from a closet, and together the two of them force the cat inside, though not without Buddy getting scratched to hell. Suzie locks the cage door, but the cat keeps up the rampage, and the cage dances around.

"What are we gonna do, Buddy?" Suzie asks, and Buddy really, really wishes he knew.

The thing's contained, sure, but it's only a matter of time before it smashes the cage around enough to break free, and then what. How do you kill something that's already dead? Buddy doesn't know, and Suzie doesn't want to think about it. "Buddy, what are we gonna do?" Suzie asks again. "The noise is gonna bring your folks down here!"

"Let me think!" Buddy slaps the sides of his head. "Let me think…" He paces around the room while Suzie keeps the cage pinned down. Everywhere Buddy goes, the cat tries to follow. It twists around in ways nothing with any concern for its well-being could. It slices chunks of flesh off against the bars and shows no pain, only hunger, as its bulging, dead eyes never break from Buddy. After a few laps around the room, Buddy notices this. He also sees that not once has it swiped at Suzie, despite her hands being far closer to it than him. "It's only interested in me," Buddy notes as the idea starts to form in his mind.

"You always said it had it in for you," Suzie says.

"It's not that," Buddy thinks aloud. "It's, I think it's like when you said something wants you to feed, right?"

"It's like a voice but not at the same time. It's inside me, but it's not me," Suzie tries to explain.

"Exactly," Buddy jumps with the conclusion he's coming to and starts looking for something sharp. "It's not you. It's not the cat. It's like what Mr. Cormac says; the brain has been hijacked." Buddy spies his fountain pen, stolen by Dash and returned to him by Suzie, sitting on the desk next to his scientific equipment. He grabs it and holds it firm with the point ready for a downward thrust.

"What does that mean?" Suzie asks, and Buddy answers her as he drives the sharp point of the pen down through the bars of the cage. He stabs the pen right between where the spine connects with the skull. The cat slumps, quietly, without fuss or pain. Suzie feels the savage strength dissipate from the creature. Feels it die, really die, and more than just physically. She feels a connection to the creature fade. She hadn't been aware of it, but its absence is glaring now that it's gone.

Buddy catches his breath, then asks Suzie to "Lift the cage up," and he takes a swab from the cat's mouth. Buddy takes it over and looks at it under the microscope, and, just like with Suzie's sample, the saliva is bursting with fertile eggs.

"Whatever gets bitten gets taken over," Buddy says. He stares at the impossible mangled remains of the cat. "It doesn't matter how dead it is. It makes more eggs and..."

Buddy doesn't finish that thought, doesn't have to. He slides off his chair, unsteady on his feet, and sits on the sofa before he falls. Shaken inside, Buddy does the math in his head and doesn't like the answer he comes up with one bit.

Suzie places the cage down as the dots start to connect for her too.

They're both so lost in thought that they jump as the basement door is pulled open.

THEY CAME IN THE STILL OF THE NIGHT

Cut to: the streets of Woodvale, where things are going to hell, and fast. The quiet little town plunged into the kind of carnage the likes of which no one could have imagined. Cut to: outside the Dairy Queen, where a child crashes into a bubblegum machine, smashes it to the ground, and sends a rainbow cavalcade of candy rattling all over the place. Pull back, and we can see the child on the run from something, but he slips and falls on marble gumballs. He looks behind him in absolute terror at the mob of bloody, bug-eyed things as they close in on him, and he screams for his mom.

All over town, scenes like that unfold and cascade into each other as the horror that grips Woodvale multiplies exponentially. Chaos superimposed over more chaos.

Back to the Day house, and as the bloodshed edges closer, Mr. Day pops into the kitchen to grab himself a little pre-dinner snack. He spots a comic book on the table and figures Buddy must have left it there by accident. The boy's usually pretty picky about looking after the things.

"*Strange Worlds*," he says and chuckles at the cover. A four-armed, orange ant-man paws at a pretty looking brunette in a sheer, skimpy gown while a raygun-wielding hero comes up from behind. He takes a good look at the girl and chuckles. "Guess I see why you like these so much."

164

It takes him back to when Buddy was just waist-high. Back to when his boy and Suzie Palmer would lay on their stomachs down in the basement, the two of them high on sugar and reading some comic books together. Buddy doing the men's voices, Suzie the women's, and the two of them trying not to pee themselves laughing as they outdo each other reading the alien dialogue in high-pitched tones.

"What are you laughing at?" Mrs. Day asks as she comes into the kitchen, and with a pat of his belly, she adds, "You better not be in here snacking before dinner." She heads over to the pot and stirs.

"Just remembering those two kids and their comics," Mr. Day says and holds up the copy of *Strange Worlds* for his wife to see. "Hey, you remember that time the two of them made costumes out of—"

Mrs. Day drops the spoon, splatters herself and the floor with sauce, and doesn't care. She holds her face in her hands, suddenly overcome with tears as the dam breaks.

"Sweetheart, what's wrong?" Mr. Day asks as he puts his hands on his wife's shoulders.

"I–it was my stupid idea," she says, and her husband doesn't know what she means. He gives her time. After a moment, she confesses to the thing that's been eating away at her all week. The reason why she was so insistent with him the other day. "I asked Jackie Palmer to scare Buddy away."

Mr. Day pulls away from his wife.

"I gave her newspapers, photos, horrible stuff," she continues, "and asked her to scare our son away from her daughter." Mrs. Day can't control herself; the tears flow, and even if her husband offered her comfort, she wouldn't take it. She knows she doesn't deserve it. "I

165

knew they'd fall in love—you could see it in their eyes, and it would be so hard on them both."

"So you never even gave them a chance?" Mr. Day asks, all the jolly candor in his voice suddenly replaced by a forcefulness unbecoming of the man.

"I just wanted to keep them safe. I didn't want them to stop being friends!"

"You had no right!" Mr. Day cuts her off.

"I'm his mother! I had every right!"

"Then go down there and tell him!" Mr. Day yells. "Go down those stairs and tell your son that because of you, because of your cowardice, he lost his best friend years before she died! You tell him!" Mr. Day storms out of the kitchen and grabs his coat.

"Where are you going?" Mrs. Day asks. "Dinner—"

"To hell with dinner! I can't be in this house with you right now!" He storms out the front door.

Mrs. Day presses against the door and lets it all out. She was right, she knows she was, but why does it feel so wrong? Why does she feel so ashamed? She was only keeping her son safe, what a mother is supposed to do. Then why?

Buddy needs to know. He can either forgive her or hate her, but she has to tell him the truth. It's the only way, for sure, to know if she did the right thing. That conviction begins to falter as she reaches the door to the basement. She pulls the door open and takes one step inside.

"Buddy?" Mrs. Day calls down into the basement.

Her son takes an awfully long time to answer.

"Yeah?"

She can't. Her nerve fails her, and Mrs. Day just can't bring herself to go down there and tell the truth. Not at this moment. "Dinner in ten, okay honey?" she covers, praying her son can't hear the guilt in her voice.

"Okay, mom," he answers, and the sound of his voice causes her to break down once more.

Cut to: the basement, where Buddy and Suzie froze like roaches in the light as the door opened. As it closes, Buddy whooshes with relief.

For some reason, unfathomable to Buddy, Suzie bursts into a fit of giggles. He just looks so funny to her, right at that moment. His eyes full of panic, his hair a riot from the tumble with the cat. He looks so adorably silly, and she can't help herself.

"What?" Buddy asks.

"B-u-ddy," Suzie teases, "come over here and sit on the floor." She takes a seat on the sofa.

"What is it?" Buddy asks again, very confused.

Suzie makes herself comfortable. "C'mere," she insists, and Buddy does what she asks. He walks over to her and she points to the floor. "Sit," she instructs, and Buddy does what he's told. "Turn around, and move back a bit." Buddy wriggles himself closer till he's right between her legs. The feel of her skin against his arms, even though she's ice-cold, fills him with an electric warmth.

"What—" Buddy starts, and Suzie shushes him as she starts to play with his hair.

"Just sit still," Suzie says as she brushes through. The touch of her fingers, the jolt of electricity when she makes contact with his skin, wipes the nightmare they just dealt with entirely from his mind, and he doesn't want this moment to end.

"There, I'm finished. Turn around," Suzie orders, and Buddy obeys. She bites her lip as she considers her handiwork, and while it's an improvement, Buddy still looks like he went nine rounds and lost. Just a little tidier. That's not what Suzie sees, though, not really. Not for the first time since last night, she sees something more than her best friend, more than the goofy nerd who makes her laugh like no one else.

"What, what is it?" Buddy asks. He feels the butt of some joke that's way over his head.

"You," Suzie says, and then she's overcome with the desire to kiss him so hard and for so long that the whole world would just disappear.

Buddy and Suzie hear the front door slam open. The ceiling shakes from the impact and sprinkles them with dust. Buddy and Suzie listen to a thud of footsteps above, and Buddy's father screams, "Buddy! Get up here right now!"

"I…" Buddy starts, "I should see what's up..." But he doesn't want to go.

"Yeah..." Suzie trails off, and she really doesn't want him to.

"Buddy!" Mr. Day screams. "Right now!"

"I wish we could just stay like this," Suzie says. "I don't want us to go anywhere."

"BUDDY!" both his parents yell.

"You ain't going anywhere," Buddy says, and he takes Suzie's hand in his. "I'm not lettin' you go anywhere this time."

Suzie smiles. "Go check on your folks, Mr. Scientist," she says. "Before they have a bird."

Buddy nods. "I'll be right back." He runs up the stairs.

Suzie looks around for something to do and settles on the small portable radio. She tunes it in and wishes she hadn't as she cuts into Rockin' Hill Billy; only he's not right. Suzie's never heard him sound so calm before, and it makes her feel the exact opposite.

This is not a prank, kids; I repeat, this is not a prank. Lock your doors, turn off your lights, and don't let anyone in. Once again, kids, this is not a prank, Clear Lake County—

Rockin' Hill Billy is cut short as Suzie drops the radio, and it smashes on the floor. Flashes of horrific images flood her eyes: a flaming car that smolders as a seared, bug-eyed driver crawls away from the wreck; a hand, not her own, around the neck of a boy as he's lifted off the ground. There's just too many. A housewife who tries to fend off her bug-eyed children with a rolling pin. A milkman who cowers in the back of his van as dozens of hands beat against the metal. It's all too much for Suzie; she faints onto the sofa as her eyes cloud over, and she blacks out. Even unconscious, she can't escape the horrors that befall the town of Woodvale.

Cut upstairs, where Buddy walks into the lounge to find his mother trembling, biting her fingers as she watches the news on TV. His father's busy locking the front windows and pulling the curtains closed. He turns around, and Buddy's never seen him so pale, so frightened, that it's even more shocking than the blood splattered across his shirt.

"What—" Buddy asks, and his mother cuts in.

"Buddy, look," she says, and Buddy turns to the TV.

It's the news. Only it doesn't look right. The newscaster, who's usually all smiles and charm, seems like he's been roughed up as he reads from a card "—doors and windows and stay together at all times. All lines to Clear Lake County Sheriff's Department are occupied, and citizens are urged not to call in unless absolutely necessary. If you can't secure your home or you can't get there, the Woodvale High Gymnasium has been designated an emergency shelter by the county—"

"What's happening?" Buddy asks, and his mother shushes him.

"Mayor Burton has asked for military intervention and is awaiting their response. No statement has been given as to the cause of the situation. Some speculate a communist attack or radioactive fallout from the nearby Weaverville Nuclear Power Plant, but nothing has been confirmed. Once again, lock your doors and windows and stay…"

Mr. Day turns to his son. "The windows open in the den?" he asks, and Buddy slowly nods. "Lock them, now!" Buddy races back down to the basement while his parents secure the upstairs.

He takes the steps two, three at a time, but when his feet hit the bottom and his eyes land on Suzie, Buddy forgets all about what he's supposed to be doing.

Suzie convulses and contorts on the sofa. Buddy rushes to her side, but she thrashes too wildly for him to get close. Her eyes race behind closed lids, and her teeth gnash at irregular intervals.

Her eyes open, only they're all cloudy and dilated. Not the serene, cool blue Buddy knows and loves. The gray fades, or rather, it withdraws, and Suzie shoots up.

"They're coming!" she cries and throws herself into Buddy's arms. He holds her tight. "I saw them!"

"Who?" Buddy asks.

A crash of glass and the solid thud of something with substantial heft hitting the floor above seems to answer Buddy's question. A scream follows.

Buddy races up the stairs with Suzie right behind him, and the first thing he sees as he bashes the door open is a pair of legs on the floor. His father lies there, near a broken window, a slice of glass buried deep in his neck.

"Dad!" Buddy skids onto his knees beside his father and takes his hand. "Dad, come on! Dad! Dad..." Buddy pleads, and Suzie can't do a thing but watch as Buddy's father bleeds out. Can't do a thing but think about how this is all her fault.

Mr. Day's hand slips from his son's, and Buddy grabs onto his arm. Buddy shakes him as tears run down his face. "Dad..."

Buddy's so overcome he doesn't hear the thing climb through the shattered window. He doesn't see it fall into the sink and slide its way down the countertop. The thing that used to be the nice old lady three doors down, whose lawn Buddy cut for pocket money every spring, reaches for him.

"Buddy, look out!" Suzie shouts as the old lady falls to the ground, awful, bug-like eyes fixed on the boy. Buddy hears her too late as the old lady grabs onto him, and as he scrambles to free himself, a cast iron frying pan connects with the old lady's face. The impact smashes her dentures and nose as it sends her crashing backward with a sickening thud and metallic clang.

Buddy casts a wide eye up at his mother, at her dress covered in blood. Breathing hard, the frying pan in her hands caked with blood and hair.

"Mom..." Buddy doesn't know what else to say.

"Get out of here!" Mrs. Day commands.

"Mom!" Buddy tries to warn her as another of the bug-eyed things comes up behind her. It used to be the Jones's son, back from college for the summer. He'd always been sweet on Mrs. Day, and yet it's without sentimentality when he bites down into her shoulder.

"No!" Buddy screams, and he reels. It's like he sees everything happening through a fisheye lens.

"Go!" Mrs. Day insists as she breaks herself free, turns, and whacks the bug-eyed thing with the frying pan. "Run!"

Suzie grabs Buddy by the hand. "C'mon Buddy, we gotta go!" It's like his feet finally hit the ground at her touch, but Buddy pushes Suzie away as soon as he gets himself together.

"I'm not going anywhere," Buddy says as he moves to get between his mother and the other bug-eyed things they can hear clambering up against the windows. Hands of all shapes, sizes, and degrees of damage push through the opening. Unconcerned with the broken glass, they wave and grasp almost, but not entirely, in tandem, like some undersea plants shifted by invisible currents.

Mrs. Day shoves her son, something she's never even come close to doing before, and the shock of it stops him in his tracks.

"Go!" she tells him with absolute authority.

"But mom—" Buddy pleads.

"Now!" his mother insists.

"No! Goddamnit, no!" Buddy stands his ground. "You're hurt, dad's...I'm not going anywhere!" He meets the fire in his mother's eyes with his own.

Suzie steps up and takes Buddy by the hand again, and Mrs. Day sees her for the first time, really sees her. Everything happened so fast it hadn't even occurred to her that someone else was there. It doesn't make any sense, but then again, nothing has in the last five minutes, except for something her husband said to her recently.

172

So Mrs. Day turns to Suzie. It doesn't matter that the girl is supposed to be dead. That Buddy must have been hiding her downstairs, lying to her face. All that matters is that she's a mother bear, and she knows she's going to die, but not before she makes sure her baby is safe. "Take him," Mrs. Day says to Suzie. "Get him out of here, you hear me?"

Suzie nods and starts to drag Buddy away.

"Goddamnit! I'm. Not. Leaving!" he insists as Suzie struggles to pull him towards the back door.

"I love you, honey," Mrs. Day says, and she pushes both kids out the door with all of her strength.

"Mom!" Buddy protests as his mother slams the door behind him and bolts it fast. She braces her back against it as Buddy bangs on it from outside—he calls for her, begs her to come with them as she slides to the floor.

She hears the front door crack and splinter, followed by moans and snarls as more and more of them pour into the house. Mrs. Day takes her husband's hand and watches the bug-eyed things come down the hall, packing the corridor tight, and she prays. Prays her husband forgives her for what she did, that she gets to see him again and tell the old fool he was right—it's better to die for love than to live without it.

"You're not gonna get through me, you sons of bitches," she growls as the bug-eyed things come down on her, and through gritted teeth, she denies them the satisfaction of a scream.

Outside the house, Buddy bangs on the door. "Mom! Mom! Goddamnit, mom!"

The bushes stir, and it's not the wind. Suzie can feel more of them closing in. She grabs Buddy by the shoulder and pulls him away from the door hard enough to throw him down the steps. He rolls on the grass and climbs to his feet.

"What the hell do you think you're doing!?" Buddy gets in her face.

"What your mom asked!" Suzie yells at him. "We have to go!"

"God damn you!" Buddy shouts back at her.

Suzie slaps him. With tears in her eyes, she slaps him hard across the face. "Whatever happened to it'll be okay, Suzie? Huh? We're gonna fix this? Huh!?"

Buddy touches the red welt on his face and knows she's right. He steps up and wraps his arms around her. "What are we gonna do?" she asks.

"I...I don't know," he tells her. Then he remembers what the newscaster said. "The school gym, they're using it as an emergency shelter."

It's not much of a plan, but it's better than nothing, so, a few seconds later, Buddy and Suzie run out into the street hand in hand. The sheer scale of the carnage halts them. Picture windows offer a preview of hell, consumed by fire and heavy, black smoke. A woman runs down the street in nothing but a nightgown, chased by more shuffling, bug-eyed things.

The sound of thunder makes Buddy and Suzie jump, and a second later, Mr. Frederickson walks across his front lawn right next to Buddy's house. He wears nothing but a housecoat, tidy whities, and his trademarked sneering mustache. A smoking double-barreled shotgun rests over his arm.

A bug-eyed thing hobbles towards him, and without so much as a how do you do, Mr. Frederickson takes aim and shoots it in the head. In an explosion of blood, bone, and hair, the thing falls backward as Mr. Frederickson breaks the gun and adds two more shells from his housecoat pocket.

"Mr. Frederickson," Buddy yells, happy to see the gun more than the man. Mr. Frederickson turns and looks towards Buddy and walks over. He halts fast, though, when he sees Suzie just behind the boy, and he raises his gun at both of them.

"Step aside, Buddy!" the man in the housecoat says as he aims. "She's one of 'em!"

Buddy pushes Suzie back and puts himself between her and the barrel of the gun. Suzie fights against it, but Buddy holds his ground. "Mr. Frederickson, no she ain't!" Buddy protests.

"She's dead," the man with the shotgun insists. "She's one of 'em! Move, or I'll shoot you both."

"No!" Buddy refuses.

Mr. Frederickson cocks the hammer. "Last chance," he states with cold-hearted certainty.

Buddy squeezes Suzie's hand and closes his eyes tight.

Just as Mr. Frederickson's finger starts to pull down on the trigger, one of the bug-eyed things lunges out of the bushes between both backyards and pushes him aside. The shotgun goes off and all but deafens Buddy and Suzie at such close range, and both rounds go wild.

A second or two passes before Buddy realizes the shot has missed, and he opens his eyes to see Mr. Frederickson on the grass as the bug-eyed thing digs in. The shotgun lies to the side with a pile of shells that must have spilled out of Mr. Frederickson's housecoat pocket.

Buddy eyes up the situation, then drops Suzie's hand, dashes down, grabs the shotgun and as many of the shells as he can, and pulls back just as the bug-eyed thing snaps at him. He rushes back to Suzie, retakes hold of her hand, and gets them running down the street.

Once they've some space between them and the chaos, they stop and Buddy tries to load the shells into the shotgun, but despite how easy Mr. Frederickson made it look, he can't get the hang of cracking it open. Suzie takes it from him, opens it up, and holds her hand out for the shells. Buddy, dumbfounded, hands two over, and she loads them into the gun.

"How?" he asks.

Suzie snaps it closed and pumps the gun. With a grin, she hands it back. "Dad always loved cowboy movies," she says, and as Buddy takes the gun from her, their fingers touch across the barrel. A gunshot goes off close by, kills the moment, and makes them both flinch.

"C'mon, we gotta get outta here," Suzie says.

"Damn right," Buddy agrees, and, hand in hand, the two of them beat feet as we pull back and see the sheer scale of the swarming nightmare devouring the suburbs behind them.

MAIN STREET, ZOMBIVILLE

Woodvale is a quiet, sleepy little town. Most people who live there are only used to combating boredom and the top button on their pants. Everything Buddy and Suzie see on their way through the neighborhood tells them that Woodvale is doomed. They run to the irregular beat of gunfire, the acrid taste of smoke fills Buddy's lungs, and both try to ignore the screams as the sun sets on Woodvale for, perhaps, the last time.

Suzie gasps as they round the corner onto Main Street and the first thing she sees is Greene's Groceries in ruins. A body hangs through the shattered storefront window, impaled on jutting shards of glass. Suzie prays Old Man Greene got out, but, well, we know different. It's just another reminder, for her, of the horror she believes she's brought to Woodvale.

Buddy tries to go on ahead, but Suzie, frozen to the spot with guilt, holds him back.

"This is awful," she says, and though she's right, Buddy can't just let her stand there and watch. A few bug-eyed things from the neighborhood have followed them. Buddy glances back; they're catching up faster than he expected.

"Suzie, we gotta—" Buddy says and pulls her, but instead of following him, her hand just slips from his then goes to cover her mouth.

"Mr. Greene," she starts but doesn't finish because another thought jumps into her head. "My parents," she says as it hits her. They just saw Buddy's father die; his mother paid for their escape with her life, but what about her folks?

"Suzie! We don't have time for this; we need to go right now!"

"What about my parents! Buddy, we need to go to my house."

"Do your folks listen to the radio? Watch TV?" Buddy asks.

"Yeah, of course," Suzie answers.

"Then they'll have heard the message and gone to the school!"

"You think?" Suzie hopes.

"I know it," Buddy reassures her, though, truth be told, how could he?

It's enough to get Suzie moving again, and the pair make off down Main just as the horde from the neighborhood reaches the far side of the intersection behind them.

What should have been a straight shot down Main Street, past the fire station and park, twenty minutes tops, turns out to be a hell of a lot more complicated when the two of them reach the smoldering ruins of a fire truck blocking the road. As if that wasn't enough, the fire and wreck have drawn a crowd, though at least their fascination with the flames keeps them from picking up on Buddy and Suzie.

There's no going through them, even with the shotgun.

"What now?" Buddy asks.

Suzie looks around and points to the laundromat. "Through there." When Buddy gives her a look, she explains. "Betty works—worked there. I used to go out back with her to smoke."

178

"I didn't know you smoked," Buddy says, and it hits his ears wrong. It's stranger to him than all the bug-eyed weirdness so far.

"Not the point," Suzie says. "There's a long alley out back on that side, and the fences are low enough to climb."

For you, Buddy reckons, and painful memories of not even making it up half the rope in gym class bubble up. It's not like he has many options, so Buddy follows her lead into the dark storefront.

Inside, even though the lights are out, there's still power. A few of the machines whirl and slosh, and at least one's been left on long enough to flood. The floor is slick and sodden with bubbles.

Buddy flicks the switch by the door, but nothing happens. At least there's light from the fire raging in the street outside, though it casts long, dancing shadows brimming with menace. He raises the shotgun and goes first, while Suzie takes hold of his shoulder and follows close behind.

With his eyes fixed ahead, and the shifting shadows making him jittery, Buddy jumps when something slams hard against the glass window of an industrial-sized machine right next to him. With the sudsy floor, he and Suzie go right on their asses, but Buddy manages to point the shotgun in the direction of whatever startled them regardless.

There's nothing there, though. Probably just the machine jumping— "Holy shit!" Buddy screams as a face pushes up against the window from inside the washer. Its teeth snap, and its dead, unblinking eyes glare at the kids. There's nothing it can do to get to them, though, no way it can open the machine from the inside.

"How the hell..." wonders Suzie.

"Must have crawled in there, thinking he'd be safe," Buddy suggests.

Suzie gets to her feet first, while Buddy stares at the trapped creature with scientific curiosity. It reminds him of something he read in *Weird Science* or *Strange Worlds*; he can't remember which. It was about two astronauts on a space station, and one of them becomes convinced the other is secretly an alien, planning to kill him. So he tricks him into going outside to repair something, then locks him out. Of course, the other astronaut is not an alien and dies a slow, horrible death as he runs out of oxygen. The whole time he presses up against the porthole, and even after he dies, his wide-eyed corpse remains there, tethered in place, tormenting and driving the lone, surviving astronaut insane.

"Let's go," Suzie says.

"Hang on," Buddy asks, and he crawls over to the machine. He gets close enough to take a good look at the thing as it scrapes its teeth across the glass.

"Buddy, this really isn't the time," Suzie insists and pulls at him.

"It's the eyes," Buddy ignores her. "It's like rapid onset cataracts. If that's even possible..." The thing's eyes bulge and never blink while Buddy examines it. Not even once. "It must be real hard for them to see. Could it be because they don't blink? Why, though, it's got control over the rest of the body. Maybe it's just easier for them?"

"Buddy!" Suzie yells. "Now!"

Responding to the urgency of her voice, Buddy climbs to his feet. "Sorry," he says, and Suzie leads him out back without further incident.

Their progress across the back lot is slow but safe. The bug-eyed things seem more drawn to the screams and chaos out front, and the back lot's relative serenity is disquieting. It feels very much like they're in the eye of the storm. At least the stench of rotting garbage, wet cardboard, and discarded cigarettes is better than the blood and smoke that's filled Buddy's lungs so far this night. He reckons he'll probably end up with asthma if he makes it through this, and his nerd cred will be confirmed. Kind of speaks to the day he's having when that thought makes him nostalgic for noogies, wedgies, and even a quaint old "kick me" sign.

Buddy and Suzie take turns hopping the fences. One goes first while the other covers with the shotgun, then they pass it over and swap. It's exhausting, at least for Buddy. So, out of breath, Buddy asks for a break before hopping the final fence that separates Dean's Hardware from the park. Suzie agrees and acts like she's tired too, but she feels nothing at all.

"Just say when you're good," Buddy pants.

"I will when you stop huffing like a train engine," Suzie says. She knows she should be tired, and it's quietly alarming her that she's not.

"We can't…all be…cheerleaders!" Buddy wheezes.

"Sure, but you got the legs for it, though."

"Oh yeah?" Buddy says. "Funny, see, here's me bustin' a gut."

After a minute, Buddy stands up, ready to go, and Suzie takes the shotgun. They both give each other a nod and hop the last fence.

They needn't have worried; the park's pretty empty, and the only bug-eyed things nearby are too busy with closer prey to bother going after them. Buddy thinks he should be out there for a moment, helping folks, but then he remembers who he's with; he needs to make sure Suzie's safe. He let her down before, and he just can't this time. Besides, a growing resentment has been building up inside him this past week. A seed of hatred for the town and the people who let this happen to her. The only thing stopping that line of thinking from taking over is knowing he, too, did nothing to save her from what happened.

The school's parking lot is full of cars all jammed in and left abandoned, like everyone who parked up was in a rush to get out and into the gym. That's a good sign; Buddy thinks it means there must be folk inside, alive and safe. Lots of them, by the look of it.

There's no sign of the Palmers' truck, though, and Buddy can't stand to watch as Suzie looks this way and that, desperate for a sign that her folks are okay. His heart sinks for her. The pain of losing his parents is still so fresh that he's barely had time to feel it, but at least he knows for sure they're dead. He has closure, that's something, at least.

Buddy and Suzie pass by a hissing, tinkling cherry-red Roadmaster, so hot that steam still wafts out from the hood.

When they get to the entrance, Buddy shoves the door, but it doesn't budge. Thinking it's stuck, he puts his back into it, and when it still doesn't move, Suzie joins in. After a good few shoves and one frustrated kick, a voice yells at them from inside.

"Go away!"

"Hello!" Buddy shouts.

"Let us in!" Suzie follows.

The two of them bang on the door, but it's no good. Whoever's inside has no intention of opening it. As Buddy and Suzie slam on the door, the sound catches the attention of a few bug-eyed things ambling around the edge of the park and the main road. They start to worm their way through the maze of abandoned cars towards the sound.

Buddy continues to bang on the door while Suzie catches sight of the incoming shamblers. She grabs his arm and pulls on it.

"What," Buddy says and gets his answer when Suzie points out to the lot. There's about six of them weaving through the cars already, and a dozen more on the outskirts. The horrendous parking jobs slow them down, but Buddy has no doubt they'll find their way through soon enough. There's enough of them, spread out so, and with more staggering in from the road that he can't see a clear way out. They'd have to climb over the cars or through the bug-eyed things, and he's not keen on either option.

"What do we do?" Suzie asks.

A commotion erupts from behind the door, and the two of them lean against the window to listen. There's an argument inside, at least three voices but maybe more. Suddenly, one voice louder than the others shouts, "Screw you all!"

The door is yanked open, and in the burst of light, all they see at first is the familiar blue and yellow of a Hornets letterman jacket. As their eyes adjust, Buddy and Suzie see, framed in a halo of fluorescent light, that their savior is none other than Gordy Garcia.

"Gordy!" Suzie says. Her heart almost beats again at seeing one of her friends alive and well.

"Suzie…" Gordy says and can't believe his eyes. "How…" It can't be, he thinks to himself. In the dark, the girl at the door looks just like Suzie Palmer. She even sounds like her, and she knows his name.

Another person, an adult, pushes Gordy aside and steps into the light. Buddy sees the revolver pointing out the door first, the barrel aimed right at Suzie. He steps between it and the girl, with the shotgun pointed ahead. It's Mr. Jessop, the bane of Johnny Freemantle's existence, the most hated teacher at Woodvale High, with a hand so jittery he could mix paint. The gun rattles like a renegade washing machine.

"Not one step," he stammers, and though he's scared, his voice still carries the same stern, stuck up do-as-I-say attitude as always. "We can't let you in! It's not safe!"

"We'll die out here," Buddy pleads. "Please, Mr. Jessop."

"Better you than us," he says, and Buddy winces as the English teacher's trigger finger twitches, but, thankfully, doesn't squeeze the trigger.

"Mr. Jessop, we gotta let them in," Gordy says as he steps up next to the teacher.

"I am not risking my life for a—" Mr. Jessop says, and Gordy cuts him off.

"For a what, huh? For a what?" Gordy gets fired up, and Mr. Jessop glares at the boy through the corner of his eye. "For a kid? For one of your students? For people in need? Huh, Mr. Jessop? Or were you going to say something else?"

Mr. Jessop panics. Having always been the self-professed liberal champion of the common man, just as long as they don't move in next door, he takes his image and what people think about him very seriously. "No, I—" The second he's distracted, Gordy socks him one on the chin and yanks the revolver out of his hand.

Gordy steps aside while Mr. Jessop staggers back and clutches his face.

Buddy and Suzie slip inside.

184

"Gordy!" Suzie says and throws her arms around him. "I'm so happy you're okay!" It is her; it really is her, Gordy realizes. Though, how? She was dead. He's kicked himself black and blue over knowing that Dash was responsible and that he said nothing, yet here she is. Sure, dead doesn't mean what it meant a day or so ago, but she's not like the bug-eyed ones outside, like the ones back at the diner. She's, well, she's Suzie.

Even under these circumstances, Buddy isn't thrilled to see Gordy again, but at least they're safe. For now. He puts the shotgun down by the door and shuts it. There's a baseball bat on the floor, and Buddy jams it back in place just as the first of the bug-eyed things reaches them. Their pounding sounds like soft slaps through the thick metal, and since the window is so small, Buddy's relatively sure they're not getting through any time soon.

There's so many of them now, way more than he could ever have imagined. They really are like ants, he thinks. For every one you see, there's exponentially more you don't.

"It's a genuine Antville out there," Gordy says as he steps up to the other window. Buddy winces instinctually at the proximity of one of his bullies. You don't know how right you are, Buddy says to himself, and when he reaches for the shotgun again, it's gone.

He hears the pump behind him and turns around to see Mr. Jessop pointing both barrels straight at Suzie. Gordy steps in between them, hands raised, and says, "Wait a minute—"

Mr. Jessop interrupts. "Get away from her," he demands. "That's Susan Palmer and, as we all know, she died. We all went to her funeral."

"She's not like them," Buddy says, but the teacher ignores him.

185

"Put the gun down, sir," Gordy pleads.

A crowd forms behind them. About a dozen or so townsfolk. Terrified eyes glazed with shock and horror. Buddy's seen that look before. In some of the books and pictures Mrs. Palmer once showed him. That's how it starts; he remembers her telling him. Then the fear builds into hate. One scared person is dangerous. More? That's a mob, and he knows what those can do. Buddy sees where this is going, and he's not about to let that happen to Suzie, so he steps around the other side, putting himself between her and the crowd.

"She's not like them," Buddy insists. "And you'll have to go through me to get her."

"Same," says Gordy, and Buddy just about forgives him for all the shit he's given him these last few years for that one act of heroism.

Meanwhile, Gordy hopes to hell nobody can tell he's just about ready to wet his pants. His whole body trembles, his mouth is ash, and every instinct he has tells him to run, but he fights that hard. For some reason, he's got a second chance to stick up for Suzie, and he couldn't live with himself if he let her down again.

"Stand aside," Mr. Jessop commands.

"No," says Buddy.

"No," says Gordy.

"Stop," yells Suzie, and she breaks down into tears. "Stop, all of you stop! Enough people have died! Enough! I won't let one more person die because of me! I won't!"

Her outburst and heartfelt plea works for the mob but not for Mr. Jessop, whose only wavering comes in his increasingly trembling hand. Even with how rattled he is, he's close enough that it'd be almost impossible to miss the shot with the spread from that shotgun.

"Buddy, Gordy, please move," she says, but neither boy relents. "I couldn't live with myself if either of you fools gets yourselves killed because of me."

"What about the closet?" asks someone in the crowd.

"Yeah, we can lock her in there so we're all safe," suggests another.

"I can't see another kid die..." another voice adds, and the nods of a few others that follow says too many of them have seen enough of that this evening.

Buddy is about to protest when Suzie agrees. "I'll go," she says. "Is that okay, Mr. Jessop?"

After a moment, the teacher nods and uses the shotgun to motion for her to move. Buddy and Gordy keep guard as the crowd parts. They're all terrified of Suzie, but there's a hint of pity there. Suzie tries to make eye contact to thank them, but no one can bring themselves to look at her. It makes the walk to the storage closet feel so much longer than it is.

As they pass across the basketball court, it's clear that there's no leadership or organization. Just huddled, scared people. At least they're alive, Suzie thinks, as she scans the room in vain for her parents.

When they reach the closet, Mr. Jessop rummages in his pocket and produces a chain of keys with a great deal of effort. He tosses them on the floor in front of Buddy. "Open it," he instructs. "And once she's inside, lock it."

Buddy picks up the keys and does what he's told. He thinks about trying something, maybe if he could get Gordy—

"Don't even think about it," the teacher says.

It always gave Buddy and just about every other kid who had Mr. Jessop for English an entire case of the heebie-jeebies the way he seemed to read their minds.

As soon as the door is open, Mr. Jessop prods Suzie inside with the shotgun, and she falls over the threshold. Buddy makes to go for Mr. Jessop, but Gordy holds him back.

"Don't," Gordy cautions, and as Suzie gets to her feet inside, she agrees.

"It'll be okay," she says, and just looking at her alone, in that dark and dusty room, makes Buddy's eyes water. How can it be, he says to himself.

"Close it," Mr. Jessop demands, and when Buddy doesn't comply, Gordy steps in and shuts the door. Buddy lets him take the keys from him, and then Gordy locks it. "Give them to me," Mr. Jessop says and holds his hand out for the keys.

"No," Gordy says and hands the keys to Buddy. Confused and astounded at his bold new ally, Buddy takes the keys.

"Yes," states Mr. Jessop, and he tilts the shotgun to make his point.

Gordy pulls back the hammer on the revolver in his hand to make one of his own, though he doesn't go as far as pointing it at the teacher. "No, we're keeping them, and I'm going to say this once: you stay the hell away from this door, and these two. You got that?"

Mr. Jessops spits. "Hooligan," he says and backs down. He heads over to the bleacher across the hall, rests the shotgun on his lap, fixes his eyes hard to the door, and watches.

NIGHT OF THE ZOMBIE CHEERLEADER

Cut to: Suzie, alone in the dark with just niggling, worrying thoughts for company. Thoughts about her parents, closer to prayers, really, that they're still alive and safe somehow; about Buddy, and how even though he just lost his parents, all he does is look after her. She thinks about Gordy, too, glad he's alive, though all it does is remind her of what she's lost. What she's done to people she loves. Like Betty.

The thing is, she's not entirely alone.

While she drowns in guilt and sorrow, another voice speaks up. One that has tried forcing itself upon her and that she's been able to keep at bay, more or less.

There's an intense droning inside her head, a sharp white-hot pain, and It speaks:

SUZIE.

Cut to: the gym hall, where Buddy and Gordy have taken up positions right by the closet door. Buddy tries to talk through the door to Suzie, but he figures the old wood's too thick since she doesn't answer.

"Rough night, huh?" asks Gordy as Buddy takes a seat. When Buddy doesn't respond, Gordy comes over and sits next to him. Despite all he's done for them this evening, Buddy is still a little uncomfortable having Gordy this close to him. One good deed doesn't easily

189

erase a learned, involuntary response, after all. He shifts, primes himself to move if he has to.

"Listen, Buddy," Gordy says. "I know this doesn't mean much, with everything else going on, but I wanna say I'm sorry."

Buddy looks up and sees an unexpected, unfamiliar sincerity in Gordy's eyes.

"I've been thinking, thinking a lot this week," he continues. "Ever since…I've been an ass, and I'm sorry. I never shoulda…it was just easier, you know? No, I guess you wouldn't. When you hang around with a guy like Dash, it's easy to lose your way."

"Then why'd you hang out with him?" Buddy asks.

"It's not that easy," Gordy tries to explain.

"Yeah. It is," Buddy challenges.

"Shit, maybe you're right, I dunno," Gordy says. "I'm a coward, Buddy. A damn yellow-bellied coward. I left some folk for dead, did nothing to stop—to save Sheriff Keyes."

Damn, Buddy thinks to himself; he can't imagine Keyes dying. He figured the Sheriff would come through by the morning with a posse of deputies and clear this whole mess. As sad as he is to hear about the lawman's fate, he can see how it haunts Gordy, and that leaves Buddy uncomfortably empathetic, especially as Gordy tears up and sobs into his hands.

"I had to—we had to run and leave my mom behind," Buddy shares in hopes that it relieves some of Gordy's guilt.

"Your dad?" Gordy asks, and Buddy just shakes his head. "Damn, that's harsh. That's, jeez, man. You're one tough mother; you know that?"

"What d'you mean?" Buddy asks, confused as hell.

"To see that happen to your mom and dad? Then still get Suzie all the way across town? That takes cojones, and you got them."

Buddy feels his cheeks flush. "It's not all that. Suzie kicked serious ass tonight herself."

"Yeah, I have no doubt," Gordy says, and his face turns grave. "Look, I gotta tell you something." Gordy leans in, and Buddy follows. "They all might think this has something to do with her being back from the dead. I don't know if it does or it doesn't, but she would never have been that way in the first place if it weren't for Dash."

Buddy's throat dries, and acid boils inside him as he asks, "What do you mean?" and doesn't know if he genuinely wants to find out.

"Dash did something. I don't know if he did it on purpose or it was an accident, but he came to me that night, all scared shitless. Begged me to lie for him, and I did."

"You piece of shit!" Buddy yells and clocks Gordy on the nose, sending him back over the bleachers and onto the floor. The fight draws stares from around the room, but no one has the spirit in them to intervene. Buddy's hand trembles and his knuckles ache, but the pain feels right. It feels glorious.

Gordy climbs back up and pinches his nose to staunch the blood. "I deserved that," he says.

"You're damn right you do," Buddy says and gets ready to give him another.

Gordy holds his hand out. "Let me finish!"

"Give me one good reason," Buddy demands, and Gordy does.

"So we can make sure Dash gets what's coming to him."

Cut to: the storage closet, where Suzie spins around as she searches for the source of the voice. "Who's there!?" she shouts. But deep down, she knows.

S-U-Z-IEEEE.

"Where are you!?"

WE ARE YOU, SUZIE.

Pain surges through her head, and a thousand white-hot pinpricks march up and down her spine in a droning, militant stampede.

"No, leave me alone!"

YOU SHOULD HAVE STAYED ASLEEP, SUZIE.

Although it's pitch dark and there's enough space for Suzie's scuffling feet to echo, she knows there's no one else in the room. It's inside her, the thing that's been inside her all this time, and it's grown. It's smarter, learned from her, and has had enough of being in the back seat.

THEY WILL ALL JOIN US, AND YOU WILL WATCH.

"No!"

YES.

Suzie falls to her knees as she's bombarded with images of the horrors so far. First, those witnessed through her own eyes. Buddy's father with a shard of glass in his neck. Greene's Groceries in flames. Then others she couldn't even imagine—a faceless child, a mountain of metal, fire, writhing torn bodies.

Then she's forced to relive the horrors she inflicted herself. Suzie sees her hand, soaked in Christina's blood as the waitress lies dead on the floor—her eyes burning with hate for her killer. Bitter to the end. She sees Betty, as the joyful smile on her face becomes a grimace of abject terror.

Then she sees through dozens of eyes pointed at Buddy's house. She sees Buddy and herself as they both run down Main Street. She sees Buddy up close, his features distorted by the glass of a washing machine window.

YOU TRUST.

"Buddy's my friend—"

Suzie's thoughts are cut short with a series of flashes, images of herself and Dash. The thing taunts her. She sees herself dance with him at the Rock 'n' Roll Ball. Smiles in his car as he wraps his Hornets jacket around her. She twirls her hair as Dash leans against the wall, his arm over her head, and watches how his muscles tense. Suzie feels his lips on hers. Then the ride out to Make-

Out Point, the look on his face as she says to take her home. Dash rips her dress—the look of panic on his face as she falls. Dash rushes away, jacket in hand, as he leaves her to die.

YOU TRUSTED THIS ONE.

"No—I…Buddy's different!"

HE WILL JOIN US.

I will not let that happen, Suzie thinks.

IT WILL.

You can read my—

WE ARE YOUR MIND, SUZIE.

You are not! Get out!

HE WILL FAIL YOU TOO. UNLESS HE BECOMES ONE OF THE FAMILY.

What does that mean? The family?

The voice goes quiet; perhaps it's said too much, she thinks. Gave away something important, and now she knows. And it knows she knows, so there's no point hiding it!

NOT ALL US ARE EQUAL.

What are you? Show me!

YOU DO NOT WANT TO SEE.

Show me!

It doesn't respond right away, and Suzie can feel its hesitation before it obliges. Suzie's mind fills with two black mandibles, attached to a head consumed by two massive bean-shaped eyes that stare into eternity with cold, ruthless inevitability. The creature is like an ant, a queen ant that's pierced her brain with its spindly, barbed legs. From all over its legs, other joints splinter off, thin as spider silk but rigid, twisted at incomprehensible angles, and they pierce different sections of her brain on all sides. Behind it, a bulbous, pulsating abdomen that curls down to her neck.

Suzie tries to hurl, but nothing comes out. The thought of this thing is a violation in every conceivable way. Even with nothing in her stomach, it tosses and heaves at the idea.

It's a queen, Suzie thinks between retches.

QUEEN! YES!

And the family?

FAMILY. BROOD. ANOINTED. WE ARE THE FOREVER.

Why am I just hearing from you now? Why haven't you spoken to me before?

It takes its time. Suzie can feel it sift through her mind, her memories, to find the answer. Like it's putting a sentence together from other people's words.

WE HAVE.

Not like this. All you've done is order me around. Try and control me. Why are you trying to reason with me now?

DOES THE MAN REASON WITH THE FOOD?

That's all we are to you? Food?

NOT ALL. YOU ARE THE MOTHER.

You need us! Like Buddy said, to carry your children? That's disgusting!

IT IS THE FOREVER.

You haven't answered me. Why are you speaking to me now?

196

FORCE IS NOT REQUIRED. SUBMIT.

Didn't expect us to fight back, huh? You picked the wrong damn world to invade!

Suzie feels the Queen rummage through her memories. It triggers flashes of newsreels and radio broadcasts, war, and violence.

WE COME IN PEACE. YOU LIVE IN WAR. THE FOREVER IS ONE. THE FOREVER IS LOVE.

The Forever can go to hell! You look through my mind and see what we did to the last gross little bug who pulled this over in Europe. You might be some freaky space ant, but we're hornets, damn it, and you just kicked the whole damn nest!

WE ARE NOT AFRAID.

No, I think you are!

Suzie backs up towards the sliver of light that comes from beneath the door to the gym.

Why talk to me now, then? Why try and reason with me?

197

SUZIE WILL SUBMIT. OR WE SHALL TEAR HIM TO PIECES!

Images of Buddy, terrified and distraught, flash through her mind.

SUZIE WILL SUBMIT!

Suzie will not!

WE ARE THE FOREVER.

No, I know what you are. I know what I am! I'm a seventeen-year-old girl who likes things she ought not to, loves people she shouldn't, and I'm good at hiding it. From my friends, from my teachers, and, most of all, from myself. So I know good and well when someone else is doing the same.

Suzie flicks the light, and the storage closet floods with a sickly, pale yellow luminescence. It's the most beautiful thing Suzie has ever seen. The sight of half-inflated basketballs, scuffed cones, and dusty, broken gymnastics equipment that stinks of rubber and flop sweat is heaven compared to what she just went through, and she collapses to the floor with a smile on her face.

They don't like light. Suzie can't wait to tell Buddy; he'll be so proud of her for figuring it out. It's the eyes; they never blink. Those damn bug eyes need it, but too much of it hurts. That's why they fog over. Why the Queen waited till it was dark to try and retake control.

This discovery leaves Suzie with two very upsetting thoughts to dwell on.

The first is that the Queen is still in there, plotting, and even if it can't seize control of Suzie, it still has some influence on the others. It sent that horde to Buddy's house, and not just for her. It knows if they get Buddy, if she causes Buddy's death too, then it'll win. There will be no fight left in her.

Then there's the revelation that these things are more effective in the dark. The sun was already going down as they made their way across town, and now that night had fallen, they were in even more danger than she could have imagined.

Cross-cut back outside the closet to the boys, completely unaware of the cosmic horror Suzie just stared down, and beat, at least for the moment.

"Is he still alive?" Buddy asks and hopes the answer is no.

"I don't know," Gordy answers. "I hope not, but it's Dash we're talking about."

"Yeah," Buddy agrees, thinking he doesn't want to have to deal with Dash as one of those bug-eyed things.

"So, here's my plan," Gordy says and lowers his voice even further. "You saw the car outside? Cherry-red Roadmaster, runs a little hot?"

"Yeah," Buddy says and waits to see where this goes.

"Nearly burned out the engine getting back into town after—shit, that doesn't matter. Anyway, I'm thinking we'll chill here tonight. Wait till the sun comes up and, if the cavalry hasn't come through yet, you, me, Suzie, and whoever else wants to come—"

"And not that piece of shit, Mr. Jessop," Buddy interrupts.

"And not that piece of shit, Mr. Jessop," Gordy agrees. "Vamoose. Sounds like a plan?"

"Yeah," Buddy says. "It does."

When Gordy sticks his hand out, Buddy takes it. It feels odd to shake hands with the same guy who kicked him off a bus just a week ago. Though, after everything, that feels like a lifetime ago for Buddy.

They agree to take turns keeping watch, so the other can rest and post up in front of the closet door. Buddy takes the first watch, and as Gordy naps next to him, Buddy places his hand against the old wood, hoping the girl on the other side can feel that he's still there for her.

After everything, Buddy doesn't think he'll ever sleep again, but as the adrenaline wears off and the exertion of the day settles in, he crashes out without even realizing.

While they rest, cut to: Christina as she makes her way through the dark, lonely halls of Woodvale High. Screams from outside call to her but every time she tries to follow, they're drowned out by a painful drone that says:

NO.

Even though she's long past using words, she knows what that means. So Christina follows the path of least resistance, guided by the invisible command of the Queen towards the gym.

She wades through unused Halloween decorations and props left ready for the big dance that never happened, though Christina halts at an orange, crepe paper ballot box decorated with black cardboard bats and spiders. This box means something to her, but the Queen will not tolerate another distraction, so the pain returns, and Christina moves on.

200

Soon she's close enough to hear the huddled whimpers and sobs of the survivors in the gym, and the voice in her head screams:

FEED!

She pushes through the curtains, then steps out onto the stage and into the light. With her gouged, lopsided skeletal grin and her torn, blood-stained uniform, it's safe to say anyone and everyone in that hall would write her in for the costume contest. That's if they were teenagers at the dance instead of terrified, aimless survivors, and if she was wearing a costume and wasn't, in fact, a pure nightmare creature. Horribly beautiful and so very, very hungry, yet, as she moves to climb off the stage and go for the nearest sleeping warm body—

NO!

It sounds, in her head, as though spoken by a thousand voices with a single mouth.

WAIT.

It's not long before the Queen's plan pays off.

One of the sleeping survivors, curled in a ball beside the stage, shifts uncomfortably at the sudden stench of blood and the gurgles of a snarling jaw soaked in fetid saliva. It's a young man, not long out of high school himself, and when he sees Christina standing there, he screams so loud he wakes up the entire hall.

It's just one of them, only Christina, yet she inspires absolute fear. Because, while she's just one, each of the traumatized survivors sees the one that destroyed their lives. They see the one that took their husbands, wives, and children from them. After what they have all been through, one may as well be a hundred—which isn't too far from the literal truth for most of the survivors. Where there is one…

Panic sets in, and screams follow. Chaos and hysteria have always been a far more potent weapon than any army, and the Queen knows this.

Some of them run towards the fire exit, and as soon as the doors are open, a sea of the bug-eyed things pour in. They descend on the desperate, stampeding survivors like snapping, famished piranhas.

Buddy and Gordy jerk awake at the screams, but both keep their cool, at least enough to not panic and run. When Buddy sees that Mr. Jessop isn't where he was when they fell asleep, it doesn't take him long to find the teacher. Despite having a loaded shotgun, the coward made a run for it like the rest and was caught by one of the bug-eyed things.

No, not just any one of them. It's Johnny Freemantle.

"No!" Buddy says. "Not Johnny, no." And in his stupor, he drops the keychain.

"Shit," Gordy says as he checks the revolver's cylinder. He only has three bullets. "I'll try to clear us a path. You get Suzie and meet me at the car."

Buddy doesn't respond. He watches as Johnny rips open their English teacher's stomach. The man must still be alive from the way his legs and arms twitch, and Buddy watches as his former friend pulls guts and what looks like undigested candy from the man's abdomen.

The bug-eyed Johnny happily shoves both into his mouth.

"Buddy!" Gordy shoves him to get his attention.

"Y-yeah?"

"You hear me? Get Suzie and get to the car. I'll clear the way. Go!" With that, Gordy races into the chaos and leaves Buddy to fumble through the keys until he finds the right one.

It takes him a minute, but as soon as Buddy gets the door open, Suzie falls into his arms.

"Buddy!" She squeezes him hard. "Thank god." Then she takes in the gym hall that has become a slaughterhouse. "What the hell's going on?"

"I think they were waiting for us to panic and run out the door," Buddy says. "There's so many, and nobody heard a peep. That doesn't make anything close to sense, though."

Yeah, it does, Suzie says to herself. It makes perfect sense, but this isn't the time to tell Buddy what she's learned.

"Gordy's gonna clear the way and then—" Buddy says, but Suzie interrupts. Christina lunges at him.

"Look out!"

Suzie pulls Buddy inside the closet, just in time, though now they're stuck with Christina blocking the door.

Looking around for something to use as a weapon, Buddy sees another door at the back and pulls Suzie towards it.

It's locked, of course, and, as Buddy cycles through the keys, trying to find the right one, Christina closes in.

If Suzie didn't know any better, she'd say Christina was enjoying this. It looks as though she's smiling, Suzie thinks, as much as you can with half your face ripped off.

Except it doesn't look half as bad as it did when she last saw Christina, when the Queen forced Suzie to look at her reflection through the dead girl's eyes. She hears a clunk as Buddy unlocks the door behind her, but instead of running, Suzie decides she's had enough.

"Christina, I'm sorry for everything," she says and punches her in the jaw so hard it visibly dislocates. What's left dangles like a fleshy sock. "But you always were a monstrous bitch!" Suzie kicks Christina so hard she stumbles back, falls on her ass, and pulls a pommel horse down on her head. The impact crushes her skull, and she explodes like a watermelon.

She didn't mean it, didn't want to kill her, but Buddy doesn't give Suzie the chance to regret her actions as he takes her by the hand and leads her through the darkened halls of the school. When they finally get outside, Suzie tries to pull away from the parking lot and make for the back end of the school, but Buddy stops her.

"Gordy said he'd meet us by his car," he explains.

"You trust him?" Suzie asks, knowing their history.

"Yeah. I do. Let's go."

Suzie lets him lead the way again, and they run back around the outside of the school, only to come face to face with a horde of bug-eyed things laced through the maze of cars.

There's no sign of Gordy, but the Roadmaster is still there.

Buddy thinks the worst when he hears a whistle from the far end of the lot, and his face lights up when he sees Gordy leap up onto the roof of a car with the shotgun in one hand and the revolver in the other.

The bug-eyed things swarm around the car. The pressure of all the bodies crushed together prevents any attempts to climb and buys Gordy the precious seconds he needs.

Gordy puts the shotgun down, tucks the revolver into his belt, and takes something out of his pocket. "Yo! Catch!" he yells and tosses the car keys across the parking lot.

Buddy steps back, puts his hand in the air, and catches them. The force of the impact stings but feels like a victory all the same.

"Good catch! You should have tried out for the team," Gordy yells. "Suzie, you're up!" Gordy hurls the shotgun over to them, and Suzie steps forward enough to catch it in both hands. "Strike two! Looks like I'm about out."

Why did he have to say that? Both Buddy and Suzie see where this is going, and neither of them likes it one bit.

"I ain't getting over there, guys. Take the Roadmaster and split," Gordy yells and almost loses his balance as the bug-eyed things rock the car even harder.

"No!" Buddy yells back just as a bunch of them push aside some cars. Bodies worm their way through the new gap. A few from the edges of Gordy's mob peel off too and push up against the last two cars that keep Buddy and Suzie from being overwhelmed.

Gordy pulls back the torn sleeve of his Hornets jacket and holds his arm up, shows Buddy and Suzie the fresh bite wound. "I've seen what happens next," Gordy yells. "So I'm gonna jump down and run my ass off as fast as I can the other way, lead as many as I can away from you guys, give you a chance to get to the car and burn rubber."

"Come on, Gordy!" Buddy yells.

"Buddy, this is happening, so get with it," Gordy insists.

Buddy is overwhelmed with conflicting emotions. He would never have thought someone like Gordy could do something so noble. The fact that he is makes Buddy ashamed of himself for thinking so little of him. Sure, Buddy had his reasons to dislike him, but perhaps there was more to him than the others. Maybe they could have even been friends.

"Thank you," Buddy says as he sheds a tear for Gordy.

"Nah, I owe you, both of you. So, maybe this makes things right," Gordy says, but it doesn't sound like he believes it.

Buddy can't bring himself to say so, but it does.

"Do me one favor, though," Gordy yells. "You see that piece of shit, Dash, you kick his ass but good!"

Buddy nods. He means to do that for sure.

"Gordy!" Suzie yells, and when Gordy looks at her, she claps three times, crosses her arms, then points sharply with her right hand while she sings, "Go, Hornets, go!"

Gordy raises a fist in the air and finishes the cheer, "Sting, sting, sting!"

And, with that, Gordy leaps from the car and lands just ahead of the mob.

By the time they turn to follow, he's already halfway across the road. Even wounded, Gordy moves like lightning. He's as fast as he ever was out on the diamond, and the last Buddy and Suzie see of him is his blue and yellow jacket vanishing as a mass of staggering bodies follow him back down Main Street.

RETURN TO MAKE-OUT
POINT

Cut to: a farmhouse, somewhere outside Woodvale, where both parents of the kid who found Suzie Palmer's body a week ago lie dead on the floor as the hulking nightmare that is Danny "Dash" Domico towers over them, and he is not satisfied. There was another here, a small but annoying creature, but it escaped him.

He steps out the front door, which hangs from one tenuous hinge and squeals as it swings in the breeze, then looks to the amber glow that burns above the nearby town. From this distance, Dash can't hear the screams, the gunfire, the hopeless weeping, and bitter struggles. The town almost looks peaceful; the fire-lit sky easily mistakable for a late summer sunset. Dash takes a few mindless, stomping strides towards town and stops when suddenly:

NO.

Dash feels something happen—a part of him wakes up, and an image is forced upon him. He sees Buddy Peter Day with Suzie Palmer in his arms, seen through Christina's eyes before that one was lost. Parts of him come alive again. Jealousy. Rage. And the functions he needs to act on them.

His teeth grit, his fists clench, and Dash turns away from the town. He moves with more speed, more coordination, and more focus than any of the other bug-eyed drones. It's a bold move, a risky gambit, but the Queen has already lost control of her host and one of her children has fallen, so it's a risk she must take.

While Dash walks away from the carnage at the farmhouse, cut in on Buddy and Suzie as they slide into the driver and passenger seats, respectively, of the Roadmaster. Only when Buddy sticks the keys in the ignition does he stop to think. An awkward pause follows. Some of the bug-eyed things manage to get over the barricade of cars and topple to the ground.

"Buddy! The hell are you waiting for!?" Suzie panics.

"I, uh, I can't drive..." he admits.

"You never took—you know what, catch!" Suzie throws him the shotgun, and Buddy grabs it just as one of the bug-eyed things reaches the car. Neither of them saw it coming, and Buddy gets such a fright that the gun goes off, taking half the bug-eyed thing's head with it.

Although he didn't mean it, Suzie doesn't know that, and to her, it looks like something out of the cowboy movies she used to watch with her father. She whoops and lifts herself onto Buddy's lap. "Nice shot!"

"What are you—"

"No time," Suzie says as she takes the wheel, turns the keys, and makes the Roadmaster roar. It kicks like it's had a lot of highly illegal work done under the hood. Suzie throws it in reverse and sends clods of dirt and grass in the air as the beast rips through the lawn like a panzer tank. A few of the bug-eyed things keep their grip, mostly on the grill, and they hang on till they either let go or lose their arms.

Soon enough, Buddy and Suzie are on the road and heading away from town.

"Uh, you mind?" Suzie says and tilts her head towards the passenger seat.

"Sure," Buddy says as Suzie lifts her backside so he can move over. He's cautious, given where she just sat, to avoid letting her know the exact effect she's had on him.

She knows, and she smirks.

"You never learned to drive?" Suzie asks, giving Buddy something less embarrassing to cover his flushed cheeks with. They're outside of town now, and since the coast is clear, as far as she can see, Suzie slows down to a steady cruise.

"I was gonna," Buddy says, all defensive. "Why we slowin' down?"

"Where are we going?" she asks. "No point in rushing if we don't know where to."

"Fair point," Buddy says. "I have no idea. You think Gordy will be okay?"

Suzie does not. "Sure," she lies. "I mean, he always was the fastest on the team. Dash hated that, never liked it when anyone said it, but it's true, so maybe..."

They both go quiet. Suzie thinks about Gordy, how soon he'll be just another one of the bug-eyed things and another name for the list of people's lives she's ruined. Buddy thinks about Dash, and if Suzie remembers what happened to her, what Gordy told him.

"Check the radio," Suzie nods. "See if there's any more news or somethin'."

Buddy flicks it on, and it's already tuned to Rockin' Hill Billy's station, except there's just dead air. "That's not good," he says.

"Maybe he ran away, though—" An idea suddenly hits Suzie; she spins the car into a screeching turn that burns the road, the tires, and Buddy's eardrums while tossing him around.

"Woah!" Buddy steadies himself. "What're you doing!?"

"We missed the turn for Make-Out Point a few minutes back," Suzie says and then, as an afterthought, "Don't get any ideas."

"You sure you wanna go back there?" Buddy asks.

"Nope. But it's the fastest way to the radio station from this side of town."

"And we're going there because—"

"Because it's built like a fortress," Suzie explains. "All concrete and metal, with just these tiny little windows all the way up. I think it used to belong to the army or something; it's the safest place in town."

Buddy wonders if it's all that given that Rockin' Hill Billy is missing in action. Maybe he has a family and went to rescue them or something. No one knows an awful lot about the guy, and most kids just assume he lives up there on the hill. "You sure know a lot about it."

"I had to go up there and do an interview after I won the dance-off. It was awkward, and Rockin' Hill Billy smelled like the back room of Greene's Groceries. That was weird."

"What does he look like?" Buddy asks.

"Hairy," Suzie laughs. "Like a total wolfman!"

"Man, wouldn't that be just what we need right now, the goddamn Wolfman!" Buddy howls like Lon Chaney Jr., and Suzie joins in. Both kids let off some steam, howling louder and louder at the moon, all the while laughing and giggling like they were back in Buddy's backyard.

After the moment passes, Buddy says, "Hey, can I ask you something?" He didn't mean it to sound so serious, but it does and, he guesses, it is.

"Sure," Suzie says, but it doesn't sound like she is.

"When did you start getting into all that stuff?" Buddy asks.

"What stuff?"

"Like dances," Buddy explains. "Getting all pretty, you know. Girly stuff."

"You think I'm pretty?" Suzie asks as she turns and gives Buddy the kind of smile that's meant to look anything but adorable—but she fails.

I sure do, Buddy thinks, while he says, "That's not what I'm saying." I always did. Goddamnit, Suzie, you're the prettiest girl there ever was, you're like sunshine in July, and I think I love you. "Like, you used to love comics and those cheesy space movies."

"I still do, Buddy," she says. "You think I didn't sneak some comics off the rack and read when it's quiet at work?"

"You did?" Buddy asks, astounded and impressed.

"A girl can be both Rita Hayworth and Fay Wray if she likes," she smirks. "Just like how a nerd can also draw like Jack Kirby."

"Who's Jack—hey, how'd you know I draw!" Buddy yells.

"He draws some romance comics, he's great. And I've watched you doodle in class," she teases. "Plus you left your sketchbook lying out while you snored on the recliner."

"I, uh, don't snore," Buddy says but realizes he can't be all that sure. Besides, as embarrassing as it is for Suzie to know that, he likes that she does. It feels intimate but in an honest, innocent way.

Ahead of them, a pair of headlights come around the bend. Good, Buddy and Suzie both think, someone else made it out too. As the lights get closer, they suddenly jerk onto the wrong side of the road, into a direct collision course with the Roadmaster.

"The hell are they doing?" Suzie wonders out loud.

"Maybe they don't see us," Buddy suggests, but when Suzie moves into the other lane, the oncoming car copies her.

"That maniac's gonna ram us!" Suzie yells as both cars dance from side to side. "Buckle up, Buddy!" And before he can, Suzie floors it; the Roadmaster screams, and small flames blast from the engine like it's a dragon just woken and ready to fly. Suzie keeps the Roadmaster on course to smash into the oncoming car. There's a wild look in her eyes, and she pokes her tongue with one of her incisors. It's a thing she does when she's super focused, which Buddy recalls, and it's the only reason he doesn't have a heart attack.

At the last second, Suzie veers to the side and lets the other car scrape past them. It passes in a blur. One that looks awfully familiar.

"It can't be," Suzie says as she glances at the rearview mirror, but it is. A 1932 Ford Deuce. It pulls off a clumsy U-turn, but the V8 inside that monster is more than enough to make up for the lost time, and it's not long before it starts to gain on them.

Suzie floors it again, but this time the Roadmaster's engine sputters and coughs. Steam pours out instead of fire, and the needle starts to dip. The Deuce gains ground, enough for both Buddy and Suzie to see Dash behind the wheel.

"Holy shit!" Buddy and Suzie yell at the same time.

212

The Deuce tailgates them. Dash's bug eyes are freakishly huge in the light cast off from the headlamps. His skeletal grin is maddeningly wide. It can't be possible, but it looks to Buddy and Suzie like he's very much enjoying this.

"Faster, must go faster!" Buddy yells.

"I can't! I think the engine's shot," Suzie yells, and the Deuce rams into the back of the Roadmaster. Suzie bumps her head on the wheel, and the car swerves hard.

"I got this," Buddy says as he pumps the shotgun. "Try and keep it steady."

I'll try, Suzie says to herself, as the Roadmaster coughs up black smoke and fills the air with the smell of burning oil.

Buddy turns and plants the shotgun on the back of his seat and lines it up with the Deuce's driver side window. The car rattles, and Buddy's rattled, but that's not the problem. Even though it's Dash, even though he's one of those things, even though their lives are on the line—Buddy doesn't know if he can. He's killed one of them, just one, and even then, it was an accident. Two, if you count the Fredericksons' cat. This, though, this will be murder. Right?

"Buddy!" Suzie yells.

Buddy jumps and pulls the trigger.

The windshield of the Deuce cracks, and shards of glass and buckshot pepper Dash's face. It makes no difference. The Deuce keeps on coming, and Dash keeps on grinning. It rams the Roadmaster again, and this time knocks the rear fender loose.

"It's not gonna work," Buddy says. "He's too far away—hey! I got it! Can you slow down, get him on our right side?"

"Clue me in?" Suzie asks.

213

"If he's close enough, I can probably blast his wheel off," Buddy explains.

"Got it," Suzie smirks and counts down. "Three, two, one," she pulls to the left, kills the gas, and the Deuce starts to take over. "Now!"

Buddy fires, pumps, and fires again, and the front left wheel of the Deuce explodes in a shower of metal and rubber.

"Yeah!" Buddy celebrates, but it's too early.

The Deuce doesn't slow down; it lands on its rim and sprays the Roadmaster with sparks so bright it blinds Buddy and causes Suzie an impossible and instant rush of pain. Like someone poured acid in her eyes.

Dash struggles to keep control as the Deuce weaves left and right. It pulls hard to the right, almost goes off the road, then cuts back in fast. The full weight of the Deuce sideswipes the Roadmaster, sends it crashing off-road, and the car spins and flips like a tossed coin.

When Suzie opens her eyes, she's alone. There's no sign of Buddy whatsoever. She's remarkably unscathed from the crash, just a ringing in her head caused by more than just the impact. As she crawls from the wreckage, at least there's no sign of Dash and the Deuce either. She climbs to her feet and has to brace herself against a tree just to stay on them.

"Buddy!" she yells. "Buddy!" But there's no answer.

Somewhere, not too far off though, there's something. Like yipping. With no other ideas for what to do, Suzie follows the sound and bounces from tree to tree as she makes her way uphill. As she gets closer, she can tell it's a dog, a small dog, and there's something familiar about its pitch.

Suzie emerges from the forest near the top of Make-Out Point, and she does, indeed, know this dog. It's little Eddie, the Jack Russell Terrier, the Wilsons' dog, trapped by his leash which has gotten hooked on a tree.

One of those bug-eyed things, a big one, stumbles after the dog. Suzie can't be sure, but there's something familiar about this one. His bulk and sluggishness work in Eddie's favor; even on the leash, he's wily and lithe enough to slip between the thing's clumsy swipes, but the little dog can't possibly keep that up forever.

"Hey!" Suzie yells. "Leave that dog alone!"

Eddie's attention snaps to Suzie, and even though he's in fight mode, he gives a little tail wag at the sight of the girl. His attacker turns towards Suzie too, and her world drops.

"Dad?"

Though his eyes, gray and unblinking, are no longer the soft green she remembers, and the last time she saw him, he didn't have three deep scratches across his face, the man is unmistakably her father.

"No..." Suzie is utterly lost. Her Pa. The man who sat her on his knee and told her stories about Deadwood Dick, Calamity Jane, and Wild Bill Hickok. Who snuck her food whenever she got sent to her room without dinner, with a wink and a hug. The big man with the bigger heart, one of those bug-eyed things. It's too much for Suzie.

Mr. Palmer steps away from the dog, and Suzie can see why her father was up at Make-Out Point. Her yearbook photo, framed, hangs from the same tree Eddie is latched to, surrounded by candles and flowers. It's a memorial. She looks around, desperate for it to be someone else, but just up the hill, there's his beat-up, blue Napco Chevy, and there's no doubt.

215

"Daddy, I'm so sorry," Suzie cries as she runs up and hugs him. Mr. Palmer doesn't react, and Suzie's too worked up to notice. She squeezes, presses her face into his chest, and waits for his big bear arms to wrap around her like they always do. They don't.

"I did—daddy, I did this. It's all my fault." She waits for him to stroke her hair and tell her she's silly in his fake cowboy accent. He doesn't.

The longer she hugs her father, the harder it is for Suzie to escape the horrible truth. He's gone. All that's left is a lifeless, bug-eyed husk of the man. Except, she woke up, right? She came back, so why not him? Deep down, she knows that's not going to happen, though.

When Suzie woke up, it was because of a pen, an innocuous item that evoked warm, deep-rooted memories of someone important to her. Someone she shared some of the happiest times of her life with. If something as dumb as a pen could do that for her, why doesn't seeing his actual daughter, back and alive, more or less, in the flesh revive Mr. Palmer?

There's something different about her, Suzie knows. It's the Queen. It's that she's the Queen. She's not Buddy, but she's no dummy either, and Suzie remembers what Mr. Cormac taught them about ants. If the Queen dies, so does the whole colony. It made a mistake, it said as much back at the school. These things have never encountered lifeforms like humans, they weren't as easy to control, and without meaning to, it brought too much of Suzie back. From the way it manipulates the others, the trap at the gym, and even Dash driving his car, it's learned though, and the Queen won't be making that mistake again.

Still, this is her dad, so Suzie hugs him even tighter. Tight enough to feel the gun tucked into the back of his

216

belt. Suzie pulls away from him, his pistol in her hand. He wasn't up here to mourn his daughter; he was up here for revenge.

What the hell was he thinking? That her killer would come back to the scene of the crime, like in those dumb detective shows? Then what?

As Suzie steps away from her father, his attention is drawn back to Eddie. The bug-eyed thing that used to be Mr. Palmer chases the little dog around the tree, significantly shortening the leash.

"Dad, no, leave him alone," Suzie begs as Mr. Palmer finally grabs hold of the dog. Eddie snarls and bares every single one of his teeth, but it does him no good. Mr. Palmer lifts the dog towards his mouth. "Dad! Stop!" The leash snaps taut, and rips free from Eddie's collar. Mr. Palmer opens his mouth. "Dad!"

A single gunshot booms. It echoes through the trees, the forest, and the very corners of Suzie's heart. "Dad..." she says as she drops the smoking gun. "I'm sorry, daddy, I'm sorry."

Both Mr. Palmer and Eddie fall to the ground. The dog distressed, but otherwise unharmed—Suzie's dad with a gunshot wound in the back of his head.

Suzie thought that not knowing what happened to her parents was the worst. That, as awful as it was for Buddy to see and hear his parents die, at least he knew. At least you wouldn't drive yourself to distraction worrying about what could be. She thought this would be better. She was wrong.

Eddie runs over to Suzie and climbs up onto her lap. He puts his paws against her chest and licks her face. He doesn't want the nice girl to be sad, so he licks harder and harder till she takes him in a hug and cuddles him tight.

"You're a good boy, Eddie," Suzie says, and even though Eddie knows this, he likes to hear it anyway.

"Suzie!" someone yells her name, and a second later, Buddy appears from the woods using the shotgun as a crutch. "Suzie! Thank god!" He runs over and then skids to a halt when he sees the body on the ground. "Oh jeez, no Suzie, no way..."

"I had to," Suzie sniffs. "He was gonna kill Eddie."

Eddie barks, fully in agreement with her.

"No one else dies because of me," Suzie says as she rises to her feet with Eddie in her arms. "Nobody. Not you, not anybody, not this dog. Nobody."

From the blackest depths of her sorrow, Suzie's found her fire. Buddy can see the change; hell, he can feel the raw determination emanating from her. It's inspiring, but they don't have time for that right now.

"Sure, but we gotta go like right now," Buddy says. "They're coming."

"Who?" Suzie asks.

"All of them."

Why Must I Be A Teenager in Love

(At End of the World)

All across Woodvale, hope dies. What survivors remain hide, huddle, and cower, for the ones brave enough to challenge the nightmares that devour their town would not be long for this world.

Cut to: a mailroom clerk tucked inside a mail cart, covered in unsorted letters. Folks who just the other day mailed packages to their relatives with a smile and a "Have a nice day" lurk and stumble around covered in blood. He's been there for what feels like hours. Had he not wet his pants at the sight of a twelve-year-old girl in pigtails clawing out his boss's throat, he'd surely happily do it in the cart instead of facing them.

Then, for no reason the clerk can figure, they all leave. Together, almost in formation, the bug-eyed things file out of the mailroom. He chooses to stay where he is, all the same.

Cut to: the town library, where the bearded beatnik librarian and a passing truck driver hammer nails through makeshift boards torn from dismantled bookshelves. Hands poke through the gaps, grasping at the two of them. The beatnik turns to grab more wood, and the second he moves, the barricade gives way, not entirely, just enough for one of the bug-eyed things to reach through and grab him.

219

"Walker, man, gonna need help like right now!" the beatnik cries.

"On it, Lee," Walker says and wastes no time. He takes a makeshift machete, made from a paper cutter, and hacks the bug-eyed thing's arm off with three mighty whacks. Even losing its arm doesn't stop the bug-eyed thing, though. The beatnik grabs a black, leather-bound book from the pile and jams it into the bug-eyed thing's snarling mouth. It staggers, though not enough, so the beatnik slams the spine of the book with the palm of his hand, drives it through the bug-eyed thing's jaw, and as it falls back, the truck driver shoves another board in place.

The two of them secure the rest of the building, much to the sheltering townsfolk's relief. Both the truck driver and the beatnik librarian are so exhausted by the end of it that neither notice as the attack subsides, and the bug-eyed things slink away like they had overdue fees they didn't want to pay.

Cut to: Sam, of the Stop-n-Go, on the roof of his apartment building. He's been there ever since those things overran the floors below. It wasn't hard for them with the heap plaster walls and even shoddier cardboard doors. Booker Heights, built for the less discerning bachelor. At least the entrance to the roof is steel, cold hard steel. There had been too many incidents with lonely, despondent men that the owners had to secure it. His only way down, the fire escape, is blocked by more of them. They reach up desperately with arms swaying like lamprey eels.

Then, almost at once, the pounding on the door subsides. Sam doesn't trust it, figures it's a trick, so he goes to the edge of the roof to see what's happening. He watches as the entire horde of the bug-eyed things march, almost like a swarm of ants. They flow from every direction towards a single point at the edge of town, to the road that leads up the hill to Make-Out Point.

From all across town, they come together. The broken, bloody, and beaten things flow into a shuffling, snarling stream that flows in one direction. Towards Buddy and Suzie—who we cut in on as they hobble uphill through the woods. Buddy's picked up a limp from the car crash, and Suzie helps him along while Eddie leads out front.

"You…you sure this is the right way?" Buddy manages to ask between gasps for air and winces of pain.

"Yeah, trust me," Suzie says and then spies the tip of the radio tower through the trees, and the little flashing light at the top. "See? Not far now."

"Yeah," Buddy says, then buckles over. "Just gimme—" Suzie doesn't let him finish. She grabs him by the hand and pulls him back up into a run. Too many people have died; not him, though. Not Buddy. She won't let that happen, and she pulls him through the rest of the woods, into the neon glow of the radio station's blue and red sign.

Eddie's already at the door by the time both Buddy and Suzie slam against it, and Buddy laughs with exhausted relief as Suzie bangs on it with her fist. "C'mon! Open up!" she demands. "Damn it. Open up!" Just as Suzie pounds on the door again, a bug-eyed thing falls around the corner of the building. Suzie doesn't notice it as she tries to pry the door open, but Buddy sure sees it.

Buddy pulls on Suzie's arm as Eddie barks. "Suzie," Buddy says as he turns her towards the sight of the biggest dead-eyed thing yet, a huge man in a bowling shirt and slicked-back hair so shiny it almost reflects the station's glowing, neon WVRK letters.

"Shit," Suzie says. "They got Rockin' Hill Billy."

"So that means," Buddy says, and the two of them finish together, "there's no one inside."

Buddy and Suzie run, and Eddie follows. But from every corner of the clearing, they come—more and more of the bug-eyed things. It doesn't matter which way they try to run; Buddy and Suzie are surrounded. A milkman with a blood-splattered apron. Boy Scouts with bite marks and slipper-wearing dads with holes in them.

"They're everywhere!" Buddy yells. He searches desperately for an escape route and his eyes lock on the ladder that leads up the radio tower on the roof of the station. "The roof! We gotta get up on the roof!"

Buddy leads Suzie around the back of the station, hoping to find a way up, only to come face to face with another mob of the dead-eyed things blocking the gate to the ladder.

Buddy aims the shotgun at the crowd, but even if he gets one with every shot, it wouldn't matter. They've only a few shells left.

Suzie grabs his arm and shouts, "Buddy, look!" She points to a small window high up on the wall. It's too high for them to climb, but right next to it, there's a dumpster.

"Yes!" Buddy yells, and he races to the dumpster and puts his back to it. Suzie joins him, and together they force the thing to scrape through the dirt close enough to the window to climb while Eddie keeps guard.

By the time they get it in place, the bug-eyed things have gotten far too close for comfort. Buddy helps Suzie up onto it first and passes her the shotgun. He starts to climb up himself and is yanked back, instantly, as one of the bug-eyed things grabs hold of the back of his shirt and pulls him away.

Buddy falls to the ground, and when his eyes open, he sees none other than Dash towering over him. The bug-eyed greaser looms a thousand times bigger than ever before, and he doesn't seem to mind all the buckshot embedded in his face one bit. Suzie's boyfriend is back, and oh boy, is Buddy in trouble.

"Holy shit," Buddy shouts as he scrambles away from Dash. He places himself square between him and the horde marching in from behind. Somehow, even though he's just one and there's a hundred or so behind him, Dash scares Buddy a hell of a lot more. It can't be right, but Dash, even though he's dead, looks like he's enjoying this. Looks like he's got a lot more than just a knuckle sandwich in mind for Buddy this time.

Eddie goes for Dash's ankle and gets a mouthful of his blood-stained jeans and tugs, but it's pointless, and Dash just kicks the dog away. The brave little guy lands in the dirt with a yelp.

Dash snarls and moves in on Buddy faster than what should be possible. Instead of just pouncing on top, Dash lifts Buddy off his feet, right into the air, and holds him like a hunter with a prized kill. Buddy struggles, but it's no use and he can't do a damn thing as the bug-eyed baseball player bears its blood-stained teeth in a hungry, twisted smile. A putrid stench wafts from its mouth, then it speaks. Somehow, it speaks.

"Bu-ddy. Su-zie. Is. Mine," the bug-eyed thing that used to be, and still partly is, Dash says. Buddy would be astounded if he wasn't watching in awe as Dash's skin creeps and closes over the buckshot wounds. These things can heal. Dear god, how are we supposed to—

Dash's head explodes in a powerful blast of meat and bone.

Buddy falls to the ground, the hulking body of Dash on top of him as the sharp burn of gunsmoke hits his lungs. He has to take his glasses off to be able to see, and it leaves Buddy with two panda-like spots of clear skin on a face otherwise coated in blood, shards of bone, and fragments of brain matter. It takes a few seconds for Buddy's vision to focus, and when it does, he sees Suzie standing over him with the smoking shotgun in one hand, her other stretched out to help him up. To Buddy, she's Grace Kelly and John Wayne all in one ginchy, shotgun-toting package.

Suzie grabs him by the hand and pulls him to his feet. "Suzie," he starts but can't find any words. Dash sure wasn't someone Buddy cared for, but, despite how much it burns him to admit it, he and Suzie had something. That couldn't have been easy, Buddy thinks. Then again, as Suzie spits on Dash's headless corpse—maybe it was.

The two of them run back to the dumpster, Suzie stopping to scoop up Eddie on the way, and they clamber up without any more immediate trouble. The thing is, the window's closed tight and doesn't so much as crack as Suzie slams the butt of the shotgun into it.

"Goddamnit!" Suzie curses and punches the wall.

"Suzie," Buddy says, and she turns to see Buddy hunched over, hands together with his back braced against the wall. "C'mon, I'll boost ya. It'll be safer up there."

Suzie nods and throws the shotgun up onto the roof and says, "Sorry, Eddie," as she hurls the little dog up. Eddie lands on the roof and shakes his head. Suzie follows the dog up with Buddy's help, and then once she's on the roof, lies on her stomach with her hand over the edge. Buddy kicks off the wall, jumps, and grabs hold of Suzie. She pulls him up, and both of them collapse onto their backs in relief. Eddie gives them both licks.

After a minute, Suzie walks to the opposite edge that overlooks the road back down the hill. The bug-eyed are everywhere, still pouring out the trees and marching up the road with a single, grim purpose. "You weren't kidding. It looks like the whole town's down there."

"We're as high as we can get," Buddy says. "We should be safe till the army or something sorts this out."

Suzie looks down into the swarm and sees a familiar face. The bouncy, short curls. The lopsided smile that in life smirked with playful, raunchy glee. Betty, the very first person she killed. She almost looks normal again. Suzie can't see any sign of the damage she did to her friend. If it wasn't for the dead bug-eyes...

"This…this is all my fault," Suzie says.

Buddy grabs hold of her. "Don't you say that!"

Suzie meets his eyes. "It is…it started with me…"

"Something did this to you! This is not your fault; you hear me?" Buddy says.

Suzie looks down at the swarm, where its mass has subsumed Dash's body, and wonders if Buddy would apply that same logic to him. Dash didn't mean to kill her. He intended to do something terrible for sure, but killing her wasn't his plan, yet it still happened. Would Buddy forgive him for that? No, he wouldn't, and she doesn't either. So why should she be forgiven for what she's brought upon this town? Dash was a bad guy, she says to herself, but I'm a real monster.

Buddy shakes her till she looks him in the eye. "You hear me? This isn't your fault!"

Suzie pulls away from him as she points to the swarm of dead things encircling them. "Look at them, Buddy!"

225

she yells. "Look at them! They're all dead! Because of me, they're all dead!"

"Suzie, no!" Buddy insists.

"Look," she says as she grabs him and forces him to look down over the edge. The closest dead things swipe up uselessly, but still. "Goddamnit, look!"

Suzie holds Buddy and waits for his eyes to open. For him to truly see and accept the scale of the horror before them. She feels his whole body, his entire being, slump when he does.

"They're here for me," Suzie says. "For what's inside me."

"We don't know that, we—" Buddy tries, but Suzie interrupts.

"I can feel them, Buddy!" Suzie says as she sweeps her arm over the swarm. "When I get really…hungry, I've seen through their eyes, and it spoke to me. Their Queen. I know what it wants."

"What do you mean? It spoke to you?"

"Back in the school, in the dark. It spoke to me, threatened me. It's so strong. I only managed to shut it up when I put the light on. They don't like light."

"Suzie…"

"It won't stop, and it's my fault…"

They're all here for me, Suzie says to herself. Just like with regular old ants, they're protecting their Queen.

 NO.

The Queen stirs. Suzie feels it squirm, and knows she's right. It's afraid.

NO.

226

It's terrified of Buddy. He's Suzie's last connection to this world, and all she has left. If it gets him, she'll give up, and once again, the Queen shall reign.

NO.

Yes! Suzie screams inside her head. *Yes, and as scared of him as you are, it's ME you should be terrified of.*

"Mr. Frederickson was right," Suzie says. "I am one of them. I am ALL of them. When you put your pen through Mr. Frederickson's cat, you didn't kill it, Buddy. It was already dead. All you did was kill the bug inside. I'm different, though. I can feel them. Feel what they want, Buddy, and it's you. All of them want to tear you apart; they won't even let you turn, not since we pissed the Queen off. They want you dead-dead." Suzie stares deep into his eyes as she says, "I'm not going to let that happen."

"Suzie, what are you saying?" Buddy asks, and he really doesn't want to hear the answer.

"You said you'd help me," Suzie says, and Buddy nods in agreement. "Said you'd fix this." Buddy nods again. "No matter the cost?" Suzie asks with steel resolve as she holds out the shotgun. "You promised," she reminds him.

"No," Buddy refuses.

"Please," she insists.

"Goddamnit, Suzie, no! No! I lost you once already..." Buddy's vision blurs with tears. "No!"

"Yes!" Suzie drops the shotgun and grabs hold of Buddy's face and forces him to meet her eyes. "You gotta. You gotta while I'm still me. What if I get hungry again? What if I can't hold it? Then where does this end, Buddy? It's taken over the town. What next, the county? The state? The country? Where does this end? It ends here, Buddy, or not at all," Suzie holds firm. "We have to kill the Queen."

"I promised I'd—" Buddy says.

"Help me!" Suzie cuts in. "You promised you'd help me, and this is how you do it." Suzie lets go of him and picks up the shotgun. "This is how you do it, Buddy. You gotta be the hero. Please. You gotta be MY hero."

Buddy pushes the gun aside and turns away from her. He walks over the edge. "I'm no goddamn hero," he says as he looks down at the swarm of the dead and thinks he'd sooner jump down and be torn apart by them than lose Suzie again.

Suzie steps up to him, takes him by the hand, and turns him around. "Buddy, I know you. You got more of a hero inside you than…than anybody I ever met. Please…"

"I'm a coward! You want to know the truth? I stopped hanging with you because I saw pictures of what happens to black boys who get friendly with white girls, and it scared me. Scared me so bad that I just ditched you so that you wouldn't get hurt 'cause of me. Now you want me to do this. Buddy yanks the gun from her. "No way in hell am I doin' that."

"You know what, I'm sick of people making my choices for me. Suzie grabs the gun. "I'll do it myself."

"No!"

"Yes! This has all gotten way out of hand. This is what I shoulda done right away," Suzie yells as they play tug-o-war with the shotgun. Eddie whimpers, tail between his legs, sensing something bad is about to happen.

228

The gun goes off, blasting one of the neon WVRK letters into a shower of sparks that lights up the roof for just a moment. It's enough to put a stop to the fight, though, and they both drop the shotgun at the same time.

Suzie sobs. "I always let other people do things for me."

"Suzie, I—"

"You don't think I should have had a say?" Even through the tears she's a force. "You think you've got the right to choose for me?"

"I didn't want you to get hurt."

"That was for me to decide, Buddy! For us to decide. Together. You can't make decisions for everyone, even if you are smarter. You just never know what's gonna happen," Suzie says, and she waves her arms at the swarm of bug-eyed things amassing like drones.

"You—you're right," Buddy says. "I'm sorry."

Suzie smiles through tears. "So, will you let me make this one?"

Buddy nods and kneels to collect the shotgun. He wipes away a tear. "I'll…I'll do us both. Together."

"Don't you dare!" Suzie is overcome with rage. "No, that's not happening."

"Suzie—"

"Don't you dare! I've caused enough death," Suzie says as Buddy refuses to meet her eyes. "Look at me, Buddy!" And he does. "You say this isn't my fault? I didn't cause this? You do that, Buddy, and I will have caused at least one death, and it's one I'll never forgive myself for."

After a moment, Buddy nods, but Suzie doesn't buy it and sticks her hands right into his pockets. She grabs the shotgun back from him and the rest of the shells too. Suzie tosses the shells over the edge before Buddy can stop her. She keeps one shell and loads it into the gun. That's enough. That's all she needs.

"Promise me," Suzie demands. "Promise me you'll live, Buddy. You'll live, grow old, get married, and have so many kids you forget all about me. Promise me you'll live, so goddamn much that it's enough for both of us!"

Buddy nods and wipes the tears as they flow without end. "I could live a thousand years, and I'd never forget you."

"Promise me!" Suzie yells.

"Okay!" he relents. "Okay."

"And make sure you look after Eddie," Suzie adds, and Eddie yips in agreement. "He's a good boy."

Buddy kicks the nearest vent pipe. "Damn it! This isn't fair!"

"Life isn't fair, Buddy." Suzie smiles and remembers something she saw in a movie with her dad, so many years ago, that stuck in her head like glue. "The thing is, it doesn't matter how bad a hand you're dealt. What's done to you. Taken from you. You have to take responsibility for yourself and do what you can with what you got."

Suzie steps up behind him and wraps her arms around his waist, rests her chin on his shoulder. His hand comes up and strokes her face.

"Where'd you get that from?" Buddy asks through tears.

"From my heart," Suzie says.

"You want the last thing you say to me to be a lie?"

"Okay, fine, it's from one of my Pa's movies. I can't remember which one."

"It feels like our lives have become some lousy movie." Buddy scoffs at the absurd truth of it. "Except the movies always have a happy ending."

"Not always," Suzie says, and the thought hangs in the air with inevitable dread.

"Why'd everything have to go and get so goddamn dark!?" Buddy says, though it's more like a prayer. He's not talking to Suzie, but to the stars, to God, to anyone who might be up there listening.

Suzie squeezes him tight. "It's okay," she says.

"Damn it all to Hell!" Buddy pulls away and spins around to face her.

"No, Buddy. It really is," Suzie says as she takes his arm and makes him point up at the night sky. She remembers something someone told her that also stuck with her all these years. Something a smartass, know-it-all boy she loves more than anything said to her one balmy summer night so long ago. "'Cause the thing about the dark is," Buddy looks up to the starry sky with her, "it lets you see what really shines."

Buddy smiles at the memory. He wishes once again that they'd had more time together. "I never should have ditched you like I did. Maybe if we were still friends, I could've—"

"You can't beat yourself up for what happened to me. Nobody made me go up to Make-Out Point with Dash," Suzie says, and though the very idea revolts him, he feels ashamed for being so selfish. "I wanted to. He liked me, and I liked him." And while Buddy's caught up with the thought that even after everything, she still carries a torch for that asshole, Suzie turns his face to hers. "But not the way you do, though. Not the way I like you." And Suzie kisses Buddy.

It's a kiss that was always meant to be. Maybe not this soon, perhaps not for years, but fate has cut all that short, so here it is, and it's a kiss that means the world to the both of them.

"I thought you didn't want your last words to me to be a lie," Buddy says.

"They're not," Suzie says. "I love you, Buddy."

Buddy smiles like he's never smiled before.

"I love you too, Suzie," Buddy says as he looks into her baby blues for the very last time.

And, with that, we pull away from the roof of the station, away from the horde gathering beneath them. We've seen a lot of horrors tonight, but you don't want to see this. It's not right. So away we go, and sometime after we lose sight of them, a single gunshot echoes through the night.

THE BOY WHO KNEW
TOO MUCH

A military convoy rumbles along the highway towards a small country town—past Norman Rockwell, postcard-perfection—except for the clouds of smoke that rise above. The closer the convoy gets, the more signs there are that something went horribly wrong. Armed troops guard hazmat-suited scientists as the convoy rattles past what used to be a roadside diner, then what once was a gas station. It passes a quaint wooden sign that reads Woodvale—Go Hornets! Sting! Sting! Sting!

The convoy makes its way through the town as, all around, troops clean up the debris and put out fires. Stacks of black, human-sized bags line one side of what used to be Main Street. It reaches the high school where a uniformed private guides each truck to a parking spot. As the vehicles file in, a single Jeep breaks from the pack. It drives up to the main doors where a Sergeant waits at attention.

Two men climb out. The first is a military man, a General, whose uniform is as sharp and pressed as his mustache. He's pristine, bar the eyepatch, which even so he wears with as much pride as any medal. The other man, dressed only in a simple black suit, possesses an otherworldly air of absolute authority. Despite the clouded skies overhead, he doesn't remove his impenetrably black shades.

The Sergeant salutes, "Sir," and breaks form to throw a glance at the Man in Black. "I was not advised—"

"He's with me," the General says with a dismissive wave.

Even with the authorization, the Sergeant doesn't like it. Especially the way the Man in Black seems to smirk. How can a man smile without so much as a twitch of his lips? Regardless, the Sergeant leads on, past the refugee camp built inside the baseball diamond. The two dozen or so townies there don't seem to care that they're under armed guard.

"How many survivors?" asks the General.

"So far, Sir, we've located around two dozen," the Sergeant says, then holds his arm out and points towards the gym hall. "If you'll follow me, Sir, we've secured the samples and the witness inside the building."

The General and the Man in Black both nod and follow.

Several steel cages, assembled inside the gym, and an opaque plastic tent at the center, sits at odds with the bleachers and half-finished Halloween decorations. Mobile lab stations are operated by more scientists, and even the soldiers in here wear hazmat suits. This makes the General feel uncomfortable and exposed, but the Sergeant's confidence assuages him. The Man in Black seems more amused than concerned.

"We have retrieved the sample from the nearby forest, and it's ready for transfer to Site B on your orders, Sir," the Sergeant tells the General, who turns to the Man in Black for approval before giving the nod.

"Show us the couple," the Man in Black says, and the Sergeant hesitates till the General ushers him on. He leads them to a steel box surrounded by four armed soldiers. The Sergeant signals for one of them to open the shutter, and when he does so, we see Betty and Teddy, sitting together with their backs against the far

234

wall of their cell. Both as docile as napping kittens. The only trace of their humanity is the way they hold each other's hand.

"Do we know why these two remain infected?" the General asks.

"Unclear, Sir," the Sergeant says. "Both were found, as passive as they are, at the epicenter alongside the witness."

"I want you to investigate," the General says. "But cautiously. We must preserve these two specimens."

"Show us this witness," the Man in Black instructs, not the least bit interested in the two catatonic lovers.

The Sergeant turns to the General, once again, for confirmation.

"Let's see the boy," the General agrees.

The Sergeant leads them out of the gym and down a corridor to the closest classroom, where two soldiers stand guard. They look through the window to see Buddy Peter Day hunched up in the corner on an army cot. Though he seems like he's been through hell, because he has, the army medics have patched him up good. He sits with his knees up, bandaged hands resting on them.

"Are we absolutely sure he's not infected?" the General asks.

"Yes, Sir," the Sergeant answers. "Based on consistent witness statements, the infection spreads via bite alone. The boys in the lab theorize it must be directly introduced to the bloodstream to take effect."

He's too busy explaining that he doesn't notice the General wasn't talking to him. Doesn't see the sideways glance to the Man in Black and the almost imperceptive nod he returns.

"What have you gotten out of him so far?" the General asks.

"Sir, there's a full report prepared for you but, permission, to be frank, Sir?"

The General nods.

"It's one of the craziest things I've ever read. It's like something out of a bad movie. The boy reckons he stopped them by killing what he calls a Queen."

The General raises his eyebrows, but when he sees the complete and utter lack of expression on the Man in Black's face, he accepts it.

"What should we do with him?" asks the Sergeant. "Shall I prepare him for transport to Site B too?"

"Might make a good scapegoat," the General suggests as he peeks through the window.

Buddy doesn't react even though he has to know they're out there, talking about his fate like it's a baseball trading-card negotiation.

"Not necessary," says the Man in Black. "Cut him a check. Cut them all checks, have them sign some papers, and let them go."

"Sir!" the Sergeant protests but then remembers his place.

"What're you suggesting?" the General asks the Man in Black. "Think of the hysteria they'll spread!?"

"No," the Man in Black states. "No one will believe them. Most won't say a word; they'll be too afraid of the mockery of their peers. The ones that do will not be believed. Especially with the work our partners are doing in Hollywood. People simply do not want to believe. They'll mock and, in their laughter, create a far more effective cover than we could ever achieve through force."

"And the town?" the Sergeant asks.

"What of it?" the Man in Black says. "Our drive through showed the main commercial district in ruins. With the heart ripped out, the rest will die. Within a few years, it'll be a ghost town. Whispers and hearsay will further mask what occurred. A dozen falsehoods will be spoken, and the truth lost among them."

"You really want us to let all these people go." The General can't believe it.

"Of course," the Man in Black says. "We're not inhuman, after all." The way he says that makes the General shudder. "Now, open the door."

"Sir?" The Sergeant is confused.

"I wish to speak with the boy. Alone," the Man in Black states.

The Sergeant hesitates but, with the urgent prompting of the General, unlocks the door. The General gives the order to load the samples for transport more to distract the Sergeant than anything else.

Inside the room, the Man in Black approaches Buddy, who does not look up or acknowledge the other man's presence. Not till he squats down next to Buddy in a way that should be painful, yet he seems effortlessly at balance.

"Hello, Buddy," the Man in Black says.

Buddy looks up at his name only to see two ragged twins of himself in the midnight black shades. "You're not with the army," he observes.

"My, you are a smart one. No, Buddy, we're not," the Man in Black answers, and Buddy's way too tired and burnt out to catch what he said.

"You look like somebody's bad impression of a spook from a movie. What are you, CIA?" Even with tear-streaked cheeks, Buddy hits out with a defiance that impresses the Man in Black. This is not the same boy his cohort observed wallowing in his sorrow just over a week ago.

"No," the Man in Black says as he slips his shades off. "We are not."

Buddy backpedals hard and pushes himself deep into the corner of the room. He sees what the Man in Black hid under those glasses: cloudy, gray eyes that stare wide without blinking. Bug eyes.

"You're one of Them!" Buddy screams, but the Man in Black only holds a finger to his lips.

"You are correct. We are one of Them, as you put it. And, as you can see, we mean you no harm, Buddy Peter Day, so please calm down." The Man in Black puts his sunglasses back on. "We have much to discuss."

As the Man in Black makes no aggressive moves and exudes an aura of perfect calm, Buddy does what he asks though keeps himself on edge. Just in case.

"What's going on?" Buddy asks.

"You are a dangerous man, Buddy Peter Day," the Man in Black says and doesn't need to state the threat. "You have uncovered a weakness in our compatibility with your kind. You have put us in great danger."

"Are you going to kill me?"

"No. If we wanted you dead, you would be."

"So, what the hell is this?"

"This," the Man in Black pauses, "is a thank-you. What you encountered was one of my kind, yes, but an insurrectionist. A zealot, what you might call a terrorist."

"A terrorist?"

"Yes, The Forever, as they call themselves, believe it is our kind's right to consume the entire universe. Our faction takes a more pragmatic approach."

"So, you don't consume people?" Buddy throws his word back at him. It feels wrong to refer to the slaughter and horror of the past twenty-four hours as something scientific and detached. So damn mundane.

"Of course we do," the Man in Black states. "But like the farmer who does not consume his entire livestock in a single season, we seed, and we nurture so that we may feed for generations."

"How long have your kind been here?" Buddy asks.

The Man in Black leans in. "Longer, much longer than yours."

How is that even possible? How could this alien race have been living on Earth since before there were humans?

"When we came, we were many—too many. Our ancestors caused much destruction: our hosts, tremendously powerful reptilian beasts, enabled this. War followed."

The dinosaurs? Have these things been here since the time of the dinosaurs? That's billions of years, and the weight of all of them hits Buddy as one.

"Few of us survived. Changes in our ways were needed. Some did not accept this. The cost of another war: too high. Those who would not accept the change—exiled back into the cold. I suspect, from the age of the rock it arrived in, that what you encountered was one such exile. There are thousands more out there, floating in their stone prisons. It's no coincidence your leaders are so obsessed with the void. We do not wish for more of them to return, and so we guide. We nurture."

"You lookin' for us to say thanks or somethin'?" Buddy spits on the Man in Black's shades. "Well, here's your thanks!"

The Man in Black removes his glasses, wipes them, and slips them back on like nothing happened. All the while, his bug eyes stare into Buddy's with quiet intensity.

"Your government could use a mind like yours, Buddy Peter Day. Your spirit. While the rest of your kind cowers, you run, fight, and, more importantly, you think."

"My folks didn't cower. Neither did Gordy. Or Suzie!"

"Is that a no?"

"You bet your damn bug ass it's a no. Now leave me alone before I go get a can of Black Flag," Buddy answers.

The Man in Black smiles.

"So what happens now?" Buddy asks. "You said you're not going to kill me, so…"

"No, we will not. As a way of saying thank you, Buddy Peter Day, for helping us avert another war. Consider this a warning, too. We have guided and shaped civilizations. We have made and killed Kings, Queens, Emperors, and Presidents. Do not attempt to expose us. Do not fight us. You will not succeed. To borrow from your current parlance, you would be aching for the breaking."

"Are you saying I'm free to go? Just like that?"

"Not quite. You sign papers promising your silence, and you will be provided for."

"Money? Jeez, isn't that just boss? Money's not going to bring back my parents. My friends, everyone else who died!"

"Consider it a bribe then. To keep our secret, and to help you keep yours."

"You—"

"We know." The Man in Black stands up. "That's all we have to say on the matter. We bid you farewell, Buddy Peter Day, and hope our paths never cross again."

As the Man in Black approaches the door, Buddy shouts, "Hey!"

The Man in Black pauses.

"What's with the eyes?" Buddy asks.

"Excuse me?" the Man in Black responds.

"If you're all so smart, how come you can't figure out how to blink? Why not close your eyes if the light is so damn dangerous? Or just rip them out?

The Man in Black doesn't answer.

"You need it, right? But too much is lethal, I'm guessing. Why, though, is that how you communicate?"

"Be careful, Buddy Peter Day, do not mistake our mercy for weakness," the Man in Black warns him. "Do not mistake our tolerance for complacency."

"One day folks will wake up, they'll fight back."

The Man in Black smiles. "And when they do, it'll be time for another mass extinction."

"You're monsters. All of you damn bugs and the ones helping you."

"Perhaps," the Man in Black says with his back to the boy. "But we, as long as the herd is docile, are benevolent ones." Then he leaves Buddy to contemplate the earth-shattering truth he's just learned.

As the sun sets on Woodvale, the convoy snakes back out of town. One trailer carries the rock that fell to Earth, another the steel cage with Betty and Teddy—still holding hands in the dark. It passes the hospital, where those bitten but not turned before the Queen's death share nightmares of gigantic, glossy black ants streaming through every orifice of their bodies. Most of them will never wake, and the ones that do will wish they hadn't.

Inside her steel cage, Betty's hand twitches.

The following morning, we fade in as the sun rises over Woodvale High. Buddy, and others, are led out the gate with plain, brown envelopes clenched in their hands. The bitter taste of signing a document stating he'd not disclose the events of the past few days in exchange for the check doesn't sit well with Buddy. He couldn't care less about the money, about the stupid paper. Part of him wants to tear it up right there, but what the Man in Black said haunts him. He knows Buddy's secret, and even if the blood of so many people—people he loved—stains the money, he'll need it all the same.

Most of the others are leaving town directly. A tall, curly-haired truck driver offers him a lift out of town, and Buddy accepts. When the man asks him where he's heading, however, Buddy tells him "Home." He has one more stop to make before he leaves Woodvale behind for good.

Their journey through town is a tour of pain and heartache for Buddy. He didn't think it was possible to ever feel such a sense of loss for a place that held as much hurt as happiness.

Fade in on what's left of Buddy's neighborhood. The few surviving families pack up what's left—what wasn't burned down or tainted with blood. The truck driver lets Buddy out and offers to wait, but Buddy declines. He watches the kid walk away, and even though he only just met him, the truck driver wishes the best for Buddy. Something tells him the kid deserves it.

Buddy walks past the ruins of homes, past windows smeared with bloody handprints, and past the blue Napco Chevy parked badly across his front lawn. He steps inside his house.

It's only been about a day and a half since Buddy was last here, but it feels like a lifetime ago. The house is silent, yet he can hear his dad laughing at his own jokes as he writes away in his office, and his mother giggling as she reads one of her romance novels on the sofa. They're still here, Buddy realizes, and always will be. All that's left, physically, are dark brown smears on the tiles, but that's not them. They are Buddy. When he threw down his life for Suzie, that was his mother's courage, and when he brought a smile to her face despite it all, that was his father's heart.

The sudden smash of something down in the basement breaks his focus. It pulls him away from the comfort of old ghosts. Buddy heads down to investigate, and he's no sooner at the bottom when Suzie throws herself onto him.

FAREWELL, WOODVALE

Flashback to that roof, to the radio station in the woods, to Buddy and Suzie surrounded by more bug-eyed things than they could count. To be clear, Buddy's a math whiz, and Suzie's never once gotten anyone's change wrong at the store, so that's a lot.

Buddy points the shotgun directly at Suzie's face. She smiles in a way that tells him this is okay.

Pull in on Buddy, and we see it's not. Buddy can't do it. Even if it means the end of the world, he just can't say goodbye to Suzie. Not again.

Sparks fly from the busted part of the neon sign. They catch Buddy's eye, and the beginning of an idea forms.

She's the only light left in his life, and he'll be damned if he's the one to put it out and—wait, the light!

Suzie closes her eyes tight and smiles.

A thunder blast from the shotgun fills Suzie's ears, but then the ringing dies, and the snarls and growls from below fade back in. Something's not right. Suzie shouldn't have even heard the gunshot, it should all be over, yet it's not.

"No!" Suzie screams. "You promised!"

Eddie barks, it seems like the thing to do.

"Yeah," Buddy shouts. "I promised I'd help you! Not kill you!"

"That's the only way!"

"No, it's not!" Buddy throws the shotgun down, and Eddie gives it a curious sniff as it smokes on the ground.

Buddy marches past Suzie. She stands, incredulous and bewildered, as Buddy tries to tear off the panel on the station's neon sign.

"Buddy?" Suzie looks for him to clue her in, but it's no good. He's gone full mad scientist again. The boy pulls the panel free, tosses it aside, and fidgets with the wires inside. "Buddy!" she tries, but he still doesn't answer.

Suzie's not having this again. If Buddy has a plan, he's going to damn well tell her, or he's going down there to get more bullets and finish the damn job. She marches over, grabs him by the shoulder, and pulls him back.

"Tell me what you're thinking or so help me—"

"The light," Buddy says like that explains it all.

"What are you talking about!?"

"Back when you said that thing, the thing I said about shining in the dark, it reminded me of what you said about the closet."

"Back at the school?"

"Yeah, you said that this thing spoke to you in the dark, but it hid when—"

"When I turned on," Suzie says and then, together, they shout, "the light!"

"So…"

"So," Buddy says as he points to the sparks and glowing neon light. "If the light's bright enough, maybe we can kill it."

"How?" Suzie is confused. "Buddy, that doesn't make any sense. It's been all kinds of bright before, and that didn't do it. Not even daylight, and I might not be a science nerd like you, but even I know there's nothin' that shines brighter than the sun!"

Not quite, Buddy says to himself as he looks into Suzie's eyes. "You didn't look right into the sun, though, did you?"

"Well, no," Suzie says. "Who does, though? That really hurts your eyes."

"Yeah," Buddy says. "That's my point. It's worth a shot."

Suzie thinks about it and remembers the intense pain the sparks from Dash's wheel rims caused. She doesn't know if it'll work, but she knows Buddy, and if anyone can think of a way out of this, it's him. "So," she says, "what's the plan, poindexter?"

"If we can rewire the junction box here." Buddy points to the mess of wires behind the sign. "So that all the power goes through one tube, then maybe it'll be bright enough to get it done."

"And that'll work?"

"Yeah, I mean, neon lights are just tubes filled with gas that glows when electricity excites it. More power should equal more excitement, and therefore more glow, right?"

"Why are you asking me? You're the nerd! I'm trusting you know what you're talking about because I sure as hell don't!"

"You know, when you call me a nerd, it doesn't sound so bad," Buddy smirks.

No, Suzi thinks, it's not. "Okay, let's do this!"

"There's a chance we could end up blinding you—"

"I don't care, Buddy. Whatever it takes to put an end to this."

Buddy turns back to the junction box. He jerks back, and sparks fly as he tries to switch the wires around.

"Would be much easier if we had some tools."

Suzie looks down at the crowd pushing up against the wall below them. Their hands sway like long, rotten grass. "Sure, I'll just run to the store, want anything else while I'm there?"

"Yeah, I could go for some Ruffles," Buddy says, then cries out as he gets a nasty shock from the junction box.

246

The zap sends him back and down onto his ass. Eddie comes over to see if he's okay and gives Buddy a lick on the chin to be sure.

Suzie steps over and takes his place at the box and says, "Tell me what to do," as Buddy gets back on his feet.

"It's no good," Buddy explains. "You'll fry."

"No, I don't think so," Suzie says as she looks at her own hands. She recalls each time something should have hurt bad, and yet not even a tickle. "I don't think I can feel pain."

"That's—how's that?"

"I don't know," Suzie tries to explain. "But none of them does." She points down to the mob of bug-eyed things. "So, tell me what to do."

Buddy trusts that Suzie's right and so she pulls at the wires with her bare hands, as sparks fly, with no reaction to the shock that floored Buddy moments ago. He talks her through the rewiring, guides her as she makes new connections, and above them, the blinking red warning light at the top of the tower goes out. Beneath them, the studio and external spotlights go dark too. Soon, all that glows are the three remaining letters that make up the station's signage.

"Okay, what now?" Suzie asks.

Buddy carefully removes one of the tubes from the sign. He holds it in both hands; the glow lights up his face like it's radioactive. "I'll hold this in front of your eyes, and see those switches? You flip them one by one. They'll divert more power to the neon and should make it brighter."

"Why not all at once? Blast it with as much light as possible," Suzie asks.

"I don't know if these tubes can take it. Too much at once, and it might explode." Buddy has no clue, but he hopes that he sounds like he does.

Suzie nods, and Buddy holds the neon tube to her eyes. "How's that feel?"

"Like a migraine wrapped in a headache," Suzie says and winces. She forces her eyes to stay open against both the natural urge to shut them tight, and the agonized writhing she can feel in the back of her head.

"Good! I mean, it's working then?"

Suzie takes a few deep breaths. She puts one hand to her forehead, uses it to pin her eyelids open, and the other goes to the first switch.

"Whatever happens, Buddy, don't let go."

Buddy nods, and Suzie flips the first switch. The effect is immediate—the tube in Buddy's hands glows brighter, and he can feel the heat grow with the hum.

"It's not enough," Suzie says through gritted teeth and pushes her eyes even closer. The glow casts mad shadows across her face, twisting her homegrown beauty into something nightmarish and maniacal. "It's hurting, but not enough."

Eddie barks.

Suzie flips the second switch, and the tube burns so bright it loses almost all hue.

NO!

The Queen speaks.

NO! WE WILL SUBMIT!

248

"The hell you will!" Suzie screams. "This is for everyone you've taken. For Buddy's mom and dad, for my Ma and Pa. For Gordy Garcia and Mr. Cormac. For Teddy Duchamp, and goddamnit, for Betty Blacker. Go. To. Hell!"

Suzie flips the final switch. The tube glows white-hot and sears Buddy's hands, giving him two round brands on each palm, but he doesn't let go.

Inside her head, Suzie feels the Queen burn; she can almost see the creature smoke and flake as the light cooks it away.

A thousand voices inside her head scream:

One voice, louder than the others, insists:

YES!

The neon tube shatters, explodes, burns the surface of Suzie's eyes, embeds glass in her face, and sends both her and Buddy to the ground.

Beneath them, the horde shudders as each bug-eyed thing falls to the ground. All except for Betty and Teddy, who stop in place and stand, statue-like, joined at hand.

Buddy gets to his feet and stumbles towards the edge. He tries to lean on a railing for support, but the burned flesh on his palms stings on contact. The sight of all the bug-eyed things, lying in an unmoving heap, brings him the saddest sense of relief.

His plan worked. They're safe, but at what cost?

"Buddy," Suzie calls as she crawls across the roof with one hand outstretched. "Buddy, where are you? I-I can't see!" She grabs her head with one hand as she cries out in pain. "Something—" Suzie screams. "Something's wrong! Oh god, it hurts!"

Buddy runs over to her and stops dead as Suzie heaves. A spurt of blood sprays onto the granite floor of the roof. Just as Suzie catches her breath and thinks it's over, another wave of pain hits her. It's like something is forcing its way through her head, and a second later, she throws up a thick glob of black and white mucus, tinged with blood. It lands on the ground with a squelching thud and, whatever it is, pulsates.

"What the hell," Buddy says as something inside the bile moves.

Sharp, spindly legs force their way out from the wet lump, and they pull behind them a broken, burned creature that looks like a gloss-black ant the size of a mouse. It's missing several legs, and squeals in utter agony, but the Queen is still alive.

"What is that!? Buddy, I can't see," Suzie panics.

"It's— Buddy goes to answer, then Eddie runs over and picks the Queen up in his mouth. The screech it makes is ear-splitting as Eddie thrashes it around and then silences the Queen for good as he bites it clean in half. "It's dead, whatever it was, it's dead," Buddy says, and Eddie gives both halves a sniff just to be sure.

Suzie falls over, and Buddy rushes to take her in his arms. "It's okay," Buddy says, "it's okay. And the two of them hold each other as tight as they can. Tears stream down Suzie's face, and even laced with blood, they're the happiest ones she's ever shed.

Eddie comes over and gives them both licks, and it's such a happy moment that neither of them even thinks for a second about what he just had in his mouth. The dog cuddles in too.

"It's going to be okay," Buddy says, and this time it's the truth.

We fade back to Buddy's basement, where the two kids hold each other tight.

"You were gone for so long, I was worried!" Suzie says and then plants a kiss as close to Buddy's lips as she can.

Eddie barks in agreement. He puts his two front legs against Buddy and gives his fingers a hello lick.

"They had a lot of questions," Buddy explains. "And they gave us all these to keep quiet." He holds up the letter, forgetting the bandage Suzie wears like a blindfold around her eyes.

Suzie punches his shoulder playfully; her accuracy is uncanny.

"Sorry," he says. "It's a check. They want to buy our silence with cash."

"Better than with a bullet," Suzie adds.

"Yeah, there's that."

Buddy lifts the bandages to see how her eyes are healing. Scorched to almost total bloodshot whiteness, her baby blues gone forever, it's unlikely Suzie will ever see again. Her face, too, scarred for life by the glass, but none of that matters to Buddy. She's Suzie, after all— she'll always be the most beautiful girl in the world to him. Hell, in the whole universe.

They kiss, and it's just right.

Buddy doesn't tell her about the Man in Black, the others, and the sheer scale of their infestation. He decides he'll tell her later, if at all. For now, he plans on taking the Man in Black's advice.

Just to be safe, the two of them wait for it to get dark before leaving. It's not like Buddy and Suzie have anywhere specific to go, and there's nowhere else either of them wants to be besides down in the basement, in each other's arms.

Eddie is fine with that, and claims the recliner as his throne.

Night falls, and under the cover of darkness, Buddy loads up Suzie's dad's truck with what little they have to take. He helps Suzie climb into the passenger seat, and Eddie leaps up onto her lap. Suzie rubs behind the dog's ears, much to his approval.

Buddy climbs in behind the wheel and tries to remember how to operate the beast.

"You need another lesson?" Suzie smirks.

"I got it," Buddy insists and he starts the engine.

"Good, 'cause you stalled so much going down the hill I thought we were on a rollercoaster!"

"Best ride at the fair!" Buddy says, and Suzie laughs. Eddie joins in with a few yips.

They drive all through the night. Away from Woodvale, past Cherry Lake, and into a new, fresh sunrise. As the car vanishes from sight, leaving behind the horror and tragedy that befell Woodvale, two words fade in from the clean, morning light:

THE END.

WOODVALE

HIGH SCHOOL

YEARBOOK
195

GO HORNETS!
STING-STING-STING!

WOODVALE
HIGH SCHOOL
Class of 1959

Christina Cole
Cheer Squad Captain, Homecoming Queen, Student Treasury

"Sometimes you just have to throw on a crown
and remind them who they're dealing with."
Marilyn Monroe

WOODVALE
HIGH SCHOOL
Class of 1955

Johnny Freemantle
Avid Fan of The Cheer Squad

"I found my thrill on Blueberry Hill."
Fats Domino

WOODVALE
HIGH SCHOOL
Class of 195

Gordy Garcia
Woodvale Hornets - Shortstop, Track Squad

"Never allow the fear of striking out keep
you from playing the game."
Babe Ruth

WOODVALE
HIGH SCHOOL
Class of 1959

Betty Blacker

Cheer Squad

"Say anything about me, darling, as long as
it isn't boring."
Tallulah Bankhead

WOODVALE
HIGH SCHOOL
Class of 1959

Teddy Duchamp
At Least He Tried

"See you later, alligator. After a while,
crocodile."
Bill Haley

WOODVALE
HIGH SCHOOL
Class of 19__

Danny "Dash" Domico
Woodvale Hornets - Captain

"Remember: Life is short, break the rules."
James Dean

WOODVALE
HIGH SCHOOL
Class of 19

Buddy Peter Day
Honor Student, Future Scientists of America

"Imagination is more important than
knowledge."
Albert Einstein

WOODVALE
HIGH SCHOOL

Class of 195

Suzie Palmer

Cheer Squad, Rock 'n' Roll Dance Queen

"The greatest treasures are those invisible to
the eye but found by the heart."
Judy Garland

WOODVALE
HIGH SCHOOL
Class of 1958

CREDITS

First things first, thank you for taking the time to read my book. I hope you enjoyed your trip to the drive-in, and if so, a kind word in a review, a share, or a recommendation can do a whole world of good for an indie author.

My Zombie Sweetheart takes place in an entirely fictional reality, one where giant insects and people-eating blobs are a distinct possibility. However, I knew I had to touch on some of the real-world horrors that you didn't see on the big screen, back in those days. *My Zombie Sweetheart* isn't about that, nor am I an expert on the subject, but I wanted it to be there because, well, it was.

I am not a scientist. Nor a historian. I'm barely even a writer, so there's bound to be mistakes here and there. I read a lot about insects, especially ants, and just like Mr. Cormac says, those things are nightmarish. In the tradition of 1950s science fiction movies, I took basic scientific facts and spun them into unbelievable hyperbole. It might not be correct, but it sure is fun. Anyway, *My Zombie Sweetheart* isn't really about all that stuff.

My Zombie Sweetheart is about second chances. About how, if you're lucky enough to get one, you have to make it count. Above all, though, it's a love story. Not just the star-crossed love shared by Buddy and Suzie, but for a whole genre that rose and fell long before I was even born. I never experienced these movies like they were meant to be, but I love them all the same. Love doesn't have to make sense; it doesn't have to be practical—just ask Buddy and Suzie. So, it's about time I showed some love myself.

First up, my mother, who made sure I was exposed to classics like *The Blob* from an early age. Your complete disregard for appropriate parenting created a monster. I hope you're proud.

Claire Dobbin, who created the logo and art for this book, is next. She floored me with the first concept sketch, and seeing Buddy and Suzie like that made this whole thing real for me. Thanks for bearing with me, considering I didn't have a clue what I was doing.

Then we have my early readers. My writing process is messy, and both Craig Walker and Max Lee (you might spot them fending off the horde at the Woodvale Library) helped make sense of the chaos and provided invaluable suggestions for changes and additions.

Now for the cheer section. Part of what gave me the confidence to get this done was the community and support I found as part of the horror community on Instagram. Derek (@horrorjunkie103178) extended a hand and involved me in so many of his projects, giving me exposure and helping build up to this. He's one of the single most helpful guys I've ever met online, even if he can't tell the difference between a lake and a river. Then there's Kaytlynn (@kaytlynn.is.conjuring), one half of This Horrible Place Podcast with her partner Jen (@jen.is.horrible). With boundless energy, she's been nothing short of a bastion of support, and I'm sure she's not a serial killer.

Special thanks to Bret Laurie for taking on the task of editing the second edition, and helping re-animate *My Zombie Sweetheart*.

And to Casey for believing in me, even when I don't.

Lastly, there's the best friend I've ever had. Dexter, my little Dachshund writing buddy whose one suggestion, "More biscuits," might not have made it into the book but helped get it written for sure.

So that's it. Thanks again, from the bottom of my heart, for giving my book a shot. It means the world to me, sincerely, and I didn't even have to resort to mind-controlling ants to make it happen. Or did I…

And, if you enjoyed your trip to Woodvale, just wait till you hear about what goes on in Cherry Lake...

About The Director

Christopher Robertson has been called the "Ryan Reynolds of Indie Horror" and "some Scottish Dr. Frankenstein." He doesn't care that they were joking. He writes cinematic horror that has been described as wholesome and gruesome in the same sentence multiple times. You can find him on Instagram as @kit_romero; he'd love it if you stalked him there.

My Zombie Sweetheart is his first book.

The October Society

Halloween approaches, and The October Society gathers.

They come to share their stories.

Tales of dark magic and crooked lies.

Of tragic pasts and wicked cruelty.

Of misguided misadventure and sinister pranks...

Collected here are the first six episodes of the spookiest show that never was. A series only found in the static between channels, that can only be watched on broken TVs in dusty attics and damp basements. Tune in, if you can, because the author of *My Zombie Sweetheart* welcomes you to *The October Society*.

Before Valentine's Day, there is… *VIRGIN NIGHT!*

In the picturesque town of Cherry Lake, the kids aren't alright.

Neither is the centuries-old undead slasher that haunts the town.

Or the all-powerful megachurch with designs of the future.

On February 13th, 1998 — *VIRGIN NIGHT* — these will collide and the town of Cherry Lake will never be the same again.

For fans of self-aware 90s slashers — *VIRGIN NIGHT* will take you back to when low-rise jeans were cool, frosted tips were a thing, and getting laid was all that mattered.

THE COTTON CANDY MASSACRE

The book you are about to read is an account of the tragedy that occurred at the reopening of Bonkin's Bonanza one day in the summer of 1989.

Some came looking for fun, like Candy Barton and her best friend, Leigh.

Others, like Rocky Rhodes and Sully Sullivan, came looking for a second chance. Instead, they would find a twisted, funfetti nightmare.

For many of the thrill-seekers and families visiting Bonkin's Bonanza, that day would be their last. And the events that unfolded would go on to become infamously known as *The Cotton Candy Massacre*.

9 798847 517034